The Nutcracker Treasury

The Nutcracker Treasury

MINT EDITIONS

The Nutcracker Treasury features work first published between 1816–1819.

ISBN 9781513201191 | E-ISBN 9781513127811

Mint Editions

MINT EDITIONS

minteditionbooks.com

Publishing Director: Jennifer Newens
Design & Production: Rachel Lopez Metzger
Project Manager: Micaela Clark
Typesetting: Mind the Margins, LLC

CONTENTS

PRINCESS PIRLIPANTINE AND THE NUTCRACKER   213
  Translated, Mutilated, and Terminated by O. Eliphaz Keat

Note from the Publisher

Many thanks to the St. Louis Public Library, without whom the publication of this book would not be possible.

The Origin of the Treasury

THE BOOK YOU ARE ABOUT to read will in some ways be repetitive—it is, after all, a collection of adaptations and reinterpretations of a single story involving a young girl and her nutcracker. There will be many similarities, overlapping details, and familiar plot points; however, in between these bouts of sameness you will also be taken on a journey of transformation.

The history of *The Nutcracker*—not to be confused with Alexandre Dumas' *The History of a Nutcracker*—is an interesting one.

Originally written by E.T.A. Hoffman in 1816, *The Nutcracker and the Mouse King* is a sort of dark fantasy that questions whether or not the story we're being told is the feverish nightmare of a young child or a legitimate journey to an alternate reality of talking toys and diabolical mice.

Dumas' retelling of the story less than three decades later, is almost identical in regard to the events that transpire, but is much kinder in its presentation of the narrative—that is to say, the reader is expected to believe that what happens to Mary *actually happens* and become swept up in the innocence of childhood romance.

By the time Pyotr Ilyich Tchaikovsky's *The Nutcracker* sees its first performance in 1892, most all the edges of Hoffman's original story and even Dumas' retelling, have been sanded away in favor of a gentler, softer more consumable Christmas fairytale full of whimsy. Which, mind you, does not take into account O. Eliphaz Keat's *Princess Pirlipantine and the Nutcracker* which takes away the main plot of the young girl receiving the Nutcracker as a Christmas gift almost entirely.

This is not to say that Alexandre Dumas, Pyotr Tchaikovsky or O. Eliphaz Keat were in any way wrong for the changes they made to Hoffman's story; rather, this treasury concerns itself—and exists—out of admiration and amazement for the story's ability to live on more than two hundred years after its original publication.

The Nutcracker Treasury is a love letter to the idea that nothing ever truly dies and that great stories will continue to be passed down from generation to generation, no matter what form they may take.

Mint Editions
Berkeley, CA

The Nutcracker

and

the Mouse King

I

Christmas Eve

URING THE LONG, LONG DAY OF the twenty-fourth of December, the children of Doctor Stahlbaum were not permitted to enter the parlor, much less the adjoining drawing room. Frederic and Maria sat nestled together in a corner of the back chamber; dusky twilight had come on, and they felt quite gloomy and fearful, for, as was commonly the case on this day, no light was brought in to them. Fred, in great secrecy, and in a whisper, informed his little sister (she was only just seven years old), that ever since morning be had heard a rustling and a rattling, and now and then a gentle knocking, in the forbidden chambers. Not long ago also he had seen a little dark man, with a large chest under his arm, gliding softly through the entry, but he knew very well that it was nobody but Godfather Drosselmeier. Upon this Maria clapped her little hands together for joy, and exclaimed, "Ah, what beautiful things has Godfather Drosselmeier made for us this time!"

Counsellor Drosselmeier was not a very handsome man; he was small and thin, had many wrinkles in his face, over his right eye he had a large black patch, and he was without hair, for which reason he wore a very nice white wig; this was made of glass however, and was a very ingenious piece of work. The Godfather himself was very ingenious also, he understood all about clocks and watches, and could even make them. Accordingly, when any one of the beautiful clocks in Doctor Stahlbaum's house was sick, and could not sing, Godfather Drosselmeier would have to attend it. He would then take off his glass wig, pull off his brown coat, put on a blue apron, and pierce the clock with sharp-pointed instruments, which usually caused little Maria a great deal of anxiety. But it did the clock no harm; on the contrary, it became quite lively again, and began at once right merrily to rattle, and to strike, and to sing, so that it was a pleasure to all who heard it. Whenever he came, he always brought something pretty in his pocket for the children, sometimes a little man who moved his eyes and made a bow, at others, a box, from which a little bird hopped out when it was opened—sometimes one thing, sometimes another.

When Christmas Eve came, he had always a beautiful piece of work prepared for them, which had cost him a great deal of trouble, and on this account it was always carefully preserved by their parents, after he had given it to them.

"Ah, what beautiful present has Godfather Drosselmeier made for us this time!" exclaimed Maria.

It was Fred's opinion that this time it could be nothing else than a castle, in which all kinds of fine soldiers marched up and down and went through their exercises; then other soldiers would come, and try to break into the castle, but the soldiers within would fire off their cannon very bravely, until all roared and cracked again. "No, no," cried Maria, interrupting him, "Godfather Drosselmeier has told me of a lovely garden where there is a great lake, upon which beautiful swans swim about, with golden collars around their necks, and sing their sweetest songs. Then there comes a little girl out of the garden down along the lake, and coaxes the swans to the shore, and feeds them with sweet cake."

"Swans never eat cake," interrupted Fred, somewhat roughly, "and even Godfather Drosselmeier himself can't make a whole garden. After all, we have little good of his playthings; they are all taken right away from us again. I like what Papa and Mamma give us much better, for we can keep their presents for ourselves, and do as we please with them." The children now began once more to guess what it could be this time. Maria thought that Miss Trutchen (her great doll) was growing very old, for she fell almost every moment upon the floor, and more awkwardly than ever, which could not happen without leaving sad marks upon her face, and as to neatness in dress, this was now altogether out of the question with her. Scolding did not help the matter in the least. Frederic declared, on the other hand, that a bay horse was wanting in his stable, and his troops were very deficient in cavalry, as his Papa very well knew.

By this time it had become quite dark. Frederic and Maria sat close together, and did not venture again to speak a word. It seemed now as if soft wings rustled around them, and very distant, but sweet music was heard at intervals. At this moment a shrill sound broke upon their ears—kling, ling—kling, ling—the doors flew wide open, and such a dazzling light broke out from the great chamber, that with the loud exclamation, "Ah! Ah!" the children stood fixed at the threshold. But Papa and Mamma stepped to the door, took them by the hand, and said, "Come, come, dear children, and see what Christmas has brought you this year."

II

The Gifts

K IND READER, OR LISTENER, WHATEVER may be your name, whether Frank, Robert, Henry,—Anna or Maria, I beg you to call to mind the table covered with your last Christmas gifts, as in their newest gloss they first appeared to your delighted vision. You will then be able to imagine the astonishment of the children, as they stood with sparkling eyes, unable to utter a word, for joy at the sight before them. At last Maria called out with a deep sigh, "Ah, how beautiful! Ah, how beautiful!" and Frederic gave two or three leaps in the air higher than he had ever done before. The children must have been very obedient and good children during the past year, for never on any Christmas Eve before, had so many beautiful things been given to them. A tall Fir tree stood in the middle of the room, covered with gold and silver apples, while sugar almonds, comfits, lemon drops, and every kind of confectionery, hung like buds and blossoms upon all its branches. But the greatest beauty about this wonderful tree, was the many little lights that sparkled amid its dark boughs, which like stars illuminated its treasures, or like friendly eyes seemed to invite the children to partake of its blossoms and fruit. The table under the tree shone and flushed with a thousand different colors—ah, what beautiful things were there! Who can describe them? Maria spied the prettiest dolls, a tea set, all kinds of nice little furniture, and what eclipsed all the rest, a silk dress tastefully ornamented with gay ribbons, which hung upon a frame before her eyes, so that she could view it on every side. This she did too, and exclaimed over and over again, "Ah, the sweet—ah, the dear, dear frock! And may I put it on? Yes, yes—may I really, though, wear it?"

In the meanwhile Fred had been galloping round and round the room, trying his new bay horse, which, true enough, he had found, fastened by its bridle to the table. Dismounting again, he said it was a wild creature, but that was nothing; he would soon break him. He then reviewed his new regiment of hussars, who were very elegantly arrayed in red and gold, and carried silver weapons, and rode upon such bright shining horses, that you would almost believe these were of pure silver also. The children had now become somewhat more composed, and turned to the picture books, which lay open on the table, where all kinds of beautiful flowers, and gayly dressed people, and boys and girls at play, were painted as natural as if they were alive. Yes, the children had just turned to these singular books, when—kling, ling, kling, ling—the bell was heard again. They knew that Godfather Drosselmeier was now about to display his Christmas gift, and ran towards a table that stood against the wall, covered by a curtain reaching from the ceiling to the floor. The curtain behind which he had remained so long concealed, was quickly drawn aside, and what saw the children then?

Upon a green meadow, spangled with flowers, stood a noble castle, with clear glass windows and golden turrets. A musical clock began to play, when the doors and windows flew open, and little men and women, with feathers in their hats, and long flowing trains, were seen sauntering about in the rooms. In the middle hall, which seemed as if it were all on fire, so many little tapers were burning in silver chandeliers, there were children in white frocks and green jackets, dancing to the sound of the music. A man in an emerald-green cloak, at intervals put his head out of the window, nodded, and then disappeared; and Godfather Drosselmeier himself, only that he was not much bigger than Papa's thumb, came now and then to the door of the castle, looked about him, and then went in again. Fred, with his arms resting upon the table, gazed at the beautiful castle, and the little walking and dancing figures, and then said, "Godfather Drosselmeier, let me go into your castle."

The Counsellor gave him to understand that that could not be done. And he was right, for it was foolish in Fred to wish to go into a castle, which with all its golden turrets was not as high as his head. Fred saw that likewise himself. After a while as the men and women kept walking back and forth, and the children danced, and the emerald man looked out at his window, and Godfather Drosselmeier came to the door, and all without the least change; Fred called out impatiently, "Godfather Drosselmeier, come out this time at the other door."

"That can never be, dear Fred," said the Counsellor.

"Well then," continued Frederic, "let the green man who peeps out at the window walk about with the rest."

"And that can never be," rejoined the Counsellor.

"Then the children must come down," cried Fred, "I want to see them nearer."

"All that can never be, I say," replied the Counsellor, a little out of humor. "As the mechanism is made, so it must remain."

"So—o," cried Fred, in a drawling tone, "all that can never be! Listen, Godfather Drosselmeier. If your little dressed up figures in the castle there, can do nothing else but always the same thing, they are not good for much, and I care very little about them. No, give me my hussars, who can manœuvre backward and forward, as I order them, and are not shut up in a house."

With this, he darted towards a large table, drew up his regiment upon their silver horses, and let them trot and gallop, and cut and slash, to his heart's content. Maria also had softly stolen away, for she too was soon tired of the sauntering and dancing puppets in the castle; but as she was very amiable and good, she did not wish it to be observed so plainly in her as it was in her brother Fred. Counsellor Drosselmeier turned to the parents, and said, somewhat angrily, "An ingenious work like this was not made for stupid children. I will put up my castle again, and carry it home." But their mother now stepped forward, and desired to see the secret mechanism and curious works by which the little figures were set in motion. The Counsellor took it all apart, and then put it together again. While he was employed in this manner he became good-natured once more, and gave the children some nice brown men and women, with gilt faces, hands, and feet. They were all made of sweet thorn, and smelt like gingerbread, at which Frederic and Maria were greatly delighted. At her mother's request, the elder sister, Louise, had put on the new dress which had been given to her, and she looked most charmingly in it, but Maria, when it came to her turn, thought she would like to look at hers a while longer as it hung. This was readily permitted.

III

The Favorite

THE TRUTH IS, MARIA WAS unwilling to leave the table then, because she had discovered something upon it, which no one had yet remarked. By the marching out of Fred's hussars, who had been drawn up close to the tree, a curious little man came into view, who stood there silent and retired, as if he were waiting quietly for his turn to be noticed. It must be confessed, a great deal could not be said in favor of the beauty of his figure, for not only was his rather broad, stout body, out of all proportion to the little, slim legs that carried it, but his head was by far too large for either. A genteel dress went a great way to compensate for these defects, and led to the belief that he must be a man of taste and good breeding. He wore a hussar's jacket of beautiful bright violet, fastened together with white loops and buttons, pantaloons of exactly the same color, and the neatest boots that ever graced the foot of a student or an officer. They fitted as tight to his little legs as if they were painted upon them. It was laughable to see, that in addition to this handsome apparel, he had hung upon his back a narrow clumsy cloak, that looked as if it were made of wood, and upon his head he wore a woodman's cap; but Maria remembered that Godfather Drosselmeier wore an old shabby cloak and an ugly cap, and still he was a dear, dear godfather. Maria could not help thinking also, that even if Godfather Drosselmeier were in other respects as well dressed as this little fellow, yet after all he would not look half so handsome as he. The longer Maria gazed upon the little man whom she had taken a liking to at first sight, the more she was sensible how much good nature and friendliness was expressed in his features. Nothing but kindness and benevolence shone in his clear green, though somewhat too prominent eyes. It was very becoming to the man that he wore about his chin a nicely trimmed beard of white cotton, for by this the sweet smile upon his deep red lips was rendered much more striking. "Ah, dear father," exclaimed Maria at last, "to whom belongs that charming little man by the tree there?"

"He shall work industriously for you all, dear child," said her father. "He can crack the hardest nuts with his teeth, and he belongs as well to Louise as to you and Fred." With these words her father took him carefully from the table, and raised up his wooden cloak, whereupon the little man stretched his mouth wide open, and showed two rows of very white sharp teeth. At her father's bidding Maria put in a nut, and—crack—the man had bitten it in two, so that the shell fell off, and Maria caught the sweet kernel in her hand. Maria and the other two children were now informed that this dainty little man came of the family of Nutcrackers, and practised the profession of his forefathers. Maria was overjoyed at what she heard, and her father said, "Dear Maria, since friend Nutcracker is so great a favorite with you, I place him under your particular care and keeping, although, as I said before, Louise and Fred shall have as much right to his services as you."

Maria took him immediately in her arms, and set him to cracking nuts, but she picked out the smallest, that the little fellow need not stretch his mouth open so wide, which in truth was not very becoming to him. Louise sat down by her, and friend Nutcracker must perform the same service for her too, which he seemed to do quite willingly, for he kept smiling all the while very pleasantly. In the mean time Fred had become tired of riding and parading his hussars, and when he heard the nuts crack so merrily, he ran to his sister, and laughed very heartily at the droll little man, who now, since Fred must have a share in the sport, passed from hand to hand, and thus there was no end to his labor. Fred always chose the biggest and hardest nuts, when all at once—crack—crack—it went, and three teeth fell out of Nutcracker's mouth, and his whole under jaw became loose and rickety. "Ah, my poor dear Nutcracker!" said Maria, and snatched him out of Fred's hands.

"That's a stupid fellow," said Fred. "He wants to be a nutcracker, and has poor teeth—he don't understand his trade. Give him to me, Maria. He shall crack nuts for me if he loses all his teeth, and his whole chin into the bargain. Why make such a fuss about such a fellow?"

"No, no," exclaimed Maria, weeping; "you shall not have my dear Nutcracker. See how sorrowfully he looks at me, and shows me his poor mouth. But you are a hard-hearted fellow; you beat your horses; yes, and lately you had one of your soldiers shot through the head."

"That's all right," said Fred, "though you don't understand it. But Nutcracker belongs as much to me as to you, so let me have him."

Maria began to cry bitterly, and rolled up the sick Nutcracker as quickly as she could in her little pocket handkerchief. Their parents now came up with Godfather Drosselmeier. The latter, to Maria's great distress, took Fred's part. But their father said, "I have placed Nutcracker expressly under Maria's protection, and as I see that he is now greatly in need of it, I give her full authority over him, and no one must dispute it. Besides, I wonder at Fred, that he should require farther duty from one who has been maimed in the service. As a good soldier, he ought to know that the wounded are not expected to take their place in the ranks."

Fred was much ashamed, and without troubling himself farther about nuts or Nutcracker, stole around to the opposite end of the table, where his hussars, after stationing suitable outposts, had encamped for the night. Maria collected together Nutcracker's lost teeth, tied up his wounded chin with a nice white ribbon which she had taken from her dress, and then wrapped up the little fellow more carefully than ever in her handkerchief, for he looked very pale and frightened. Thus she held him, rocking him in her arms like a little child, while she looked over the beautiful pictures of the new picture book, which she found among her other Christmas gifts. Contrary to her usual disposition, she showed some ill-temper towards Father Drosselmeier, who kept continually laughing at her, and asked again and again how it was that she liked to caress such an ugly little fellow. That singular comparison with Drosselmeier, which she made when her eyes first fell upon Nutcracker, now came again into her mind, and she said very seriously: "Who knows, dear godfather, if you were dressed like my sweet Nutcracker, and had on such bright little boots—who knows but you would then be as handsome as he is!" Maria could not tell why her parents laughed so loudly at this, and why the Counsellor's face turned so red, and he, for his part, did not laugh half so heartily this time as he had done more than once before. It is likely there was some particular reason for it.

IV

WONDERS UPON WONDERS

IN THE SITTING ROOM OF THE Doctor's house, just as you enter the room, there stands on the left hand, close against the wall, a high glass case, in which the children preserve all the beautiful things which are given to them every year. Louise was quite a little girl when her father had the case made by a skilful joiner, who set in it such large, clear panes of glass, and arranged all the parts so well together, that every thing looked much brighter and handsomer when on its shelves than when it was held in the hands. On the upper shelf, which Maria and Fred were unable to reach, stood all Godfather Drosselmeier's curious machines. Immediately below this was a shelf for the picture books; the two lower shelves Maria and Fred filled up as they pleased, but it always happened that Maria used the lower one as a house for her dolls, while Fred, on the contrary, cantoned his troops in the one above.

And so it happened today, for while Fred set his hussars in order above, Maria, having laid Miss Trutchen aside, and having installed the new and sweetly dressed doll in her best furnished chamber below, had invited herself to tea with her. I have said that the chamber was well furnished, and it is true; here was a nice chintz sofa and several tiny chairs, there stood a tea table, but above all, there was a clean, white little bed for her doll to repose upon. All these things were arranged in one corner of the glass case, the sides of which were hung with gay pictures, and it will readily be supposed, that in such a chamber the new doll, Miss Clara, must have found herself very comfortable.

It was now late in the evening, and night, indeed, was close at hand, and Godfather Drosselmeier had long since gone home, yet still the children could not leave the glass case, although their mother repeatedly told them that it was high time to go to bed. "It is true," cried Fred at last; "the poor fellows (meaning his hussars) would like to get a little rest, and as long as I am here, not one of them will dare to nod—I know that." With these words he went up to bed, but Maria begged very hard, "Only leave me here a little while, dear mother. I have two or three things to attend to, and when they are done I will go immediately to bed." Maria was a very good and sensible child, and therefore her mother could leave her alone with her playthings without anxiety. But for fear she might become so much interested in her new doll and other presents as to forget the lights which burned around the glass case, her mother blew them all out, and left only the lamp which hung clown from the ceiling in the middle of the chamber, and which diffused a soft, pleasant light. "Come in soon, dear Maria, or you will not be up in time tomorrow morning," called her mother, as she went up to bed. There was something Maria had at heart to do, which she had not told her mother, though she knew not the reason why; and as soon as she found herself alone she went quickly about it. She still carried in her arms the wounded Nutcracker, rolled up in her pocket handkerchief. Now she laid him carefully upon the table, unrolled the handkerchief softly, and examined his wound. Nutcracker was very pale, but still he smiled so kindly and sorrowfully that it went straight to Maria's heart. "Ah! Nutcracker, Nutcracker, do not be angry at brother Fred because he hurt you so, he did not mean to be so rough; it is the wild soldier's life with his hussars that has made him a little hard-hearted, but otherwise he is a good fellow, I can assure you. Now I will tend you very carefully until you are well and merry again; as to fastening in your teeth and setting your shoulders, that Godfather Drosselmeier must do; he understands such things."

But Maria was hardly able to finish the sentence, for as she mentioned the name of Drosselmeier, friend Nutcracker made a terrible wry face, and there darted something out of his eyes like green sparkling flashes. Maria was just going to fall into a dreadful fright, when behold, it was the sad smiling face of the honest Nutcracker again, which she saw before her, and she knew now that it must be the glare of the lamp, which, stirred by the draught, had flared up, and distorted Nutcracker's features so strangely.

"Am I not a foolish girl," she said, "to be so easily frightened, and to think that a wooden puppet could make faces at me? But I love Nutcracker too well, because he is so droll and so good tempered; therefore he shall be taken good care of as he deserves."

With this Maria took friend Nutcracker in her arms, walked to the glass case, stooped down, and said to her new doll, "Pray, Miss Clara, be so good as to give up your bed to the sick and wounded Nutcracker, and make out as well as you can with the sofa, Remember that you are well and hearty, or you would not have such fat red cheeks, and very few little dolls have such nice sofas."

Miss Clara, in her gay Christmas attire, looked very grand and haughty, and would not even say "Muck." "But why should I stand upon ceremony?"

said Maria, and she took out the bed, laid little Nutcracker down upon it softly, and gently rolled a nice ribbon which she wore around her waist, about his poor shoulders, and then drew the bedclothes over him snugly, so that there was nothing to be seen of him below the nose. "He shan't stay with the naughty Clara," she said, and raised the bed with Nutcracker in it to the shelf above, and placed it close by the pretty village, where Fred's hussars were quartered. She locked the case, and was about to go up to bed, when—listen children—when softly, softly it began to rustle, and to whisper, and to rattle round and round, under the hearth, behind the chairs, behind the cupboards and glass case. The great clock whir—red louder and louder, but it could not strike. Maria turned towards it, and there the large gilt owl that sat on the top, had dropped down its wings, so that they covered the whole face, and it stretched out its ugly head with the short crooked beak, and looked just like a cat. And the clock whirred louder in plain words. "Dick—ry, dick—ry, dock—whirr, softly clock, Mouse-King has a fine ear—prr—prr—pum—pum—the old song let him hear—prr—prr—pum—pum—or he might—run away in a fright—now clock strike softly and light." And pum—pum, it went with a dull deadened sound twelve times. Maria began now to tremble with fear, and she was upon the point of running out of the room in terror, when she beheld Godfather Drosselmeier, who sat in the owl's place on the top of the clock, and had hung down the skirts of his brown coat just like wings. But she took courage, and cried out loudly, with sobs, "Godfather Drosselmeier, Godfather Drosselmeier, what are you doing up there? Come down, and do not frighten me so, you naughty Godfather Drosselmeier!"

Just then a wild squeaking and whimpering broke out on all sides, and then there was a running, trotting and galloping behind the walls, as if a thousand little feet were in motion, and a thousand little lights flashed out of the crevices in the floor. But they were not lights—no—they were sparkling little eyes, and Maria perceived that mice were all around, peeping out and working their way into the room. Presently it went trot—trot—hop—hop about the chamber, and more and more mice, in greater or smaller parties galloped across, and at last placed themselves in line and column, just as Fred was accustomed to place his soldiers when they went to battle. This Maria thought was very droll, and as she had not that aversion to mice which most children have, her terror was gradually leaving her, when all at once there arose a squeaking so terrible and piercing, that it seemed as if ice-cold water was poured down her back. Ah, what now did she see!

I know, my worthy reader Frederic, that thy heart, like that of the wise and brave soldier Frederic Stahlbaum, sits in the right place, but if thou hadst seen what Maria now beheld, thou wouldst certainly have run away; yes, I believe that thou wouldst have jumped as quickly as possible into bed, and then have drawn the covering over thine ears much farther than was necessary to keep thee warm. Alas! Poor Maria could not do that now, for—listen children—close before her feet, there burst out sand and lime and crumbled wall stones, as if thrown up by some subterranean force, and seven mice-heads with seven sparkling crowns rose out of the floor, squeaking and squealing terribly. Presently the mouse's body to which these seven heads belonged, worked its way out, and the great mouse crowned with the seven diadems, squeaking loudly, huzzaed in full chorus, as he advanced to meet his army, which at once set itself in motion, and hott—hott—trot—trot it went—alas, straight towards the glass case—straight towards poor Maria who stood close before it!

Her heart had before beat so terribly from anxiety and fear, that she thought it would leap out of her bosom, and then she knew she must die; but now it seemed as if the blood stood still in her veins. Half fainting, she tottered backward, when clatter—clatter—rattle—rattle it went—and a glass pane which she had struck with her elbow fell in pieces at her feet. She felt at the moment a sharp pain in her left arm, but her heart all at once became much lighter, she heard no more squeaking and squealing, all had become still, and although she did not dare to look, yet she believed that the mice, frightened by the clatter of the broken glass, had retreated into their holes. But what was that again! Close behind her in the glass case a strange bustling and rustling began, and little fine voices were heard. "Up, up, awake—arms take—awake—to the fight—this night—up, up—to the fight." And all the while something rang out clear and sweet like little bells. "Ah, that is my clear musical clock!" exclaimed Maria joyfully, and turned quickly to look.

She then saw how it flashed and lightened strangely in the glass case, and there was a great stir and bustle upon the shelves. Many little figures crossed up and down by each other, and worked and stretched out their arms as if they were making ready. And now, Nutcracker raised himself all of a sudden, threw the bedclothes clear off, and leaped with both feet at once out of bed, crying aloud, "Crack—crack—crack—stupid pack—drive mouse back—stupid pack—crack—crack—mouse—back—crick—crack—stupid pack."

With these words he drew his little sword, flourished it in the air, and exclaimed, "My loving vassals, friends and brothers, will you stand by me in the hard fight?" Straightway three Scaramouches, a Harlequin, four Chimney sweepers, two Guitar players and a drummer cried out,

"Yes, my lord, we will follow you with fidelity and courage—we will march with you to battle—to victory or death," and then rushed after the fiery Nutcracker, who ventured the dangerous leap down from the upper shelf.

Ah, it was easy enough for them to perform this feat, for beside the fine garments of thick cloth and silk which they wore, the inside of their bodies were made of cotton and tow, so that they came down plump, like bags of wool. But poor Nutcracker had certainly broken his arms or his legs, for remember, it was almost two feet from the shelf where he stood to the floor, and his body was as brittle as if it had been cut out of Linden wood. Yes, Nutcracker would certainly have broken his arms or his legs, if, at the moment when he leaped, Miss Clara had not sprung quickly from the sofa, and caught the hero with his drawn sword in her soft arms.

"Ah, thou dear, good Clara," sobbed Maria, "how I have wronged thee! Thou didst certainly resign thy bed willingly to little Nutcracker."

But Miss Clara now spoke, as she softly pressed the young hero to her silken bosom. "You will not, oh, my lord! Sick and wounded as you are, share the dangers of the fight. See how your brave vassals assemble themselves, eager for the affray, and certain of conquest. Scaramouch, Harlequin, Chimney sweepers, Guitar players, Drummer, are all ready drawn up below, and the china figures on the shelf stir and move strangely! Will yon not, oh, my lord! Repose upon the sofa, or from my arms look down upon your victory?" Thus spoke Clara, but Nutcracker demeaned himself very ungraciously, for he kicked and struggled so violently with his legs, that Clara was obliged to set him quickly down upon the floor. He then, however, dropped gracefully upon one knee, and said, "Fair lady, the recollection of thy favor and condescension will go with me into the battle and the strife."

Clara then stooped so low that she could take him by the arm, raised him gently from his knees, took off her bespangled girdle, and was about to throw it across his neck, but little Nutcracker stepped two paces backward, laid his hand upon his breast, and said very earnestly, "Not so, fair lady, lavish not thy favors thus upon me, for—" he stopped, sighed heavily, tore off the ribbon which Maria had bound about his shoulders, pressed it to his lips, hung it across him like a scarf, and then boldly flourishing his bright little blade, leaped like a bird over the edge of the glass case upon the floor. You understand my kind and good readers and listeners, that Nutcracker, even before he had thus come to life, had felt very sensibly the kindness and love which Maria had shown towards him, and it was because he had become so partial to her, that he would not receive and wear the girdle of Miss Clara, although it shone and sparkled so brightly. The true and faithful Nutcracker preferred to wear Maria's simple ribbon. But what will now happen? As soon as Nutcracker had leaped out, the squeaking and whistling was heard again. Ah, it is under the large table, that the hateful mice have concealed their countless bands, and high above them all towers the dreadful mouse with seven heads! What will now happen!

V

The Battle

"**B**EAT THE MARCH, TRUE VASSAL DRUMMER!**" screamed Nutcracker very loudly, and immediately the drummer began to rattle and to roll upon his drum so skilfully, that the windows of the glass case trembled and hummed again. Now it rustled and clattered therein, and Maria perceived that the covers of the little boxes in which Fred's army were quartered, were bursting open, and now the soldiers leaped out, and then down again upon the lowest shelf, where they drew up in fine array.

Nutcracker ran up and down, speaking inspiring words to the troops— "Let no dog of a trumpeter blow or stir!" he cried angrily, for he was afraid he should not be heard, and then turned quickly to Harlequin, who had grown a little pale, and chattered with his long chin. "General," he said, earnestly, "I know your courage and your experience; there is need now for a quick eye, and skill to seize the proper moment. I intrust to your command all the cavalry and artillery. You do not need a horse, for you have very long legs, and can gallop yourself tolerably well. I look to see you do your duty." Thereupon Harlequin put his long, thin fingers to his mouth, and crowed so piercingly, that it sounded as if a hundred shrill trumpets were blown merrily.

Then it stirred again in the glass case—a neighing, and a whinnying, and a stamping were heard, and see! Fred's cuirassiers and dragoons, but above all, his new splendid hussars marched out, and halted close by the case. Regiment after regiment now defiled before Nutcracker, with flying colors and warlike music, and ranged themselves in long rows across the floor of the chamber. Before them went Fred's cannon rattling along, surrounded by the cannoniers, and soon bom—bom it went, and Maria could see how the mice suffered by the fire, how the sugar plums plunged into their dark, heavy mass, covering them with white powder, and throwing them more than once into shameful disorder. But the greatest damage was done them by a heavy battery that was mounted upon mamma's footstool, which—pum, pum—kept up a steady fire of caraway seeds against the enemy, by which a great many of them fell. The mice, notwithstanding, came nearer and nearer, and at last mastered some of the cannon, but then it went prr—prr—and Maria could scarcely see what now happened for the smoke and dust. This however was certain, that each corps fought with the greatest animosity, and the victory was for a long time doubtful. The mice kept deploying more and more forces, and the little silver shot, which they fired very skilfully, struck now even into the glass case. Clara and Trutchen ran around in despair.

"Must I die in the blossom of youth?" said Clara. "Have I so well preserved myself for this, to perish here in these walls?" cried Trutchen. Then they fell about each, other's necks, and screamed so terribly, that they could be heard above the mad tumult of the battle.

Of the scene that now presented itself you can have no idea, good reader. It went prr—prr—puff—piff—clitter—clatter—bom, burum—bom, burum—bom—in the wildest confusion, while the Mouse-King and mice squeaked and screamed, and now and then the mighty voice of Nutcracker was heard, as he gave the necessary orders, and he was seen striding along through the battalions in the hottest of the fire. Harlequin had made some splendid charges with his cavalry, and covered himself with honor, but Fred's hussars were battered by the enemy's artillery, with odious, offensive balls, which made dreadful spots in their red jackets, for which reason they would not move forward. Harlequin ordered them to draw off to the left, and in the enthusiasm of command headed the movement himself, and the cuirassiers and dragoons followed; that is, they all drew off to the left, and galloped home. By this step the battery upon the footstool was exposed to great danger, and it was not long before a strong body of very ugly mice pushed on with such determined bravery, that the footstool, cannons, cannoniers and all were overthrown by their headlong charge. Nutcracker seemed a little disturbed at this, and gave orders that the right wing should make a retreating movement. You know very well, oh my military reader Frederic, that to make such a movement is almost the same thing as to run away, and you are now grieving with me at the disaster which impends over the army of Maria's darling Nutcracker.

But turn your eyes from this scene, and view the left wing, where all is still in good order, and where there is yet great hope, both for the general and the army. During the hottest of the fight, large masses of mice cavalry had debouched softly from under the settee, and amid loud and hideous squeaking had thrown themselves with fury upon the left wing; but what an obstinate resistance did they meet with there! Slowly, as the difficult nature of the ground required—for the edge of the glass case had to be traversed—the china figures had advanced, headed by two Chinese emperors, and formed themselves into a hollow square. These brave, motley, but noble troops, which were composed of Gardeners, Tyrolese, Bonzes, Friseurs, Merry-andrews, Cupids, Lions, Tigers, Peacocks, and

Apes, fought with coolness, courage, and determination. By their Spartan bravery this battalion of picked men would have wrested the victory from the foe, had not a bold major rushed madly from the enemy's ranks, and bitten off the head of one of the Chinese emperors, who in falling dashed to the ground two Bonzes and a Cupid. Through this gap the enemy penetrated into the square, and in a few moments the whole battalion was torn to pieces. Their brave resistance, therefore, was of no avail to Nutcracker's army, which, once having begun to retreat, retired farther and farther, and at every step with diminished numbers, until the unfortunate Nutcracker halted with a little band close before the glass case. "Let the reserve advance! Harlequin—Scaramouch—Drummer—where are you?"

Thus cried Nutcracker, in hopes of new troops which should deploy out of the glass case. And there actually came forth a few brown men and women, made of sweet thorn, with golden faces, and caps, and helmets, but they fought around so awkwardly, that they did not hit one of the enemy, and at last knocked the cap off their own general's head. The enemies' chasseurs, too, bit off their legs before long, so that they tumbled over, and carried with them to the ground some of Nutcracker's best officers. Nutcracker, now completely surrounded by the foe, was in the greatest peril. He tried to leap over the edge, into the glass case, but found his legs too short. Clara and Trutchen lay each in a deep swoon,—they could not help him—hussars, dragoons sprang merrily by him into safe quarters, and in wild despair, he cried, "A horse—a horse—a kingdom for a horse!" At this moment two of the enemies' tirailleurs seized him by his wooden mantle, and the Mouse-King, squeaking from his seven throats, leaped in triumph towards him. Maria could no longer control herself.

"Oh, my poor Nutcracker!" she cried, sobbing, and without being exactly conscious of what she did, grasped her left shoe, and threw it with all her strength into the thickest of the mice, straight at their king. In an instant, all seemed scattered and dispersed, but Maria felt in her left arm a still sharper pain than before, and sank in a swoon to the floor.

VI

The Sickness

WHEN MARIA WOKE OUT OF HER deep and deathlike slumber, she found herself lying in her own bed, with the sun shining bright and sparkling through the ice-covered windows into the chamber. Close beside her sat a stranger, whom she soon recognized, however, as the Surgeon Wendelstern. He said softly, "She is awake!" Her mother then came to the bedside, and gazed upon her with anxious and inquiring looks. "Ah, dear mother," lisped little Maria, "are all the hateful mice gone, and is the good Nutcracker safe?"

"Do not talk such foolish stuff," replied her mother; "what have the mice to do with Nutcracker? You naughty child, you have caused us a great deal of anxiety. But so it always is, when children are disobedient and do not mind their parents. You played last night with your dolls until it was very late. You became sleepy, probably, and a stray mouse may have jumped out and frightened you; at all events, you broke a pane of glass with your elbow, and cut your arm so severely, that neighbor Wendelstern, who has just taken the piece of glass out of the wound, declares that it came very near cutting a vein, in which case you might have had a stiff arm all your life, or perhaps have bled to death. It was fortunate that I woke about midnight, and not finding you in your bed, got up and went into the sitting room. There you lay in a swoon upon the floor, close by the glass case, the blood flowing in a stream. I almost fainted away myself at the sight. There you lay, and scattered around, were many of Frederic's leaden soldiers, broken China figures, gingerbread men and women and other playthings, and not far off your left shoe."

"Ah! Dear mother, dear mother," exclaimed Maria, interrupting her, "those were the traces of that dreadful battle between the puppets and the mice, and what frightened me so was the danger of poor Nutcracker, when the mice were going to take him prisoner. Then I threw my shoe at the mice, and after that I don't know what happened."

Surgeon Wendelstern here made a sign to the mother, and she said very softly to Maria, "Well, never mind about it, my dear child, the mice are all gone, and little Nutcracker stands safe and sound in the glass case." Doctor Stahlbaum now entered the chamber, and spoke for a while with Surgeon Wendelstern, then he felt Maria's pulse, and she could hear very plainly that he said something about a fever. She was obliged to remain in bed and take physic, and so it continued for some days, although except a slight pain in her arm, she felt quite well and comfortable. She knew little Nutcracker had escaped safe from the battle, and it seemed to her that she sometimes heard his voice quite plainly, as if in a dream, saying mournfully, "Maria, dearest lady, what thanks do I not owe you! But you can do still more for me." Maria tried to think what it could be, but in vain; nothing occurred to her. She could not play very well on account of the wound in her arm, and when she tried to read or look at her picture books, a strange glare came across her eyes, so that she was obliged to desist. The time, during the day, always seemed very long to her, and she waited impatiently for evening, as her mother then usually seated herself by her bedside, and read or related some pretty story to her.

One evening she had just finished the wonderful history of prince Fackardin, when the door opened, and Godfather Drosselmeier entered, saying, "I must see now for myself how it goes with the sick and wounded Maria." As soon as Maria saw Godfather Drosselmeier in his brown coat, the image of that night in which Nutcracker lost the battle against the mice, returned vividly to her mind, and she cried out involuntarily, "Oh Godfather Drosselmeier, you have been very naughty; I saw you as you sat upon the clock, and covered it with your wings, so that it should not strike loud, to scare away the mice. I heard how you called out to the Mouse-King. Why did you not come to help us; me, and the poor Nutcracker? It is all your fault, naughty Godfather Drosselmeier, that I must he here sick in bed." Her mother was quite frightened at this, and said, "What is the matter with you, dear Maria?"

But Godfather Drosselmeier made very strange faces, and said in a grating, monotonous tone, "Pendulum must whirr—whirr—whirr—this way—that way—clock will strike—tired of ticking—all the day—softly whirr—whirr—whirr—strike kling—klang—strike klang—kling—bing and bang and bang and bing—'twill scare away the Mouse-King. Then Owl in swift flight comes at dead of night. Pendulum must whirr—whirr—Clock will strike kling—klang—this way—that way—tired of ticking all the day—bing—bang—and Mouse-King scare away—whirr—whirr—prr—prr." Maria stared at Godfather Drosselmeier, for he did not look at all as he usually did, but appeared much uglier, and he moved his right arm backward and forward, like a puppet pulled by wires. She would have been afraid of him, if her mother had not been present, and if Fred had not slipped in, in the meanwhile, and interrupted him with loud laughter.

"Ha, ha! Godfather Drosselmeier," cried Fred, "you are today too droll again—you act just like my Harlequin that I threw into the lumber room long ago." But their mother was very serious, and said, "Dear Counsellor, this is very strange sport—what do you really mean by it?"

"Gracious me," replied Drosselmeier, laughing, "have you forgotten then my pretty watchmaker's song? I always sing it to such patients as Maria." With this he drew his chair close to her bed, and said, "Do not be angry that I did not pick out the Mouse-King's fourteen eyes—that could not be—but instead, I have in store for you a very agreeable surprise." The Counsellor with these words put his hand in his pocket, drew something out slowly, and behold it was—Nutcracker with his lost teeth nicely fastened in, and his lame chin well set and sound. Maria cried aloud with joy, while her mother smiled, and said, "You see now, Maria, that Godfather Drosselmeier meant well by your little Nutcracker."

"But still you must confess," Maria, said the Counsellor, "that Nutcracker's figure is none of the finest, neither can his face be called exactly handsome. How this ugliness came to be hereditary in the family, I will now relate to you, if you will listen. Or perhaps you know already the story of the Princess Pirlipat and the Lady Mouserings, and the skilful Watchmaker?"

"Look here, Godfather Drosselmeier," interrupted Fred, "Nutcracker's teeth you have fastened in very well, and his chin is no longer lame and rickety, but why has he no sword? Why have you not put on his sword?"

"Ah," replied the Counsellor, angrily, "you must always meddle and make, you rogue. What is Nutcracker's sword to me? I have cured his wounds, and he may find a sword for himself as he can."

"That's true," said Fred, "he is a brave fellow, and will know how to get one."

"Tell me then, Maria," continued the Counsellor, "have you heard the story of the Princess Pirlipat?"

"I hope, dear Counsellor," said the mother, "that your story will not be frightful, as those that you narrate usually are."

"By no means, dearest madam," replied Drosselmeier, "on the contrary, what I have this time the honor to relate is droll and merry."

"Begin, begin then, dear Godfather!" cried the children, and the Counsellor began as follows.

VII

The Story of the Hard Nut

Pirlipat's mother was the wife of a king, and therefore a queen, and Pirlipat straightway at the moment of her birth a true princess. The king was beside himself with joy, when he saw his beautiful daughter, as she lay in the cradle. He shouted aloud, danced, jumped about upon one leg, and cried again and again, "Ha! Ha! Was there ever any thing seen more beautiful than my little Pirlipat?" Thereupon all the ministers, generals, presidents and staff officers jumped about upon one leg like the king, and cried aloud, "No, never!"

And it was so, in truth, for as long as the world has been standing, a lovelier child was never born, than this very Princess Pirlipat. Her little face seemed made of lilies and roses, delicate white and red; her eyes were of living sparkling azure, and it was charming to see how her little locks curled in bright golden ringlets. Besides this, Pirlipat had brought into the world two rows of little pearly teeth, with which two hours after her birth, she bit the high chancellor's finger, as he was examining her features too closely, so that he screamed out, "Oh, Gemini!" Others assert that he screamed out, "Oh, Crickee!" but on this point authorities are at the present day divided.

Well, little Pirlipat bit the high chancellor's finger, and the enraptured land knew now that some sense dwelt in Pirlipat's beautiful body. As has been said, all were delighted. The queen alone was very anxious and uneasy, and no one knew wherefore, but every body remarked with surprise, the care with which she watched Pirlipat's cradle. Besides that the doors were guarded by soldiers, and not counting the two nurses, who always remained close by the cradle, six maids night after night sat in the room to watch. But what seemed very foolish, and no one could understand the meaning of it, was this; each of these six maids must have a cat upon her lap, and stroke it the whole night through, and thus keep it continually purring. It is impossible that you, dear children, can guess why Pirlipat's mother made all these arrangements, but I know, and will straightway tell you.

It happened that once upon a time many great kings and fine princes were assembled at the court of Pirlipat's father, on which occasion much splendor was displayed, the theatres were crowded, balls were given, and tournaments held almost every day. The king, in order to show plainly that he was in no want of gold and silver, was resolved to take a good handful out of his royal treasury, and expend it in a suitable manner. Therefore as soon as he had been privately informed by the overseer of the kitchen, that the court astronomer had predicted the right time for killing, he ordered a great feast of sausages, leaped into his carriage, and went himself to invite the assembled kings and princes to take a little soup with him, in order to enjoy the agreeable surprise which he had prepared for them. Upon his return, he said very affectionately to the queen, "You know, my dear, how extremely fond I am of sausages."

The queen knew at once what he meant by that, and it was this, that she should take upon herself, as she had often done before, the useful occupation of making sausages. The lord treasurer must straightway bring to the kitchen the great golden sausage kettle, and the silver chopping knives and stew pans. A large fire of sandal wood was made, the queen put on her damask apron, and soon the sweet smell of the sausage meat began to steam up out of the kettle. The agreeable odor penetrated even to the royal council chamber, and the king, seized with a sudden transport, could no longer restrain himself, "With your permission, my lords," he cried, and leaped up, ran as fast as he could into the kitchen, embraced the queen, stirred a little with his golden sceptre in the kettle, and then his emotion being quieted, returned calmly to the council.

The important moment had now arrived when the fat was to be chopped into little pieces, and browned gently in the silver stew pans. The maids of honor now retired, for the queen, out of true devotion and reverence for her royal spouse, wished to perform this duty alone. But just as the fat began to fry, a small wimpering, whispering voice was heard, "Give me a little of the fat, sister—I should like my part of the feast—I too am a queen—give me a little of the fat." The queen knew very well that it was Lady Mouserings who said this. Lady Mouserings had lived these many years in the king's palace. She maintained that she was related to the royal family, and that she was herself a queen in the kingdom of Mousalia, for which reason she held a great court under the hearth. The queen was a kind and benevolent lady, and although she was not exactly willing to acknowledge Lady Mouserings as a true queen and sister, yet she was very ready to allow her a little banquet on this great holiday. She answered, therefore, "Come out, then, Lady Mouserings, you are welcome to a little of the fat." Upon this, Lady Mouserings leaped out very quickly and merrily, jumped upon the hearth, and seized with her dainty little paws, one piece of fat after the other as the queen reached it to her. But now, all the cousins and aunts of the Lady Mouserings came running out, besides her seven sons, rude and forward rogues, who all fell at once upon the fat, and the terrified queen could not drive them away. But as good fortune would have it, the chief maid of honor came in at this moment, and chased away the intruding guests, so that a little of the fat was left. The king's mathematician being summoned, demonstrated very clearly that there was enough, remaining to season all the sausages, if distributed with the nicest judgment and skill.

Drums and trumpets were now heard without, and all the invited potentates and princes, some on white palfreys, some in crystal carriages, came in splendid apparel to the sausage feast. The king received them kindly and graciously, and then, adorned with crown and sceptre, as became the monarch of the land, seated himself at the head of the table. Already in the first course, that of the sausage balls, it was observed that he grew pale and paler; raised his eyes to heaven; gentle sighs escaped from his bosom, and he seemed to undergo great inward suffering. But in the second course, which consisted of the long sausages, he sank back upon his throne, sobbing and moaning, held both hands to his face, and at last wept and groaned aloud. All sprang up from the table, the royal physician tried in vain to feel the pulse of the unhappy monarch, a deep-seated, unknown torture appeared to agitate him. At last, after much anxiety, and after the application of some very strong remedies, the king seemed to come a little to himself, and stammered out scarce audibly the words, "*Too little fat!*"

Then the queen threw herself in despair at his feet, and sobbed out, "Oh, my poor, unhappy, royal husband! Alas, how great must be the suffering which you endure! But see the guilty one at your feet; punish, punish her without mercy. Alas! Lady Mouserings with her seven sons, and aunts and cousins, *have eaten up the fat, and—*" with these words she fell right over backwards in a swoon. Then the king, full of rage, leaped up and cried out, "Chief maid of honor, how happened that?" The chief maid of honor told the story, as much as she knew of it, and the king resolved to take vengeance upon Lady Mouserings and her family for having eaten up the fat of his sausages. The privy council was called, and it was resolved to summon Lady Mouserings to trial, and confiscate all her estates. But as the king was of opinion that in the meanwhile she might eat up more of his sausage fat, the affair was placed at last in the hands of the royal watchmaker and mechanist.

This man (whose name was the same as mine, to wit, Christian Elias Drosselmeier) engaged, by means of a very singular and deep political scheme, to drive Lady Mouserings and her family from the palace forever. He invented therefore several curious little machines, in which a piece of toasted fat was fastened to a thread, and these Drosselmeier placed around lady Mouserings' dwelling. Lady Mouserings was much too wise not to see through Drosselmeier's craft, but all her warnings, all her entreaties were of no avail, every one of her seven sons, and many of her cousins and aunts, went into Drosselmeier's machines, and, as they tried to snap away the fat, were caught by an iron grating, which fell suddenly down behind them, and were afterwards miserably slaughtered in the kitchen. Lady Mouserings, with the little remnant of her family, forsook the dreadful place. Grief, despair, revenge filled her bosom. The court revelled in joy at this event, but the queen was very anxious, for she knew the disposition of Lady Mouserings, and was very sure that she would not suffer the death of her sons to go unavenged. In fact, Lady Mouserings appeared one day, when the queen was in the kitchen, preparing a harslet hash for her royal husband, a dish of which he was very fond, and said, "My sons, my cousins and aunts are destroyed; take care queen, that Mouse-Queen does not bite thy little princess in two—take good care." With this she disappeared, and was not seen again; but the queen was so frightened that she let the hash fall into the fire; and thus a second time Lady Mouserings spoiled a favorite dish for the king, at which he was very angry.

"But this, dear children," said Drosselmeier, "is enough for tonight—the rest at another time."

Maria, who had her own thoughts about this story, begged Godfather Drosselmeier very hard to go on, but she could not prevail upon him. He rose, saying, "Too much at once is bad for the health—the rest tomorrow." As the Counsellor was just stepping out of the room, Fred called out, "Tell me, Godfather Drosselmeier, is it then really true that you invented mousetraps?"

"How can you ask such a silly question?" said his mother, but the Counsellor smiled mysteriously, and said in an under tone, "Am I a skilful watchmaker, and yet not able to invent a mousetrap?"

The Story of the Hard Nut Continued

YOU KNOW NOW, CHILDREN, COMMENCED COUNSELLOR Drosselmeier, on the following evening, why the queen took such care in guarding the beautiful Princess Pirlipat. Was it not to be feared that Lady Mouserings would execute her threat, that she would come again, and bite the little princess to death? Drosselmeier's machines were not the least protection against the wise and prudent Lady Mouserings, but the court astronomer, who was at the same time private stargazer and fortune-teller to his majesty, declared it to be his opinion that the family of Baron Purr would be able to keep Lady Mouserings from the cradle. Most of that name were secretaries of legation at court, with little to do, though always at hand for an embassy to a foreign power, but they must now render themselves useful at home. And thus it came that each of the waiting-women must hold a son of that family upon her lap, and by continual and attentive fondling, lighten the severe public duties which fell to their lot.

Late one night the two chief nurses who sat close by the cradle, started up out of a deep sleep. All around lay in quiet slumber—no purring—the stillness of the grave! Even the death-watch could be heard ticking! And what was the terror of the two chief waiting-women, as they just saw before them a large, dreadful mouse, which stood erect upon its hind feet, and had laid its ugly head close against the face of the princess. With a cry of terror they jumped up; all awoke, but in a moment Lady Mouserings (for the great mouse by Pirlipat's cradle was no one but she) ran as fast as she could to the corner of the chamber. The secretaries of legation leaped after her, but too late—she had disappeared through a hole in the chamber floor.

Little Pirlipat awoke at the noise and wept bitterly. "Thank heaven," cried the nurse, "she lives—she lives!" But how great was their terror, when they looked at Pirlipat, and saw what a change had taken place in the sweet beautiful child. Instead of the white and red face with golden locks, a large, ill-shaped head sat upon her thin shrivelled body, her azure blue eyes were changed into green staring ones, and her little mouth had stretched itself from ear to ear. The queen was brought to death's door by grief and sorrow, and it was found necessary to hang the king's library with thick wadded tapestry, for again and again he ran his head against the wall, crying out at every time in lamentable tones, "Ah, me, unhappy monarch!" He might now have seen how much better it would have been to eat his sausages without fat, and to leave Lady Mouserings and her family at peace under the hearth; but Pirlipat's royal father did not think about this, he laid all the blame upon the court watch-maker and mechanist, Christian Elias Drosselmeier of Nuremburg. He therefore wisely decreed that Drosselmeier should restore the Princess Pirlipat to her former condition within four weeks, or at least find out some certain and infallible method of effecting this, otherwise he should suffer a shameful death under the axe of the executioner.

Drosselmeier was not a little terrified, but he had great confidence in his skill and good fortune, and began immediately the first operation which he thought useful. He took little Princess Pirlipat apart with great dexterity, unscrewed her little hands and feet, and carefully examined her inward structure; but he found, alas, that the princess would grow uglier as she grew bigger, and knew not what to do or what to advise. He put the princess carefully together again, and sank down by her cradle in despair, for he was not allowed to leave it. The fourth, week had commenced—yes, Thursday had come, when the king looked in with flashing eyes, and shaking his sceptre at him, cried, "Christian Elias Drosselmeier, cure the princess, or thou must die." Drosselmeier began to weep bitterly, but the Princess Pirlipat lay as happy as the day, and cracked nuts. Pirlipat's uncommon appetite for nuts now occurred for the first time to the mechanist, and the fact likewise that she had come into the world with teeth.

In truth, immediately after her transformation, she had screamed continually until a nut accidentally came in her way, which she immediately put into her mouth, cracked it, ate the kernel, and then became quite composed. Since that time her nurses found that nothing pleased her so well as to be supplied with nuts. "Oh, sacred instinct of Nature! Eternal, inexplicable sympathy of existence!" cried Christian Elias Drosselmeier. "Thou pointest me to the gates of this mystery. I will knock, and they will open." He begged straightway for permission to speak with the royal astronomer, and was led to his apartment under a strong guard. They embraced with many tears, for they had been warm friends, then retired into a private cabinet, and examined a great many books which treated of instinct, of sympathies, and antipathies, and other mysterious things. Night came on; the astronomer looked at the stars, and with the aid of Drosselmeier, who had great skill in such matters, set up the horoscope of

Princess Pirlipat. It was a great deal of trouble, for the lines grew all the while more and more intricate; but at last—what joy!—At last it became clear, that the Princess Pirlipat, in order to be freed from the magic which had deformed her, and to regain her beauty, had nothing to do but to eat the kernel of the nut Crackatuck.

Now the nut Crackatuck had such a hard shell, that an eight-and-forty pounder might be wheeled over it without breaking it. This hard nut must be cracked with the teeth before the princess, by a man who had never been shaved, and had never worn boots. The young man must then hand her the kernel with closed eyes, and must not open them again until he had marched seven steps backward without stumbling. Drosselmeier and the astronomer had labored together, without cessation, for three days and nights, and the king was seated at dinner on Sunday afternoon, when the mechanist, who was to have been beheaded early Monday morning, rushed in with joy and transport, and proclaimed that he had found out a method of restoring to the Princess Pirlipat her lost beauty. The king embraced him with great kindness, and promised him a diamond sword, four orders of honor, and two new Sunday suits. "Immediately after dinner we will go to work," he added; "and see to it, dear mechanist, that the unshorn young man in shoes is ready at hand with the nut Crackatuck; and take care that he drinks no wine beforehand, for fear he should stumble as he goes the seven steps backward, like a crab; afterward he may drink like a fish." Drosselmeier was very much discomposed at these words; and, after much stuttering and stammering, said, that the method was discovered, indeed, but that the nut Crackatuck and the young man to crack it were yet to be sought after, and that it was quite doubtful whether nut or nutcracker would ever be found.

The king in great anger swung his sceptre about his crowned head, and roared with the voice of a lion, "Then off goes thy head!" It was very fortunate for the unhappy Drosselmeier, that the kind's dinner had been cooked better than usual this day, so that he was in a pleasant humor, and disposed to listen to reason, while the good queen, who was moved by the hard fate of the mechanist, used her influence to soothe him. Drosselmeier then after a while took courage, and represented to the monarch, that he had performed his task in discovering the means to restore the princess to her beauty, and thus by the terms of the royal decree had secured his safety. The king said that was all trash, stupid stuff and nonsense, but resolved at last, that the watchmaker should leave the court instantly, accompanied by the royal astronomer, and never return without the nut Crackatuck in his pocket. By the intercession of the queen, he consented that the nutcracker might be summoned by a notice in all the home and foreign newspapers and journals.

Here the Counsellor broke off again, and promised to narrate the rest on the following evening.

IX

Conclusion of the Story of the Hard Nut

THE NEXT EVENING AS SOON as the candles were lighted, Godfather Drosselmeier appeared, and continued his story as follows:

Drosselmeier and the astronomer had been fifteen years on their journey without seeing the least signs of the nut Crackatuck. It would take me a month, children, to tell where they went, and what strange things happened to them. I must pass them over, and commence where Drosselmeier sank at last into despondency, and felt a great desire to see his dear native city, Nuremburg. This desire came upon him all at once, as he was smoking a pipe of tobacco with his friend in the middle of a great wood in Asia. "Oh, sweet city," he cried, "sweet native city, sweet Nuremberg! He who has never seen thee, though he may have travelled to London, Paris, Rome, if his heart is not dead to emotion, must continually desire to visit thee—thee, oh Nuremberg, sweet city, where there are so many beautiful houses with windows!" As Drosselmeier grieved in such a sorrowful manner, the astronomer was moved with sympathy, and began to cry and howl so pitifully that it was heard far and wide through. Asia. He soon composed himself again, wiped the tears out of his eyes, and said: "But why, my respected colleague, why sit here and howl? Why should we not go to Nuremberg? Is it not all the same, wherever we seek after this miserable nut, Crackatuck?"

"That is true," replied Drosselmeier, greatly consoled. Both arose, knocked out their pipes, and went straightforward out of the wood in the middle of Asia, right to Nuremburg. They had scarcely arrived there, when Drosselmeier ran to his brother, Christopher Zacharias Drosselmeier, puppetmaker, varnisher, and gilder, whom he had not seen for these many years. The watchmaker told him the whole story of the Princess Pirlipat, Lady Mouserings, and the nut Crackatuck, so that he struck his hands together, over and over again with astonishment, and exclaimed: "Ei, ei, brother, brother, what strange things are these!" Drosselmeier then related the history of his travels: how he had passed two years with King Date, how coldly he had been received by Prince Almond, and how he had sought information to no purpose of the Natural Society in Squirrelberg—in short, how his search everywhere had been in vain to find even the least signs of the nut Crackatuck.

During this account, Christopher Zacharias had often snapped his fingers, turned about on one foot, winked, laughed, clucked with his tongue, and then called out: "Hi—hem—ei—oh!—If it should!—" At last, he tossed his hat and wig up in the air, clasped his brother round the neck, and cried: "Brother, brother, you are safe!—Safe, I say; for I must be wonderfully mistaken if I have not that nut Crackatuck at this very moment in my possession!" He then drew a little box from his pocket, and took out of it a gilded nut of moderate size. "See," he said, "this nut fell into my hands in this way. Many years ago, a stranger came here at Christmas time with, a sack full of nuts, which, he offered for sale cheap. Just as he passed my shop, he got into a quarrel with a nut-seller of this city, who did not like to see a stranger come hither to undersell him, and for this reason attacked him. The man put down his sack upon the ground, the better to defend himself, and at the same moment, a heavily-laden wagon passed directly over it; all the nuts were cracked in pieces except this one, which the stranger, with a singular smile, offered me, for a bright dollar of the year 1720. I thought that strange, but as I found in my pocket just such a dollar as the man wanted, I bought the nut, and gilded it over, without exactly knowing why I bought the nut so dear, or why I set so much store by it.

All doubt, whether this nut was actually the long-sought nut, Crackatuck, was instantly removed, when the astronomer was called, who carefully scraped off the gold, and found upon the rind the word Crackatuck, engraved in Chinese characters. The joy of the travellers was beyond bounds, and the brother the happiest man under the sun, for Drosselmeier assured him that his fortune was made, since he would have a considerable pension for the rest of his days, and then there was the gold which had been scraped off—he might keep that for gilding. The mechanist and the astronomer had both put on their night-caps, and were getting into bed as the latter commenced: "My worthy colleague, good fortune never comes single. Take my word for it, we have found, not only the nut Crackatuck, but also the young man who is to crack it, and hand the kernel to the princess. I mean nobody else than your brother's son. I cannot sleep; no, this very night I must cast the youth's horoscope." With these words, he threw the night-cap off his head, and began straightway to take an observation.

The brother's son was in truth a handsome, well grown young man, who had never been shaved, and who had never worn boots. In his early youth he had on Christmas nights gone around as a Merry Andrew, but this could not be seen in his behavior in the least, so well had his manners been formed by his fathers care. On Christmas days he wore a handsome red coat trimmed with gold, a sword, a hat under his arm, and a curling wig. In this fine dress he would stand in his father's shop, and out of gallantry crack nuts for the young girls, for which reason he was called the handsome Nutcracker.

On the following morning the astronomer was in raptures: he fell upon the mechanist's neck, and cried, "It is he—we have him—he is found! But there are two things, worthy colleague, which we must see to. In the first place, we must braid for your excellent nephew a stout wooden queue, which shall be joined in such a way to his lower jaw, that it can move it with great force. In the next place, when we arrive at the king's palace, we must let no one know that we have brought the young man with us who is to crack the nut Crackatuck. It is best that he should not be found for a long time. I read in his horoscope, that after many young men have broken their teeth to no purpose, the king will promise to him who cracks the nut, and restores to the princess her lost beauty, the princess herself, and the succession to the throne as a reward."

His brother, the puppetmaker, was highly delighted to think that his son might marry the Princess Pirlipat, and become a prince and king, and he gave him up entirely into the hands of the two travellers. The queue which Drosselmeier fastened upon his young and hopeful nephew, answered admirably, so that he made a series of the most successful experiments, even upon the hardest peach stones. As Drosselmeier and the astronomer had sent immediate information to the palace, of the discovery of the nut Crackatuck, suitable notices had been published, and when the travellers arrived, many handsome young men, and among them some handsome princes, had appeared, who trusting to their sound teeth, were ready to undertake the disenchantment of the princess. The travellers were not a little terrified when they beheld the princess again. Her little body, with its tiny hands and feet, was hardly able to carry her great misshapen head, and the ugliness of her face was increased by a white cotton beard, which had spread itself around her mouth, and over her chin. All happened as the astronomer had read in the horoscope. One youth in shoes after another, bit upon the nut Crackatuck until his teeth and jaws were sore, and as he was led away, half swooning, by the physician in attendance, sighed out, "That was a hard nut."

When the king, in the anguish of his heart, had promised his daughter and his kingdom to him who should effect the disenchantment, the handsome young Drosselmeier stepped forward, and begged for permission to begin the experiment. And no one had pleased the fancy of Princess Pirlipat as well as young Drosselmeier; she laid her little hand upon her heart, and sighed deeply, "Ah, if this might be the one who is to crack the nut Crackatuck, and become my husband!" After young Drosselmeier had gracefully saluted the king and queen, and then the Princess Pirlipat, he received the nut Crackatuck from the hands of the master of ceremonies, put it without hesitation between his teeth, pulled his queue very hard, and crack—crack—the shell broke into many pieces. He then nicely removed the little threads and broken bits of shell that hung to the kernel, and reached it with a low bow to the princess, after which he shut his eyes, and began to walk backwards. The princess straightway swallowed the kernel, and behold! Her ugly shape was gone, and in its place appeared a most beautiful figure, with a face of roses and lilies, delicate white and red, eyes of living, sparkling azure, and locks curling in bright golden ringlets.

Drums and trumpets mingled their sounds with the loud rejoicings of the people. The king and his whole court danced, as at Pirlipat's birth, upon one leg; and the queen had to be carefully tended with Cologne water, because she had fallen into a swoon from delight and rapture. Young Drosselmeier, who had still his seven steps to perform, was a good deal discomposed by the tumult, but he kept firm, and was just stretching back his right foot for the seventh step, when Lady Mouserings rose squeaking and squealing out of the floor; down came his foot upon her head, and he stumbled, so that he hardly kept himself from falling. Alas! What a hard fate! As quick as thought, the youth was changed to the former figure of the princess. His body became shrivelled up, and was hardly able to support his great misshapen head, his eyes turned green and staring, and his mouth was stretched from ear to ear. Instead of his queue, a narrow wooden cloak hung down upon his back, with which he moved his lower jaw.

The watchmaker and astronomer were benumbed with terror and affright, while Lady Mouserings rolled bleeding and kicking upon the floor. Her malice did not go unpunished, for young Drosselmeier had trodden upon her neck so heavily with the sharp heel of his shoe that she could not survive. When Lady Mouserings lay in her last agonies, she squeaked and whimpered in a piteous tone: "Oh, Crackatuck! Hard nut—hi, hi!—Of thee I now must die!—Que, que—son with seven crowns will bite—Nutcracker—at night—hi, hi—que, que—and revenge his mother's death—short breath—must I—hi, hi—die, die—so young—que, que—oh, agony!—Queek!" With this cry, Lady Mouserings died, and the royal oven-heater carried out her body. As for young Drosselmeier, no one troubled himself any farther about him, but the princess put the king in mind of his promise, and he commanded that they should bring the young hero before him. But when the unfortunate youth approached, the princess held both hands before her face, and cried, "Away, away with the ugly Nutcracker!" The court marshal immediately took him by the shoulders, and pushed him out of doors. The king was full of anger, because they had wished to give him a Nutcracker for a son-in-law, and he put all the blame upon the mechanist and astronomer, and banished them forever from the kingdom. This did not stand in the horoscope which the astronomer had set up at Nuremberg, but he did not allow himself to be discouraged. He straightway took another observation, and declared that he could read in the stars, that young Drosselmeier would conduct himself so well in his new station, that in spite of his deformity, he would yet become a prince and a king; and that his former beauty would return, as soon as the son of Lady Mouserings, who had been born with seven heads, after the death of her seven sons, had fallen by his hand, and a maiden had loved him, notwithstanding his ugly shape. And they say that young Drosselmeier has actually been seen about Christmas time in his father's shop at Nuremberg, as a Nutcracker, it is true, but, at the same time, as a prince.

This, children, is the story of the Hard Nut; and you know now why people say so often, "That was a hard nut!" and whence it comes that Nutcrackers are so ugly.

The Counsellor thus concluded his narration. Maria thought that the Princess Pirlipat was an ill-natured, ungrateful thing; and Fred declared, that if Nutcracker were any thing of a man, he would not be long in settling matters with the Mouse-King, and would get his old shape again very soon.

X

The Uncle and the Nephew

I F ANY ONE OF MY GOOD readers has ever had the misfortune to cut himself with glass, he knows how it hurts, and how long a time it takes to heal. Whenever Maria tried to get up, she felt very dizzy, and so it continued for a whole week, during which time she was obliged to remain in bed; but at last she became entirely well, and could play about the chamber as merrily as ever. Every thing in the glass case looked prettily, for the trees, flowers, and houses, and beautiful puppets, stood there as new and bright as ever. But, best of all, Maria found her dear Nutcracker again. He stood on the second shelf, and smiled upon her with a good, sound set of teeth. In the midst of all the pleasure which she felt in gazing at her favorite, a pang went through her heart, when she thought that Godfather Drosselmeier's story had been nothing else but the history of the Nutcracker, and of his quarrel with Lady Mouserings and her son. She knew well enough that her Nutcracker could be none other than the young Drosselmeier of Nuremberg—Godfather Drosselmeier's agreeable, but now, alas! Enchanted, nephew. For, that the skilful watchmaker at the court of Pirlipat's father was the Counsellor Drosselmeier himself, she did not doubt for an instant, even while he was telling the story.

"But why was it that your uncle did not help you?—Why did he not help you?" complained Maria, as it became clearer and clearer to her mind, that in that battle which she saw, Nutcracker's crown and kingdom were at stake. "Were not all the other puppets subject to him, and is it not plain that the prophecy of the astronomer has been fulfilled, and that young Drosselmeier is prince and king of the puppets?" While the shrewd Maria explained and arranged all this so well in her mind, she believed, since she had seen Nutcracker and his vassals in life and motion, that they actually did live and move. But that was not so; every thing in the glass case remained stiff and lifeless; yet Maria, far from giving up her conviction, cast all the blame upon the magic of Lady Mouserings and her seven-headed son. "But, if you are not able to move, or to talk to me, dear Master Drosselmeier," she said aloud to the Nutcracker, "yet I know well enough that you understand me, and know what a good friend I am to you. You may depend upon my help, and I will beg of your uncle to bring his skill to your assistance, whenever you have need of it." Nutcracker remained still and motionless, but it seemed to Maria as if a gentle sigh was breathed in the glass case, so that the panes trembled, scarce audibly indeed, but with a strange, sweet tone; and a voice rang out, like a little bell: "Maria mine—I'll be thine—and thou mine—Maria mine!" Maria felt, in the cold shuddering that crept over her, a singular pleasure.

Twilight had come on; the doctor, with Godfather Drosselmeier, entered the sitting room; and it was not long before Louise had arranged the tea table, and all sat around, talking cheerfully of various things. Maria had very quietly taken her little arm-chair, and seated herself close at Godfather Drosselmeier's feet. During a moment when they were all silent, she looked up with her large blue eyes in the Counsellor's face, and said: "I know, dear Godfather Drosselmeier, that my Nutcracker is your nephew, the young Drosselmeier, of Nuremberg, and he has become a prince, or king rather, as your companion, the astronomer, foretold. All has turned out exactly so. You know now that he is at war with the son of Lady Mouserings—with the hateful Mouse-King. Why do you not help him?" Maria then related the whole course of the battle, just as she had seen it, and was often interrupted by the loud laughter of her mother and Louise. Fred and Drosselmeier only remained serious. "Where does the child get all this strange stuff in her head?" said the doctor.

"She has a lively imagination," replied the mother; "in fact, they are nothing but dreams caused by her violent fever."

"That story is not true," said Fred. "My red hussars are not such cowards as that. If I thought so—swords and daggers!—I would make a stir among them!"

But Godfather Drosselmeier, with a strange smile, took little Maria upon his lap, and said in a softer tone than he was ever heard to speak in before: "Ah, dear Maria, more power is given to thee than to me, or to the rest of us. Thou, like Pirlipat, art a princess born, for thou dost reign in a bright and beautiful kingdom. But thou hast much to suffer, if thou wouldst take the part of the poor misshapen Nutcracker, for the Mouse-King watches for him at every hole and corner. I cannot, thou—thou alone canst rescue him; be firm and true." Neither Maria nor any one else knew what Drosselmeier meant by these words; and they appeared so singular to Doctor Stahlbaum, that he felt the Counsellor's pulse, and said: "Worthy friend, you have some violent congestion about the head; I will prescribe something for you." But the mother shook her head thoughtfully, and spoke: "I feel what it is that the Counsellor means, but I cannot express it in words."

XI

THE VICTORY

NOT LONG AFTER, MARIA WAS awaked one moonlight night by a strange rattling, that seemed to come out of a corner of the chamber. It sounded as if little stones were thrown and rolled about; and every now and then there was a terrible squeaking and squealing. "Ah! The mice—the mice are coming again!" exclaimed Maria, in affright; and she was about to wake her mother, but her voice failed her, and she could stir neither hand nor foot, for she saw the Mouse-King work his way out of a hole in the wall, then run, with sparkling eyes and crowns, around and around the chamber, when, at last, with a desperate leap, he sprang upon the little table that stood close by her bed. "Hi—hi—hi—must give me thy sugar plums—thy gingerbread—little thing—or I will bite thy Nutcracker—thy Nutcracker!" So squeaked the Mouse-King, and snapped and grated hideously with his teeth, then sprang down again, and away through the hole in the wall. Maria was so distressed by this occurrence that she looked very pale in the morning, and was scarcely able to say a word. A hundred times she was going to inform her mother or Louise of what had happened, or at least to tell Fred, but she thought: "No one will believe me, and I shall only be laughed at." This, at least, was very clear, that if she wished to save little Nutcracker, she must give up her sugar plums and her gingerbread. So, in the evening, she laid all that she had—and she had a great deal—down before the foot of the glass case.

The next morning:, her mother said: "It is strange what brings the mice all at once into the sitting room. See, poor Maria, they have eaten up all your gingerbread." And so it was. The ravenous Mouse-King had not found the sugar plums exactly to his taste, but he had gnawed them with his sharp teeth, so that they had to be thrown away. Maria did not grieve about her cake and sugar plums, for she was greatly delighted to think that she had saved little Nutcracker. But what was her terror, when the very next night she heard a squeaking and squealing close to her ear! Ah, the Mouse-King was there again, and his eyes sparkled more dreadfully, and he whistled and squeaked much louder than before: "Must give me thy sugar puppets—chocolate figures—little thing—or I will bite thy Nutcracker—thy Nutcracker!" And with this, the terrible Mouse-King sprang down, and ran away again. Maria was very sad; she went the next morning to the glass case, and gazed with the most sorrowful looks at her sugar and chocolate figures, And her grief was reasonable, for thou canst not imagine, my attentive reader, what beautiful figures of sugar and chocolate little Maria Stahlbaum possessed. A pretty shepherd and shepherdess watched a whole flock of milk-white lambs, while a little dog frisked about them; next came two letter carriers, with letters in their hands; and then four neat pairs of nicely-dressed boys and girls, with gay ribbons, rocked at see-saw upon as many boards, white and smooth as marble. Behind some dancers, stood Farmer Caraway and the Maid of Orleans—these Maria did not care so much about; but close in a corner stood her darling, a little red-cheeked baby, and now the tears came into her eyes.

"Ah, dear Master Drosselmeier," she said, turning to Nutcracker, "there is nothing that I will not do to save you, but this is very hard!" Nutcracker looked all the while so sorrowfully, that Maria, who felt as if she saw the Mouse-King open his seven mouths, to devour the unhappy youth, resolved to sacrifice them all. So at evening, she placed all her sugar figures down at the foot of the glass case, just as she had done before with her sugar plums and cake. She kissed the shepherd, and the shepherdess, and the lambs, and at last took her darling, the little red-cheeked baby out of the corner, and placed it down behind all the rest; Farmer Caraway and the Maid of Orleans must stand in the first row.

"Well, that is too bad!" said her mother, the next morning. "A mouse must have got into the glass case, for all poor Maria's sugar figures are gnawed and bitten in pieces." Maria could not keep from shedding tears, but she soon smiled again, and said to herself: "That is nothing, if Nutcracker is only saved." In the evening, her mother told the Counsellor of the mischief which, the mouse had been doing in the glass case, and said: "It is provoking that we cannot destroy this fellow that makes such havoc with Maria's sugar toys."

"Ha!" cried Fred, merrily. "The baker opposite has a fine, gray secretary of legation; suppose I bring him over? He will soon make an end of the thing; he will have the mouse's head off, very quickly, even if it be Lady Mouserings herself, or her son, the Mouse-King."

"And jump about the tables and chairs," said his mother, laughing, "and throw down cups and saucers, and do all kinds of mischief."

"Ah, no indeed," said Fred; "the baker's secretary of legation is a light, careful fellow. I wish I could walk on the roof of a house as well as he!"

"Let us have no cats in the night," said Louise, who could not bear them.

"Fred's plan is the best," said the doctor, but we will try a trap first. Have we got one?"

"Godfather Drosselmeier can make them best," said Fred, "for he invented them."

All laughed; and, when the mother said that there was no mousetrap in the house, the Counsellor assured her that he had a number in his possession, and immediately sent for one. In a short time it was brought, and a very excellent mousetrap it seemed to be. The story of the Hard Nut now came vividly to the minds of the children. As the cook toasted the fat, Maria shook and trembled. Her head was full of the story and its wonders, and she said to her old friend Dora: "Ah, great Queen, take care of Lady Mouserings and her family!" But Fred had drawn his sword, and cried: "Let them come on!—Let them come on! I will scatter them!" But all remained still and quiet under the hearth. As the Counsellor tied the fat to a fine piece of thread, and set the trap softly, softly down by the glass case, Fred cried out: "Take care, Godfather Mechanist, or Mouse-King will play you a trick!"

Ah, but what a night did Maria pass! Something cold as ice tapped here and there against her arm; and crept, rough and hideous, upon her cheek, and squeaked and squealed in her ear. The hateful Mouse-King sat upon her shoulder. He opened his seven blood-red mouths, and, grating and snapping his teeth, he squeaked and hissed in her ear: "Wise mouse—wise mouse—goes not into the house—goes not to the feast—likes sugar things best—craft set at naught—will not be caught—give, give all—new frock—picture books—all the best—or shall have no rest.—I will tear and bite—Nutcracker at night—hi, hi—que, que!" Maria was full of sorrow and anxiety. She looked very pale and disturbed on the following morning, when Fred told her that the mouse had not been caught, so that her mother thought that she was grieving for her sugar things, or perhaps was afraid of the mouse. "Do not grieve, dear child," she said; "we will soon get rid of him. If the trap does not answer, Fred shall bring his gray secretary of legation."

As soon as Maria was alone in the sitting room, she stepped to the glass case, and said, sobbing, to Nutcracker: "Ah, my dear, good Mr. Drosselmeier, what can I—poor, unhappy maiden—do? For, if I should give up all my picture books, and even my new, beautiful frock, to the hateful mouse, he will ask more and more. And, when I have nothing left to give him, he will at last want me, instead of you, to bite in pieces."

As little Maria grieved and sorrowed in this way, she observed a large spot of blood on Nutcracker's neck, which had been there ever since the battle. Now, after Maria had known that her Nutcracker was young Drosselmeier, the Counsellor's nephew, she did not carry him anymore in her arms, nor hug and kiss him, as she used to do; indeed, she would very seldom move or touch him; but when she saw the spot of blood, she took him carefully from the shelf, and commenced rubbing it with her pocket-handkerchief. But what was her astonishment, when she felt that he suddenly grew warm in her hand, and began to move! She put him quickly back upon the shelf again, when—behold!—His little mouth began to work and twist, and move up and down, and at last, with a great deal of labor, he lisped out: "Ah, dearest, best Miss Stahlbaum—excellent friend, how shall I thank you? No! No picture books, no Christmas frock!—Get me a sword—a sword. For the rest, I—" Here speech left him, and his eyes, which had begun to express the deepest sympathy, became staring and motionless.

Maria did not feel the least terror; on the contrary, she leaped for joy, for she had now found a way to rescue Nutcracker without any more painful sacrifices. But where should she obtain a sword for him? Maria at last resolved to ask advice of Fred; and in the evening, when their parents had gone out, and they sat alone together in the chamber by the glass case, she told him all that had happened to Nutcracker and Mouse-King, and then begged him to furnish the little fellow with a sword. Upon no part of this narration did Fred reflect so long and so earnestly as upon the poor account which she gave him of the bravery of his hussars. He asked once more very seriously, if it were so. Maria assured him of it upon her word, when Fred ran quickly to the glass case, addressed his hussars in a very moving speech, and then, as a punishment for their cowardice, cut their military badges from their caps, and forbade them for a year to play the Hussar's Grand March. After this, he turned again to Maria, and said: "As to a sword, I can easily supply the little fellow with one. I yesterday permitted an old colonel of the cuirassiers to retire upon a pension, and consequently he has no farther use for his fine sharp sabre." The aforesaid colonel was living on the pension which Fred had allowed him, in the farthest corner of the third shelf. He was brought out, his fine silver sabre taken from him, and buckled about Nutcracker.

Maria could scarcely get to sleep that night, she was so anxious and fearful. About midnight, it seemed to her as if she heard a strange rustling, and rattling, and slashing, in the sitting room. All at once, it went "Queek!" "The Mouse-King!—The Mouse-King!" cried Maria, and sprang in her fright out of bed. All was still; but presently she heard a gentle knocking at the door, and a soft voice was heard: "Worthiest, best, kindest Miss Stahlbaum, open the door without fear—good tidings!" Maria knew the voice of the young Drosselmeier, so she threw her frock about her, and opened the door. Little Nutcracker stood without, with a bloody sword in his right hand, and a wax taper in his left. As soon as he saw Maria, he bent down on one knee, and said: "You, oh lady—you alone it was, that filled me with knightly courage, and gave this arm strength to contend with the presumptuous foe who dared to disturb your slumber. The treacherous Mouse-King is overcome; he lies bathed in his blood. Scorn not to receive the tokens of victory from a knight who will remain devoted to your service until death." With these words, Nutcracker took off the seven crowns of the Mouse-King, which he had hung upon his left arm, and reached them to Maria, who received them with great joy. Nutcracker then arose, and said: "Best, kindest Miss Stahlbaum, you know not what beautiful things I could show you at this moment while my enemy lies vanquished, if you would have the condescension to follow me for a few steps. Oh, will you not be so kind? Will you not be so good, best, kindest Miss Stahlbaum?"

XII

The Puppet Kingdom

I BELIEVE THAT NONE OF YOU, children, would have hesitated for an instant to follow the good, honest Nutcracker, who could never have meditated any evil. Maria consented to follow him, so much the more readily, because she knew what claims she had upon his gratitude, and because she was convinced that he would keep his word, and show her many beautiful things. "I will go with you, Master Drosselmeier," she said; "but it must not be far, and it must not be long, for as yet I have hardly had any sleep."

"I will choose, then," replied Nutcracker, the nearest, though a more difficult way." He went onward, and Maria followed him, until he stopped before a large, antique wardrobe, which stood in the hall. Maria perceived, to her astonishment, that the doors of this wardrobe, which were always kept locked, now stood wide open, so that she could see her father's fox-furred travelling coat, which hung in front. Nutcracker clambered very nimbly up by the carved figures and ornaments, until he could grasp the large tassel which hung down the back of the coat, and was fastened to it by a thick cord. As soon as Nutcracker pulled upon the tassel, a neat little stairs of cedar wood stretched down from the sleeve of the travelling-coat to the floor. "Ascend, if you please, dearest Miss," cried Nutcracker. Maria did so; but scarcely had she gone up the sleeve—scarcely had she seen her way out at the collar, when a dazzling light broke forth upon her, and all at once she stood upon a sweet-smelling meadow, surrounded by millions of sparks, which darted up like flashing jewels. "We are now upon Candy Meadow," said Nutcracker; "but we will directly pass through, yonder gate." When Maria looked up, she saw the beautiful gate, which stood a few steps before them upon the meadow. It seemed built of variegated marble, of white, brown, and raisin color; but when Maria came nearer, she perceived that the whole mass consisted of sugar, almonds and raisins, kneaded and baked together, for which reason the gate, as Nutcracker assured her when they passed through it, was called the Almond and Raisin Gate. Upon a gallery built over the gate, made apparently of barley sugar, there were six apes, in red jackets, who struck up the finest Turkish music which was ever heard, so that Maria scarcely observed that they were walking onward and onward, over a rich mosaic, which was nothing else than a pavement of nicely-inlaid lozenges. Very soon the sweetest odors streamed around them, which were wafted from a wonderful little wood, that opened on each side before them. There it shone and sparkled so, among the dark leaves, that the golden and silvery fruit could plainly be seen hanging from their gayly-colored stems, while the trunks and branches were ornamented with ribbons and nosegays; and when the orange perfume stirred and moved like a soft breeze, how it rustled anions the boughs and leaves, and the golden fruit rocked and rattled in merry music, to which the bright, dancing sparkles kept time! "Ah, how delightful it is here!" cried Maria, entranced in happiness.

"We are in Christmas Wood, best miss," said Nutcracker.

"Ah, if I could but linger here a while," cried Maria. "Oh, it is too, too charming!"

Nutcracker clapped his hands, and some little shepherds and shepherdesses, and hunters and huntresses came near, who were so delicate and white, that they seemed made of pure sugar. They brought a dainty little armchair, all of gold, laid upon it a green cushion of candied citron, and invited Maria very politely to sit down. She did so, and immediately the shepherds and shepherdesses danced a very pretty ballet, while the hunters very obligingly blew their horns, and then all disappeared again in the bushes. "Pardon, pardon, kindest Miss Stahlbaum," said Nutcracker, "the dance was miserably performed, but the people all belong to our company of wire dancers, and they can do nothing but the same, same thing; they are deficient in variety. And the hunters blew so dull and lazily—but shall we not walk a little farther?"

"Ah, it was all very pretty, and pleased me very much," said Maria, as she rose, and followed Nutcracker.

They now walked along by a soft, rustling brook, out of which all the sweet perfumes seemed to arise which filled the whole wood. "This is the Orange Brook," said Nutcracker, "but its fine perfume excepted, it cannot compare either in size or beauty with Lemonade River, which like it empties into Orgeat Lake." In fact Maria very soon heard a louder rustling and dashing, and then beheld the broad Lemonade River, which rolled in proud cream-colored billows, between banks covered with bright green bushes. A refreshing coolness arose out of its noble waves.

Not far off, a dark yellow stream dragged itself lazily along, but it gave forth a very sweet odor, and a great number of little children sat on the shore angling for little fish, which they ate up as soon as caught. When Maria came nearer she observed that these fish were shaped almost like peanuts.

At a distance there was a very neat little village, on the borders of this stream; houses, churches, parsonages, barns, were all dark brown, but many of the roofs were gilded, and some of the walls were painted so strangely, that it seemed as if little sugar plums and bits of citron were stuck upon them. "That is Gingerbreadville," said Nutcracker, "which lies on Molasses River. Very pretty people live in it, but they are a little ill-tempered, because they suffer a good deal from the toothache, and so we will not visit it."

At this moment Maria observed a little town in which the houses were clear and transparent, and of different colors, which was a very pretty sight to look at. Nutcracker went straight forward towards it, and now Maria heard a busy, merry clatter, and saw a thousand tiny little figures, collected around some heavily laden wagons, which had stopped in the market. These they unloaded, and what they took out looked like sheets of colored paper and chocolate cakes. "We are now in Bonbon Town," said Nutcracker. "An importation has just arrived from Paper Land, and from King Chocolate. The poor people of Bonbon Town are often terribly threatened by the armies of Generals Fly and Gnat, for which reason they fortify their houses with stout materials from Paper Land, and throw up fortifications of the strong bulwarks, which King Chocolate sends to them. But, worthiest Miss Stahlbaum, we will not visit all the little towns and villages of this land. To the capital—to the capital!"

Nutcracker hastened forward, and Maria followed full of curiosity. It was not long before a sweet odor of roses enveloped them, and every thing around was touched with a soft rose-colored tint. Maria soon observed that this was the reflection of the red glancing lake, which rustled and danced before them, with charming and melodious tones in little rosy waves. Beautiful silver-white swans with golden collars, swam over the lake singing sweet tunes, while little diamond fish dipped up and down in the rosy water, as if in the merriest dance. "Ah," exclaimed Maria, ardently, this is then the lake which Godfather Drosselmeier was once going to make for me, and I myself am the maiden, who is to fondle and caress the dear swans."

Nutcracker laughed in a scornful manner, such as Maria had never observed in him before, and then said: "Godfather Drosselmeier can never make any thing like this. You—you yourself, rather, sweetest Miss Stahlbaum—but we will not trouble our heads about that. Let us sail across the Rose Lake to the capital."

XIII

The Capital

NUTCRACKER CLAPPED HIS LITTLE HANDS together again, when the Rose Lake began to dash louder, the waves rolled higher, and Maria perceived a car of shells, covered with bright, sparkling, gay-colored jewels, moving toward them in the distance, drawn by two golden-scaled dolphins. Twelve of the loveliest little Moors, with caps and aprons braided of humming-bird's feathers, leaped upon the shore, and carried, first Maria, and then Nutcracker, with a soft, gliding step, over the waves, and placed them in the car, which straightway began to move across the lake. Ah, how delightful it was as Maria sailed along, with the rosy air and the rosy waves breathing and dashing around her! The two golden-scaled dolphins raised up their heads, and spouted clear, crystal streams out of their nostrils, high, high in the air, which fell down again in a thousand quivering, flashing rainbows, and it seemed as if two small silver voices sang out: "Who sails upon the rosy lake? The little fairy—awake, awake! Music and song—bim-bim, fishes—sim-sim, swans—tweet-tweet, birds—whiz-whiz, breezes!—Rustling, ringing, singing, blowing!—A fairy o'er the waves is going! Rosy billows, murmuring, playing, dashing, cooling the air!—Roll along, along."

But the singing of the falling fountains did not seem to please the twelve little Moors, who were seated up behind the car, for they shook their parasols so hard that the palm leaves of which they were made rattled and clattered, and they stamped with their feet in very strange time, and sang, "Klapp and klipp, and klipp and klapp, backward and forward, up and down!" "Moors are a merry folk," said Nutcracker, somewhat disturbed, "but they will make the whole lake rebellious." And very soon there arose a confused din of strange voices, which seemed to float in the sea and in the air; but Maria did not heed them, for she was gazing in the sweet-scented, rosy waves, out of which the face of a charming little maiden smiled up upon her. "Ah!" she cried joyfully, and struck her hands together. "Look, look, dear Master Drosselmeier! There is the Princess Pirlipat down in the water! Oh, how sweetly she smiles upon me!"

Nutcracker sighed quite sorrowfully, and said: "Oh, kindest Miss Stahlbaum, that is not the Princess Pirlipat—it is you, you—it is your own lovely face that smiles so sweetly out of the Rose Lake." Upon this, Maria drew her head back very quickly, put her hands before her face, and blushed very much. At this moment, she was lifted out of the car by the twelve Moors, and carried to the shore. They now found themselves in a little thicket, which was perhaps more beautiful even than the Christmas Wood, it was so bright and sparkling. What was most wonderful in it were the strange fruits that hung upon the trees, which were not only curiously colored, but gave out also every kind of sweet odor. "We are in Sweetmeat Grove," said Nutcracker, "but yonder is the Capital."

And what a sight! How can I venture, children, to describe the beauty and splendor of the city which now displayed itself to Maria's eyes, upon the broad, flowery meadow before them? Not only did the walls and towers glitter with the gayest colors, but the style of the buildings was like nothing else that is to be found in the world. Instead of roofs, the houses had diadems set upon them, braided and twisted in the daintiest manner; and the towers were crowned with variegated trellis-work, and hung with festoons the most beautiful that ever were seen. As they passed through the gate, which looked as if it were built of macaroons and candied fruits, silver soldiers presented arms, and a little man in a brocade dressing-gown threw himself upon Nutcracker's neck, with the words: "Welcome, best prince! Welcome to Confectionville!"

Maria was not a little astonished to hear young Drosselmeier called a prince by such a distinguished man. But she now heard such a hubbub of little voices, such a huzzaing and laughter, such a singing and playing, that she could think of nothing else, and turned to Nutcracker to ask him what it all meant. "Oh, worthiest Miss Stahlbaum, it is nothing uncommon. Confectionville is a populous and merry city; thus it goes here every day. Let us walk farther, if you please."

They had only gone a few steps, when they came to the great market-place, which presented a wonderful sight. All the houses around were of sugared filigree work; gallery was built over gallery, and in the middle stood a tall obelisk of white and red sugared cream, while four curious, sweet fountains played in the air, of orgeat, lemonade, mead, and soda-water, and in the great basin were soft bruised fruits, mixed with sugar and cream, and touched a little by the frost.

But prettier than all this were the charming little people, who, by thousands, pushed and squeezed, knocked their heads together, huzzaed, laughed, jested, and sang—who had raised indeed that merry din which Maria had heard at a distance. Here were beautifully-dressed men and women, Armenians and Greeks, Jews and Tyrolese, officers and soldiers, preachers, shepherds, and harlequins—in short, all the people that can possibly be found in the world. On one corner the tumult increased; the people rocked and reeled to clear the way, for just at that moment the Grand Mogul was carried by in a palanquin, attended by ninety-three grandees of the kingdom, and seven hundred slaves. Now, on the opposite corner, the fishermen, five hundred strong, were marching in procession; and it happened, very unfortunately, that the Grand Turk took it into his head just then to ride over the marketplace with three thousand Janissaries, besides which a loner train came from the Festival of Sacrifices, with sounding music, singing: "Up, and thank the mighty sun!" and pushed straight on for the obelisk. Then what a squeezing, and a pushing, and a rattling, and a clattering. By and by, a screaming was heard, for a fisherman had knocked off a Brahmin's head in the crowd, and the Great Mogul was almost run over by a Harlequin. The tumult grew wilder and wilder, and they had commenced to beat and strike each other, when the man in the brocade dressing gown, who had called Nutcracker a prince at the gate, clambered up by the obelisk, and having thrice pulled a little bell, called out three times: "Confiseur! Confiseur! Confiseur!"

The tumult was immediately appeased; each one tried to help himself as well as he could; and, after the confused trains and processions were set in order, and the dirt upon the Great Mogul's clothes was brushed off, and the Brahmin's head put on again, the former hubbub began anew. "What do they mean by 'Confiseur,' good Master Drosselmeier?" asked Maria.

"Ah, best Miss Stahlbaum," replied Nutcracker, "by 'Confiseur' is meant an unknown but very fearful power, which they believe can do with them as he pleases; it is the Fate that rules over this merry little people, and they fear it so much, that the mere mention of the name is able to still the greatest tumult. Each one then thinks no longer of any thing earthly—of cuffs, and kicks, and broken heads, but retires within himself, and says: 'What are we, and what is our destiny?'"

Maria could not refrain from a loud exclamation of surprise and wonder, as all at once they stood before a castle glimmering with rosy light, and crowned with a hundred airy towers. Beautiful nosegays of violets, narcissuses, tulips, and dahlias, were hung about the walls, and their dark, glowing colors only heightened the dazzling, rose-tinted, white ground upon which they were fastened. The large cupola of the centre building and the sloping roofs of the towers were spangled with a thousand gold and silver stars. "We are now in front of Marchpane Castle," said

Nutcracker. Maria was completely lost in admiration of this magic palace, yet it did not escape her that one of the large towers was without a roof, while little men were moving around it upon a scaffolding of cinnamon, as if busied in repairing it. But before she had time to inquire about it, Nutcracker continued: "Not long ago, this beautiful castle was threatened with serious injury, if not with entire destruction. The Giant Sweet-tooth came this way, and bit off the roof of yonder tower, and was gnawing upon the great cupola, when the people of Confectionville gave up to him a full quarter of the city, and a considerable portion of Sweetmeat Grove, as tribute, with which he contented himself, and went his way."

At this moment soft music was heard, the doors of the palace opened, and twelve little pages marched out with lighted cloves, which they carried in their hands like torches. Each of their heads was a pearl; their bodies were made of rubies and emeralds; and they walked upon feet cast out of pure gold. Four ladies followed them, almost as tall as Maria's Clara, but so richly and splendidly dressed, that she saw in a moment that they were princesses born. They embraced Nutcracker in the tenderest manner, and cried with joyful sobs: "Oh, my prince, my best prince! Oh, my brother!"

Nutcracker seemed very much moved; he wiped the tears out of his eyes; then took Maria by the hand, and said with great emotion: "This is Miss Maria Stahlbaum, the daughter of a much-respected and very worthy physician, and she is the preserver of my life. Had she not thrown her shoe at the right time—had she not supplied me with the sword of a pensioned colonel, I should now be lying in my grave, torn and bitten to pieces by the terrible Mouse-King. View her—gaze upon her, and tell me, if Pirlipat, although a princess by birth, can compare with her in beauty, goodness, and virtue? No, I say no!"

And all the ladies cried out "No!" and then fell upon Maria's neck, exclaiming: "Ah, clear preserver of the prince, our beloved brother! Charming Miss Maria Stahlbaum!" She now accompanied these ladies and Nutcracker into the castle, and entered a room, the walls of which were of bright, colored crystal. But of all the beautiful things which Maria saw here, what pleased her most were the nice little chairs, sofas, secretaries, and bureaus, with which the room was furnished, and which were all made of cedar or Brazil wood, and ornamented with golden flowers. The princesses made Maria and Nutcracker sit down, and said that they would immediately prepare something for them to eat. They then brought out a great many little cups and saucers, and plates and dishes, all of the finest porcelain, and spoons, knives, and forks, graters, kettles, pans, and other kitchen furniture, all of gold and silver.

Then they brought the finest fruits and sugar things, such as Maria had never seen before, and began in the nicest manner to squeeze the fruits with their little snow-white hands, and to pound the spice, and grate the sugar-almonds, in short, so to turn and handle every thing, that Maria could see how well the princesses had been brought up, and what a delicious meal they were preparing. As she desired very much to learn such things, she could not help wishing to herself that she might assist the princesses in their labor. The most beautiful of Nutcracker's sisters, as if she had guessed Maria's secret thoughts, reached her a little golden mortar, saying: "Oh, sweet friend, dear preserver of my brother, will you not pound a little of this sugar candy?"

While Maria pounded in the mortar, Nutcracker began to give a full account of his adventures, of the dreadful battle between his army and that of the Mouse-King, and how he had lost it by the cowardice of his troops; how the terrible Mouse-King lay in wait to bite him in pieces, and how Maria, to preserve him, gave up many of his subjects, who had entered her service, and all just as it had happened. During this narration, it seemed to Maria, as if his words became less and less audible, and the pounding of her mortar also sounded more and more distant, until she could scarcely hear it; presently, she saw a silver gauze before her, in which the princesses, the pages, Nutcracker, and herself, too, were all enveloped. A singular humming, and rustling, and singing was heard, which seemed to die away in the distance; and now Maria was raised up, as if upon mounting waves, higher and higher—higher and higher—higher and higher!

XIV

The Conclusion

PRR—PUFF IT WENT! MARIA FELL down from an immeasurable height. That was a fall! But she opened her eyes, and there she lay upon her little bed; it was bright day, and her mother stood by her, saying: "How can you sleep so long? Breakfast has been ready this great while." You now perceive, kind readers and listeners, that Maria, completely confused by the wonderful things which she had seen, had at last fallen asleep in the room at Marchpane Castle, and that the Moors, or the pages, or perhaps even the princesses themselves must have carried her home, and laid her softly in bed. "Oh, mother, dear mother, you cannot think where young Master Drosselmeier led me last night, and what beautiful things I have seen!" And then she began and told the whole, almost as accurately as I have related it, while her mother listened in astonishment.

When she had finished, her mother said: "You have had a long and very beautiful dream, but now drive it all out of your head." Maria insisted upon it that she had not dreamed, but had actually seen what she had related, when her mother led her into the sitting room, to the glass case; took Nutcracker out, who was standing, as usual, upon the second shelf, and said: "Silly child, how can you believe that this wooden Nuremberg puppet can have life or motion?"

"But, dear mother," replied Maria, "I know little Nutcracker is young Master Drosselmeier, of Nuremberg, Godfather Drosselmeier's nephew." Then her father and mother both laughed very heartily. "Ah, dear father," said Maria, almost crying, "you should not laugh so at my Nutcracker; he has spoken very well of you; for when we entered Marchpane Castle, and he presented me to his sisters, the princesses, he said that you were a much respected and very worthy physician." At this the laughter was still louder, and Louise, and even Fred, joined in. Maria then ran into the other chamber, took the seven crowns of the Mouse-King out of her little box, brought them in, and handed them to her mother, saying: "See here, dear mother, here are the seven crowns of the Mouse-King, which young Master Drosselmeier gave me last night, as a token of his victory." Her mother examined the little crowns in great astonishment; they were made of a strange but very shining metal, and were so delicately worked, that it seemed impossible that mortal hands could have formed them. Her father, likewise, could not gaze enough at them, and he insisted very seriously that Maria should confess how she obtained them. But she could give no other account of them, and kept firm to what she had said; and, as her father spoke very harshly to her, and even called her a little storyteller, she began to cry bitterly, and said: "Oh, what, what then shall I say?"

At this moment the door opened. The Counsellor entered, and exclaimed: "What's this? What's this?" The doctor told him of all that had happened, and showed him the little crowns. As soon as the Counsellor cast his eyes on them, he laughed and cried: "Stupid pack—stupid pack! These are the very crowns which I used to wear on my watch-chain, years ago, and which I gave to little Maria, on her birthday, when she was two years old. Don't you remember them?" Neither father nor mother could remember them; but when Maria saw that her parents had forgotten their anger, she ran to Godfather Drosselmeier, and said: "Ah, you know all about it, Godfather Drosselmeier. Tell them yourself, that my Nutcracker is your nephew, young Master Drosselmeier, of Nuremberg, and that it was he who gave me the crowns!"

The Counsellor's face turned very dark and grave, and he muttered: "Stupid pack—stupid pack!" Upon this, the doctor took little Maria upon his knee, and said very seriously: "Listen to me, Maria. Once for all, drive your foolish dreams and nonsense out of your head. If I ever hear you say again, that the silly, ugly Nutcracker is the nephew of your Godfather Drosselmeier, I will throw him out of the window, and all the rest of your puppets, Miss Clara not excepted."

Poor Maria durst not now speak of all these wonders, but she thought so much the more. Her whole soul was full of them; for you may imagine, that things so fine and beautiful as those which she had seen are not easily forgotten. Even Fred turned his back upon his sister, whenever she spoke of the wonderful kingdom in which she had been so happy; and, it is said, that he sometimes would mutter between his teeth: "Silly goose!" But that I can hardly believe of so amiable and good-natured a fellow. This is certain, however, he no longer believed a word of what Maria had told him. He made a formal apology to his hussars, on public parade, for the injustice which he had done them; stuck in their caps feathers of goose-quill, much finer and taller than those of which they had been deprived; and permitted them again to blow the Hussar's Grand March. Ah, ha! We know best how it stood with their courage, when those hateful balls spotted their red coats!

Maria was not allowed, then, to speak any more of her adventures, but the images of that wonderful fairy kingdom played about her in sweet, rustling tones. She could bring them all back again, whenever she fixed her thoughts steadfastly upon them, and hence it came, that, instead of playing, as she formerly did, she would sit silent and thoughtful, musing within herself, for which reason the rest would often scold her, and call her a little dreamer. Some time after this, it happened that the Counsellor was busy, repairing a clock in Doctor Stahlbaum's house. Maria sat close by the glass case, and, lost in her dreams, was gazing at Nutcracker, when the words broke from her lips involuntarily: "Ah, dear Master Drosselmeier, if you actually were living, I would not behave like Princess Pirlipat, and slight you, because for my sake you had ceased to be a handsome young man!"

At this, the Counsellor screamed: "Hey—hey—stupid pack!" Then there was a clap, and a knock, so loud, that Maria sank from her chair in a swoon. When she came to herself, her mother was busied about her, and said: "How came such a great girl to fall from her chair? Here is Godfather Drosselmeier's nephew, just arrived from Nuremberg! Come—behave like a little woman!"

She looked up; the Counsellor had put on his glass wig again, and his brown coat; he was smiling very pleasantly, and he held by the hand a little but very well-shaped young man. His face was as white as milk, and as red as blood; he wore a handsome red coat, trimmed with gold, and shoes and white silk stockings; in his buttonhole was stuck a nosegay; his hair was nicely powdered and curled; and down his back there hung a magnificent queue. The sword by his side seemed to be made of nothing but jewels, it flashed and sparkled so brightly, and the little hat which he carried under his arm looked as if it were overlaid with soft, silken flakes. It very soon appeared how polite and well-bred the young man was, for he had brought Maria a great many handsome playthings—the nicest gingerbread, and the same sugar figures which the Mouse-King had bitten to pieces; and for Fred he had brought a splendid sabre. At table, the little fellow cracked nuts for the whole company—the hardest could not resist him; with the right hand he put them in his mouth; with the left, he pulled hard upon his queue, and—crack—the nut fell in pieces! Maria had turned very red when she first saw the handsome young man; and she became still redder, when, after dinner, young Drosselmeier invited her to go with him into the sitting room to the glass case. "Play prettily together, children; I have nothing against it, since all my clocks are going," cried the Counsellor.

Scarcely was Maria alone with young Drosselmeier, when he stooped upon one knee, and said: "Oh, my very best Miss Stahlbaum, you see here at your feet the happy Drosselmeier, whose life you saved on this very spot. You said most amiably, that you would not slight me, like the hateful Princess Pirlipat, if I had become ugly for your sake. From that moment, I ceased to be a miserable Nutcracker, and resumed again my old—and, I hope, not disagreeable—figure. Oh, excellent Miss Stahlbaum, make me happy with your dear hand; share with me crown and kingdom; rule with me in Marchpane Castle, for there I am still king!"

Maria raised the youth, and said softly: "Dear Master Drosselmeier, you are a kind, good-natured young man; and, since you rule in such a charming land, among such pretty, merry people, I will be your bride." With this, Maria immediately became Drosselmeier's betrothed bride.

After a year and a day, he came, as I have heard, and carried her away in a golden chariot, drawn by silver horses. There danced at the wedding two-and-twenty thousand of the most splendid figures, adorned with pearls and diamonds; and Maria, it is said, is at this hour queen of a land, where sparkling Christmas woods, transparent Marchpane Castles—in short, where the most beautiful, the most wonderful things can be seen by those who will only have eyes for them.

THE END

The History

of

a Nutcracker

I

GODFATHER DROSSELMAYER

IN THE CITY OF NUREMBERG lived a much-respected Chief Justice called Judge Silberhaus, which means, "house of silver." He had two children, a nine-year-old boy, Fritz, and a daughter Mary who was seven and a half years old. They were both very attractive children but so different in appearance and nature that one would have never have taken them for brother and sister. Fritz was a fine big boy, chubby, blustering and frolicsome, stamping his foot at the least opposition, convinced that all things in the world were created for his pleasure and whims. He would continue in this conviction until his father, irritated by the shouting and stamping, would emerge from his study and lifting the index finger of his right hand to the level of his frowning eyebrow, would remark, "Monsieur *Fritz!*"

Then Fritz would want to sink under the floor.

As to his mother, it goes without saying that no matter how high she raised her finger or even her hand, Fritz paid not the slightest attention.

Mary, on the other hand, was a delicate pale child, with long curling ringlets falling over her little shoulders like a moving sheaf of gold. She was modest, sweet, affable, sympathetic to all troubles, even those of her dolls, obedient to the slightest sign from her mother and never gave trouble to Miss Trudchen, the governess. Consequently, everyone loved Mary.

Now, in the year 17— came the twenty-fourth day of December. You may not know, my dear children, that the twenty-fourth of December is the day before Christmas, being the day when the Infant Jesus was born in a manager between a donkey and a cow. I must now explain one thing to you.

The most ill-informed ones among you have heard it said that each country has its customs; the best informed ones doubtless know already that Nuremberg is a German city is renowned for its toys, dolls, and polichinelles, which are sent in well-filled cases to all the countries of the world. The children of Nuremberg therefore should be the happiest children on earth. At least they are not like the inhabitants of Ostend who have an abundance of oysters only to see them wasted. Thus Germany, quite a different country than France, has likewise different customs. In

France, the first day of the New Year is the day for exchanging presents. In Germany the gift day is the twenty-fourth of December, that is to say, the night before Christmas. Across the Rhine gifts are given in this way: a large tree is installed on a low table in the living room and its branches are hung with toys. Those too large for the branches are put on the table; them the children are reminded that the good little angel had given them some of the presents which he received from the three wise kings. This is not wholly untrue because you know it is from the Infant Jesus that all good things of this world come.

I do not need to tell you that among the fortunate children of Nuremberg, I mean those who at Christmas receive many toys of all kinds, were the little boy and girl of Judge Silberhaus. Besides their parents who adored them, they had a godfather called Godfather Drosselmayer who adored them also. I must describe briefly this illustrious personage who occupied in the City of Nuremberg a position almost as distinguished as that of Judge Silberhaus. Godfather Drosselmayer, Medical Commissioner, was not at all a good-looking fellow; far from it. He was a tall, spare man, about five feet, eight inches high. He was so round-shouldered and stooped that in spite of his long limbs he could pick up a handkerchief without seeming to bend over. His face was like a wrinkled apple touched by April frost. In the place of his right eye was a large black plaster; he was perfectly bald, a drawback which was offset by a luxuriant and curly wig, an ingenious work of his own, made of spun glass. On account of this remarkable head-covering he always carried his hat under his arm. The one remaining eye, however, was alive and brilliant, seeming to perform the functions of its missing comrade as well as its own, so rapidly did it make the rounds of a room wherein Godfather Drosselmayer wished to take in all details at one glance, or focus itself steadily upon people whose inmost thoughts he desired to know.

Godfather Drosselmayer, through the study of men and animals, had become familiar with all the resources of machinery so that he made men who walked, saluted, presented arms; women who danced, played the harpsichord and the violin; dogs which fetched, carried and barked; birds which flew, hopped and sang; fish which swam and ate. He had finally succeeded in making dolls and polichinelles pronounce in a harsh and monotonous voice a few words, simple ones it is true, like papa and mamma. Nevertheless, in spite of all these dubious attempts, Godfather Drosselmayer did not despair but insisted that someday he would succeed in making real men, women, dogs, birds and fish. It goes without saying that his two godchildren, to whom he had promised his first experiments in this field, were always full of pleasant anticipations.

You can clearly see that Godfather Drosselmayer's mechanical skills made him a very useful friend. When a clock got out of order in the house of Judge Silberhaus and in spite of attempts on the part of ordinary clockmakers its hands ceased indicating the hour, its *tick tock* subsided, its movement stopped, they sent for the godfather. He would arrive on a run, having, like all true artists, a real affection for his hobby. Taken to the lifeless timepiece he would lift out the movement and place it between his knees. Ten, tongue sticking out, his one eye glowing like a carbuncle, his glass wig on the floor beside him, he would draw form his pocket a collection of miscellaneous small instruments made by himself for purposes known only to himself, choose the sharpest ones and plunge them into the clock. This operation, while it worried Mary who could not believe that the clock did not suffer, nevertheless restored the patient so that, once replaced in its case, it would begin to stir and strike more beautifully than ever. Then the room appeared to live once more.

On one occasion, touched by the coaxing of Mary, who was sadly watching their dog as he laboriously turned the kitchen spit, Godfather Drosselmayer had condescended, from the heights of his scientific knowledge, to make an automatic dog. Thereafter, Turk, sensitive to the cold, after three years of working so near the fire, warmed his nose and paws before the blaze like a veritable gentleman with nothing to do but watch his successor who, once started, would keep at his task indefinitely. After the Judge, his wife, Fritz and Mary, Turk was certainly the member of the household who most loved and venerated Godfather Drosselmayer. He made a great fuss every time he saw him arrive, announcing by joyous barks and the wagging of his tail that the quaint old man was near even before he touched the knocker.

On this Christmas Eve just as dusk was falling Fritz and Mary, who had not been allowed in the drawing room, were sitting in one corner of the dining room. While Miss Trudchen, their governess, was knitting near the window to catch the last rays of the sun, the children were seized with a sort of vague uneasiness because the lights had not yet been brought in. They were speaking in low voices to each other as people do when a little frightened.

"Fritz," said Mary, "surely mother and father are busy with the Christmas tree for ever since morning I have been hearing things being moved about in the drawing room."

"Yes," said Fritz, "and about ten minutes ago I realized from the way Turk was barking that Godfather was coming."

"Oh gracious!" cried Mary, clapping her hands, "what do you suppose that the good godfather will bring us? I think it will be a beautiful garden all planted with trees, along which will run a lovely river, its grassy banks bordered with flowers. On this river, maybe there will be silver swans with golden collars and a young girl feeding them marzipan which they will eat out of her apron."

"In the first place," said Fritz in the superior tone peculiar to him, which his parents regarded as one of his gravest faults, "you should know, Miss Mary, that swans do not eat marzipan."

"I believe you," said Mary, "but as you are a year and a half older than I you ought to know more about such things."

Fritz swaggered a bit and resumed: "I think I can say that if Godfather Drosselmayer brings anything it will be a fortress with soldiers to guard, cannons to defend, and enemies to attack it. There will be splendid battles."

"I do not like battles," said Mary. "If he brings a fortress, as you think, it will be for you; except that I want to nurse the wounded ones."

"Whatever he brings," said Fritz, "you know that it will be neither for you nor for me, because, with the excuse that his presents are true works of art, they will be taken away as soon as we get them and put on the top shelf of the big glass cupboard which even father can reach only by standing on a chair. That is why I like our other toys better than those that Godfather Drosselmayer brings. We can have them to play with at least until they are broken."

"Yes, I do too," replied Mary, "only it is not necessary to repeat this to Godfather."

"Why?"

"Because it would hurt his feelings to know that we do not like his toys as well as the others. He thinks they make us happy. We must not let him know that he is mistaken."

"Oh, bah!" said Fritz.

"Miss Mary is right, Master Fritz," said Miss Trudchen, who ordinarily kept silent, only speaking when she felt the occasion demanded it.

"See here," said Mary in an animated tone to prevent Fritz from replying rudely to the governess, "let us try to guess what we will get. I have confided to mother that Miss Rose, my doll, is getting more and more awkward in spite of my constant scoldings, and keeping falling on her nose. As this never happens without leaving disagreeable traces, it is impossible to take her out anymore; her face goes badly with her pretty clothes."

"I have reminded father," said Fritz, "that a big chestnut horse would be fine in my stable. I told him, too, that there can be no well-organized army without light cavalry and that I need a squadron of hussars to complete my division."

At this point Miss Trudchen considered it time to speak again. "Monsieur Fritz and Miss Mary," she said, "you know every well that it is the good angel who gives and blesses all these beautiful toys. Do not choose in advance what you want. He knows much better than you what will please you."

"Oh!" cried Fritz; "and yet last year he sent me foot soldiers, although, as I have just said, I should have been better satisfied with a squadron of hussars."

"For my part I have only to thank my good angel," said Mary; "for I did but ask for a doll last year, and I not only had the doll, but also a beautiful white dove, with red feet and beak."

In the meantime the night had altogether drawn in, and the children, who by degrees spoke lower and lower and grew closer and closer together, fancied that they heard the wings of their guardian angels fluttering near them, and a sweet music in the distance, like that of an organ accompanying the Hymn of Nativity, beneath the gloomy arches of a cathedral. Presently a sudden light shone upon the wall for a moment, and Fritz and Mary believed that it was their guardian angel, who, after depositing the toys in the drawing room, flew away in the midst of a golden lustre to visit other children who were expecting him with the same impatience as themselves.

Immediately afterwards a bell rang—the door was thrown violently open—and so strong a light burst into the apartment that the children were dazzled, and uttered cries of surprise and alarm.

The judge and his wife then appeared at the door, and took the hands of their children, saying, "Come, little dears, and see what the guardian angels have sent you."

The children hastened to the drawing room; and Miss Trudchen, having placed her work upon a chair, followed them.

II

The Christmas Tree

M Y DEAR CHILDREN, YOU ALL know the beautiful toy stalls in the
Soho Bazaar, the Pantheon, and the Lowther Arcade; and your
parents have often taken you there, to permit you to choose whatever
you liked best. Then you have stopped short, with longing eyes and open
mouth; and you have experienced a pleasure which you will never again
know in your lives—no, not even when you become men and acquire
titles or fortunes. Well, that same joy was felt by Fritz and Mary when
they entered the drawing room and saw the great tree growing as it were
from the middle of the table, and covered with blossoms made of sugar,
and sugar plums instead of fruit—the whole glittering by the light of a
hundred Christmas candles concealed amidst the leaves. At that beautiful
sight Fritz leapt for joy, and danced about in a manner which showed how
well he had attended to the lessons of his dancing master. On her side,
Mary could not restrain two large tears of joy which, like liquid pearls,
rolled down her countenance, that was open and smiling as a rose in June.

But the children's joy knew no bounds when they came to examine all
the pretty things which covered the table. There was a beautiful doll, twice
as large as Miss Rose; and there was also a charming silk frock, hung on
a stand in such a manner that Mary could walk round it. Fritz was also
well pleased; for he found upon the table a squadron of hussars, with red
jackets and gold lace, and mounted on white horses; while on the carpet,
near the table, stood the famous horse which he so much longed to see
in his stables. In a moment did this modern Alexander leap upon the
back of that brilliant Bucephalus, which was already saddled and bridled;
and, having ridden two or three times round the table, he got off again,
declaring that though the animal was very spirited and restive, he should
soon be able to tame him in such a manner that ere a month passed the
horse would be as quiet as a lamb.

But at the moment when Fritz set his foot upon the ground, and when
Mary was baptising her new doll by the name of Clara, the bell rang a
second time; and the children turned towards that corner of the room
whence the sound came.

They then beheld something which had hitherto escaped their
attention, so intent had they been upon the beautiful Christmas tree. In

fact, the corner of the room of which I have just spoken, was concealed, or cut off as it were, by a large Chinese screen, behind a which there was a certain noise accompanied by a certain sweet music, which proved something unusual was going on in that quarter. The children then recollected that they had not yet seen the doctor; and they both exclaimed at the same moment, "Oh! Godpapa Drosselmayer!"

At these words—and as if it had only waited for that exclamation to put itself in motion—the screen opened inwards, and showed not only Godfather Drosselmayer, but something more!

In the midst of a green meadow, decorated with flowers, stood a magnificent country seat, with numerous windows, all made of real glass, in front, and two gilt towers on the wings. At the same moment the jingling of bells was heard from within—the doors and windows opened—and the rooms inside were discovered lighted up by wax-tapers half an inch high. In those rooms were several little gentlemen and ladies, all walking about: the gentlemen splendidly dressed in laced coats, and silk waistcoats and breeches, each with a sword by his side, and a hat under his arm; the ladies gorgeously attired in brocades, their hair dressed in the style of the eighteenth century, and each one holding a fan in her hand, wherewith they all fanned themselves as if overcome by the heat.

In the central drawing room, which actually seemed to be on fire, so splendid was the lustre of the crystal chandelier, filled with wax candles, a number of children were dancing to the jingling music; the boys all in round jackets, and the girls all in short frocks. At the same time a gentleman, clad in a furred cloak, appeared at the window of an adjoining chamber, made signs, and then disappeared again; while Godfather Drosselmayer himself, with his drab frock coat, the patch on his eye, and the glass wig—so like the original, although only three inches high, that the puppet might be taken for the doctor, as if seen at a great distance—went out and in the front door of the mansion with the air of a gentleman, inviting those who were walking outside to enter his abode.

The first moment was one of surprise and delight for the two children; but, having watched the building for a few minutes with his elbows resting on the table, Fritz rose and exclaimed, "But, Godpapa Drosselmayer, why do you keep going in and coming out by the same door? You must be tired of going backwards and forwards like that. Come, enter by that door there, and come out by this one here."

And Fritz pointed with his finger to the doors of the two towers.

"No, that cannot be done," answered Godfather Drosselmayer.

"Well, then," said Fritz, "do me the pleasure of going up those stairs, and taking the place of that gentleman at the window: then tell him to go down to the door."

"It is impossible, my dear Fritz," again said the doctor.

"At all events the children have danced enough: let them go and walk, while the gentlemen and ladies who are now walking, dance in their turn."

"But you are not reasonable, you little rogue," cried the godpapa, who began to grow angry: "the mechanism must move in a certain way."

"Then let me go into the house," said Fritz.

"Now you are silly, my dear boy," observed the judge: "you see that it is impossible for you to enter the house, since the vanes on the top of the towers scarcely come up to your shoulders."

Fritz yielded to this reasoning and held his tongue; but in a few moments, seeing that the ladies and gentlemen kept on walking, that the children would not leave off dancing, that the gentleman with the furred cloak appeared and disappeared at regular intervals, and that Godfather Drosselmayer did not leave the door, he again broke silence.

"My dear godpapa," said he, "if all these little figures can do nothing more than what again, you may take them away they are doing over and over tomorrow, for I do not care about them; and I like my horse much better, because it runs when I choose—and my hussars, because they maneuvre at my command, and wheel to the right or left, or march forward or backward, and are not shut up in any house like your poor little people who can only move over and over in the same way.

With these words he turned his back upon Godfather Drosselmayer and the house, hastened to the table, and drew up his hussars in battle array.

As for Mary, she had slipped away very gently, because the motions of the little figures in the house seemed to her to be very tiresome: but, as she was a charming child, she said nothing, for fear of wounding the feelings of Godpapa Drosselmayer. Indeed, the moment Fritz had turned his back, the doctor said to the judge and his wife, in a tone of vexation, "This masterpiece is not fit for children; and I will put my house back again into the box, and take it away."

But the judge's wife approached him, and, in order to atone for her son's rudeness, begged Godfather Drosselmayer to explain to her all the secrets of the beautiful house, and praised the ingenuity of the mechanism to such an extent, that she not only made the doctor forget his vexation, but put him into such a good humour, that he drew from the pockets of his drab coat a number of little men and women, with horn complexions, white eyes, and gilt hands and feet. Besides the beauty of their appearance, these little men and women sent forth a delicious perfume, because they were made of cinnamon.

At this moment Miss Trudchen called Mary, and offered to help her to put on the pretty little silk frock which she had so much admired on first entering the drawing room; but Mary, in spite of her usual politeness, did not answer the governess, so much was she occupied with a new person age whom she had discovered amongst the toys, and to whom, my dear children, I must briefly direct your attention, since he is actually the hero of my tale, in which Miss Trudchen, Mary, Fritz, the judge, the judge's lady, and even Godfather Drosselmayer, are only secondary characters.

III

The Little Man with the Wooden Cloak

I told you that Mary did not reply to the invitation of Miss Trudchen, because she had just discovered a new toy which she had not before perceived.

Indeed, by dint of making his hussars march and counter march about the table, Fritz had brought to light a charming little gentleman, who, leaning in a melancholy mood against the trunk of the Christmas tree, awaited, in silence and polite reserve, the moment when his turn to be inspected should arrive. We must pause to notice the appearance of this little man, to whom I gave the epithet "charming" somewhat hastily; for, in addition to his body being too long and large for the miserable little thin legs which supported it, his head was of a size so enormous that it was quite at variance with the proportions indicated not only by nature, but also by those drawing-masters who know much better than even Nature herself.

But if there were any fault in his person, that defect was atoned for by the excellence of his toilette, which denoted at once a man of education and taste. He wore a braided frock coat of violet-coloured velvet, all frogged and covered with buttons; trousers of the same material; and the most charming little Wellington boots ever seen on the feet of a student or an officer. But there were two circumstances which seemed strange in respect to a man who preserved such elegant taste: the one was an ugly narrow cloak made of wood, and which hung down like a pig's tail from the nape of his neck to the middle of his back; and the other was a wretched cap, such as peasants sometimes wear in Switzerland, upon his head. But Mary, when she perceived those two objects which seemed so unsuitable to the rest of his costume, remembered that Godfather Drosselmayer himself wore above his drab coat a little collar of no better appearance than the wooden cloak belonging to the little gentleman in the military frock; and that the doctor often covered his own bald head with an ugly—an absolutely frightful cap, unlike all other ugly caps in the world—although this circumstance did not prevent the doctor from being an excellent godpapa. She even thought to herself that were Godpapa Drosselmayer to imitate altogether the dress of the little gentleman with the wooden cloak, he could not possibly become so genteel and interesting as the puppet.

You can very well believe that all these reflections on the part of Mary were not made without a close inspection of the little man, whom she liked from the very first moment that she saw him. Then, the more she looked at him, the more she was struck by the sweetness and amiability which were expressed by his countenance. His clear green eyes, which were certainly rather goggle, beamed with serenity and kindness. The frizzled beard of white cotton, extending beneath his chin, seemed to become him amazingly, because it set off the charming smile of his mouth, which was rather wide perhaps; but then, the lips were as red as vermilion!

Thus was it that, after examining the little man for upwards of ten minutes, without daring to touch it, Mary exclaimed, "Oh! Dear papa, whose is that funny figure leaning against the Christmas tree?"

"It belongs to no one in particular," answered the judge; "but to both of you together."

"How do you mean, dear papa? I do not understand you."

"This little man," continued the judge, "will help you both; for it is he who in future will crack all your nuts for you; and he belongs as much to Fritz as to you, and as much to you as to Fritz."

Thus speaking, the judge took up the little man very carefully, and raising his wooden cloak, made him open his mouth by a very simple motion, and display two rows of sharp white teeth. Mary then placed a nut in the little man's mouth; and crack—crack—the shell was broken into a dozen pieces, and the kernel fell whole and sound into Mary's hand. The little girl then learnt that the dandified gentleman belonged to that ancient and respectable race of Nutcrackers whose origin is as ancient as that of the town of Nuremberg, and that he continued to exercise the honourable calling, of his forefathers. Mary, delighted to have made this discovery, leapt for joy; whereupon the Judge said, "Well, my dear little Mary, since the Nutcracker pleases you so much, although it belongs equally to Fritz and yourself, it is to you that I especially trust it. I place it in your care."

With these words the judge handed the little fellow to Mary, who took the puppet in her arms, and began to practise it in its vocation, choosing, however—so good washer heart—the smallest nuts, that it might not be compelled to open its mouth too wide, because by so doing its face assumed a most ridiculous expression. Then Miss Trudchen drew near to behold the little puppet in her turn; and for her also did it perform its duty in the most unassuming and obliging manner in the world, although she was but a dependent.

While he was employed in training his horse and parading his hussars, Master Fritz heard the crack-crack so often repeated, that he felt sure something new was going on. He accordingly looked up and turned his large inquiring eyes upon the group composed of the judge, Mary, and Miss Trudchen; and, when he observed the little man with the wooden cloak in his sister's arms, he leapt from his horse, and, without waiting to put the animal in its stable, hastened towards Mary. Then what a joyous shout of laughter burst from his lips as he espied the funny appearance of the little man opening his large mouth, Fritz also demanded his share of the nuts which the puppet cracked; and this was of course granted. Next he wanted to hold the little man while he cracked the nuts; and this wish was also gratified. Only, in spite of the remonstrances of his sister, Fritz chose the largest and hardest nuts to cram into his mouth; so that at the fifth or sixth c-r-r-ack! And out fell three of the poor little fellow's teeth. At the same time his chin fell and became tremulous like that of an old man.

"Oh! My poor Nutcracker!" cried Mary, snatching the little man from the hands of Fritz.

"What a stupid fellow he is!" cried the boy: "he pretends to be a nutcracker, and his jaws are as brittle as glass. He is a false nutcracker, and does not understand his duty. Give him to me, Mary; I will make him go on cracking my nuts, even if he loses all his teeth in doing so, and his chin is dislocated entirely. But how you seem to feel for the lazy fellow!"

"No—no—no!" cried Mary, clasping the little man in her arms: "no—you shall not have my Nutcracker! See how he looks at me, as much as to tell me that his poor jaw is hurt. Fie, Fritz! You are very ill-natured—you beat your horses; and the other day you shot one of your soldiers."

"I beat my horses when they are restive," said Fritz, with an air of importance; "and as for the soldier whom I shot the other day, he was a wretched scoundrel that I never have been able to do anything with for the last year, and who deserted one fine morning with his arms and baggage—a crime that is punished by death in all countries. Besides, all these things are matters of discipline which do not regard women. I do not prevent you from boxing your doll's ears; so don't try to hinder me from whipping my horses or shooting my soldiers. But I want the Nutcracker."

"Papa—papa! Help—help!" cried Mary, wrapping the little man in her pocket handkerchief: "Help! Fritz is going to take the Nutcracker from me!"

At Mary's cries, not only the judge drew near the children; but his wife and Godfather Drosselmayer also ran towards them. The two children told their stories in their own way—Mary wishing to keep the Nutcracker, and Fritz anxious to have it again. But to the astonishment of Mary, Godfather Drosselmayer a smile that seemed perfectly frightful to the little girl, decided in favour of Fritz. Happily for the poor Nutcracker, the judge and his wife took Little Mary's part.

"My dear Fritz," said the judge, "I trusted the Nutcracker to the care of your sister; and as far as my knowledge of surgery goes, I see that the poor creature is very unwell, and requires attention. I therefore give him over solely to the care of Mary, until he is quite well; and no one must say a word against my decision. And you, Fritz, who stand up so firmly in behalf of military discipline, when did you ever hear of making a wounded soldier return to his duty? The wounded always go to the hospital until they are cured; and if they be disabled by their wounds, they are entitled to pensions."

Fritz was about to reply; but the judge raised his forefinger to a level with his right eye, and said, "Master Fritz!"

You have already seen what influence those two words had upon the little boy:—thus, ashamed at having drawn upon himself the reprimand conveyed in those words, he slipped quietly off, without giving any answer, to the table where his hussars were posted: then, having placed the sentinels in their stations, he marched off the rest to their quarters for the night.

In the meantime, Mary picked up the three little teeth which had fallen from the Nutcracker's mouth, and kept the Nutcracker himself well wrapped up in the pocket handkerchief; she had also bound up his chin with a pretty white ribbon which she cut from the frock. On his side, the little man, who was at first very pale and much frightened, seemed quite contented in the care of his protectress, and gradually acquired confidence, when he felt himself gently rocked in her arms.

Then Mary perceived that Godfather Drosselmayer watched with mocking smiles the care which she bestowed upon the little man with the wooden cloak; and it struck her that the single eye of the doctor had acquired an expression of spite and malignity which she had never before seen. She therefore tried to get away from him; but Godfather Drosselmayer burst out laughing, saying, "Well my dear god daughter, I am really astonished that a pretty little girl like you can be so devoted to an ugly little urchin like that."

Mary turned round; and, much as she loved her godfather, even the compliment which he paid her did not make amends for the unjust attack he made upon the person of her Nutcracker. She even felt—contrary to her usual disposition—very angry; and that vague comparison which she had before formed between the little man with the wooden cloak and her godfather, returned to her memory.

"Godpapa Drosselmayer," she said, "you are unkind towards my little Nutcracker, whom you call an ugly urchin. Who knows whether you would even look so well as he, even if you had his pretty little military coat, his pretty little breeches, and his pretty little boots!"

At these words Mary's parents burst out laughing; and the doctor's nose grew prodigiously longer. Why did the doctor's nose grow so much longer? Mary, surprised by the effect of her remark, could not guess the reason.

But as there are never any effects without causes, that reason no doubt belonged to some strange and unknown cause, which we must explain.

IV

Wonderful Events

I DO NOT KNOW, MY DEAR little friends, whether you remember that I spoke of a certain large cupboard, with glass windows, in which the children's toys were locked up. This cupboard was on the right of the door of the judge's own room. Mary was still a baby in the cradle, and Fritz had only just began to walk, when the judge had that cupboard made by a very skilful carpenter, who put such brilliant glass in the frames, that the toys appeared a thousand times finer when ranged on the shelves than when they were held in the hand. Upon the top shelf of all, which neither Fritz nor Mary could reach, the beautiful pieces of workmanship of Godfather Drosselmayer were placed. Immediately beneath was the shelf containing the picture books; and the two lower shelves were given to Fritz and Mary, who filled them in the way they liked best. It seemed, however, to have been tacitly agreed upon between the two children, that Fritz should hold possession of the higher shelf of the two, for the marshalling of his troops, and that Mary should keep the lower shelf for her dolls and their households. This arrangement was entered into on the eve of Christmas Day. Fritz placed his soldiers upon his own shelf; and Mary, having thrust Miss Rose into a corner, gave the bedroom, formed by the lowest shelf, to Miss Clara, with whom she invited herself to pass the evening and enjoy a supper of sugar plums. Miss Clara, on casting her eyes around, saw that everything was in proper order; her table well spread with sugar plums and conserved fruits, and her nice white bed with its white counterpane, all so neat and comfortable. She therefore felt very well satisfied with her new apartment.

While all these arrangements were being made, the evening wore away: midnight was approaching—Godfather Drosselmayer had been gone a long time—and yet the children could not be persuaded to quit the cupboard.

Contrary to custom, it was Fritz that yielded first to the persuasion of his parents, who told him that it was time to go to bed.

"Well," said he, "after all the exercise which my poor hussars have had today, they must be fatigued; and as those excellent soldiers all know their duty towards me—and as, so long as I remain here, they will not close their eyes—I must retire."

With these words—and having given them the watchword, to prevent them from being surprised by a patrol of the enemy—Fritz went off to bed.

But this was not the case with Mary; and as her mamma, who was about to follow her husband to their bed-chamber, desired her to tear herself away from the dearly beloved cupboard, little Mary said, "Only one moment, dear mamma—a single moment: do let me finish all I have to do here. There are a hundred or more important things to put to rights; and the moment I have settled them, I promise to go to bed."

Mary requested this favour in so touching and plaintive a tone,—she was, moreover, so glad and obedient a child—that her mother did not hesitate to grant her request. Nevertheless, as Miss Trudchen had already gone up stairs to get Mary's bed ready, the judge's wife, thinking that her daughter might forget to put out the candles, performed that duty herself, leaving only a light in the lamp hanging from the ceiling.

"Do not be long before you go to your room, dear little Mary," said the judge's wife; "for if you remain up too long, you will not be able to rise at your usual hour tomorrow morning."

With these words the lady quitted the room and closed the door behind her.

The moment Mary found herself alone, she bethought herself, above all things, of her poor little Nutcracker; for she had contrived to keep it in her arms, wrapped up in her pocket handkerchief. She placed him upon the table very gently, unrolled her handkerchief, and examined his chin. The Nutcracker still seemed to suffer much pain, and appeared very cross.

"Ah! My dear little fellow," she said in a low tone, "do not be angry, I pray, because my brother Fritz hurt you so much. He had no evil intention, rest well assured; only his manners have become rough, and his heart is a little hardened by his soldier's life. Otherwise he is a very good boy, I can assure you; and I know that when you are better acquainted with him, you will forgive him. Besides, to atone for the injury which he has done you, I will take care of you; which I will do so attentively that in a few days you will be quite well. As for putting in the teeth again and fastening your chin properly, that is the business of Godpapa Drosselmayer, who perfectly understands those kind of things."

Mary could say no more; for the moment she pronounced the name of her Godfather Drosselmayer, the Nutcracker, to whom this discourse was addressed, made so dreadful a grimace, and his eyes suddenly flashed so brightly, that the little girl stopped short in affright, and stepped a pace back. But as the Nutcracker immediately afterwards resumed its amiable expression and its melancholy smile, she fancied that she must have been the sport of an illusion, and that the flame of the lamp, agitated by a current of air, had thus disfigured the little man. She even laughed at herself, saying, "I am indeed very foolish to think that this wooden puppet could make faces to me. Come, let me draw near the poor fellow, and take that care of him which he requires."

Having thus mused within herself, Mary took the puppet once more in her arms, drew near the cupboard, knocked at the glass door, which Fritz had closed, and said to the new doll, "I beg of you, Miss Clara, to give up your bed to my poor Nutcracker, who is unwell, and to shift for yourself on the sofa tonight. Remember that you are in excellent health yourself, as your round and rosy cheeks sufficiently prove. Moreover, a night is soon passed; the sofa is very comfortable; and there will not be many dolls in Nuremberg as well lodged as yourself."

Miss Clara, as you may very well suppose, did not utter a word; but it struck Mary that she seemed very sulky and discontented; but Mary whose conscience, told her that she had treated Miss Clara in the most considerate manner, used no farther ceremony with her, but, drawing the bed towards her, placed the Nutcracker in it, covering him with the clothes up to the very chin: she then thought that she knew nothing, as yet of the real disposition of Miss Clara, whom she had only seen for a few hours; but that as Miss Clara had appeared to be in a very bad humour at losing her bed, some evil might happen to the poor invalid if he were left with so insolent a person.

She therefore placed the bed, with the Nutcracker in it, upon the second shelf, close by the ridge where Fritz's cavalry were quartered: then, having laid Miss Clara upon the sofa, she closed the cupboard, and was about to rejoin Miss Trudchen in the bed chamber, when all round the room the poor little girl heard a variety of low scratching sounds, coming from behind the chairs, the store, and the cupboard. The large clock which hung against the wall, and which was surmounted by a large gilt owl, instead of a cuckoo, as is usual with old German clocks, began that usual whirring sound which gives warning of striking; and yet it did not strike. Mary glanced towards it, and saw that the immense gilt owl had drooped its wings in such a way that they covered the entire clock, and that the bird thrust forward as far as it could its hideous cat-like head, with the round eyes and the crooked beak. Then the whirring sound of the clock became louder and louder, and gradually changed into the resemblance of a human voice, until it appeared as if these words issued from the beak of the owl: "Clocks, clocks, clocks! Whir, whir, whirl in a low tone! The king of the mice has a sharp ear! Sing him his old song! Strike, strike, strike, clocks all: sound his last hour—for his fate is nigh at hand!"

And then, dong-dong-dong—the clock struck twelve in a hollow and gloomy tone.

Mary was very much frightened. She began to shudder from head to foot; and she was about to run away from the room, when she beheld Godfather Drosselmayer seated upon the clock instead of the owl, the two skirts of his coat having taken the place of the drooping wings of the bird. At that spectacle, Mary remained nailed as it were to the spot with astonishment; and she began to cry, saying, "What are you doing up there, Godpapa Drosselmayer? Come down here, and don't frighten me like that, naughty Godpapa Drosselmayer."

But at these words there began a sharp whistling and furious kind of tittering all around: then in a few moments Mary heard thousands of little feet treading behind the walls; and next she saw thousands of little lights through the joints in the wainscot. When I say little lights, I am wrong—I mean thousands of little shining eyes. Mary full well perceived that there was an entire population of mice about to enter the room. And, in fact, in the course of five minutes, thousands and thousands of mice made their appearance by the creases of the door and the joints of the floor, and began to gallop hither and thither, until at length they ranged themselves in order of battle, as Fritz was wont to draw up his wooden soldiers. All this seemed very amusing to Mary; and as she did not feel towards mice that absurd alarm which so many foolish children experience, she thought she should divert herself with the sight, when there suddenly rang through the room a whistling so sharp, so terrible, and so long, that a cold shudder passed over her.

At the same time, a plank was raised up by some power underneath, and the king of the mice, with seven heads all wearing gold crowns, appeared at her very feet, in the midst of the mortar and plaster that was broken up; and each of his seven mouths began to whistle and scream horribly, while the body to which those seven heads belonged forced its way through the opening. The entire army advanced towards the king, speaking with their little mouths three times in chorus. Then the various regiments marched across the room, directing their course towards the cupboard, and surrounding Mary on all sides, so that she began to beat a retreat.

I have already told you that Mary was not a timid child; but when she thus saw herself surrounded by the crowds of mice, commanded by that monster with seven heads, fear seized upon her, and her heart began to beat so violently, that it seemed as if it would burst from her chest. Her blood appeared to freeze in her veins, her breath failed her; and, half fainting, she retreated with trembling steps. At length pir-r-r-r! and the pieces of one of the panes in the cupboard, broken by her elbow which knocked against it, fell upon the floor. She felt at the moment an acute pain in the left arm; but at the same time her heart grew lighter, for she no longer heard that squeaking which had so much frightened her.

Indeed, everything had again become quiet around her; the mice had disappeared; and she thought that, terrified by the noise of the glass which was broken, they had sought refuge in their holes.

But almost immediately afterwards, a strange noise commenced in the cupboard; and numerous little sharp voices exclaimed, "To arms! To arms! To arms!" At the same time the music of Godfather Drosselmayer's country house, which had been placed upon the top shelf of the cupboard, began to play; and on all sides she heard the words, "Quick! Rise to arms! To arms!"

Mary turned round. The cupboard was lighted up in a wondrous manner, and all was bustle within. All the harlequins, the clowns, the punches, and the other puppets scampered about; while the dolls set to work to make lint and prepare bandages for the wounded. At length the Nutcracker himself threw off—all the clothes, and jumped off the bed, crying, "Foolish troop of mice! Return to your holes, or you must encounter me!"

But at that menace a loud whistling echoed through the room; and Mary perceived that the mice had not returned to their holes; but that, frightened by the noise of the broken glass, they had sought refuge beneath the chairs and tables, whence they were now beginning to issue again.

On his side, Nutcracker, far from being terrified by the whistling, seemed to gather fresh courage.

"Despicable king of the mice," he exclaimed; "it is thou, then! Thou acceptest the death which I have so long offered you? Come on, and let this night decide between us. And you, my, good friends—my companions, my brethren, if it be indeed true that we are united in bonds of affection, support me in this perilous contest! On! On!—Let those who love me, follow!"

Never did a proclamation produce such an effect.

Two harlequins, a clown, two punches, and three other puppets, cried out in a loud tone, "Yes, my lord, we are your's in life and death! We will conquer under your command, or die with you!"

At these words, which proved that there was an echo to his speech in the heart of his friends, Nutcracker felt himself so excited, that he drew his sword, and without calculating the dreadful height on which he stood, leapt from the second shelf. Mary, upon perceiving that dangerous leap, gave a piercing cry; for Nutcracker seemed on the point of being dashed to pieces; when Miss Clara, who was on the lower shelf, darted from the sofa and received him in her arms.

"Ah! My dear little Clara," said Mary, clasping her hands together with emotion: "how have I mistaken your disposition!"

But Miss Clara, thinking only of the present events, said to the Nutcracker, "What! My lord—wounded and suffering as you are, you are plunging head long into new dangers! Content yourself with commanding the army, and let the others fight! Your courage is known; and you can do no good by giving fresh proof of it!"

And as she spoke, Clara endeavoured to restrain the gallant Nutcracker by holding him tight in her arms; but he began to struggle and kick in such a manner that Miss Clara was obliged to let him glide down. He slipped from her arms, and fell on his knees at her feet in a most graceful manner, saying, "Princess, believe me, that although at a certain period you were unjust towards me, I shall always remember you, even in the midst of battle!"

Miss Clara stooped as low down as possible, and, taking him by his little arm, compelled him to rise: then taking off her waistband all glittering with spangles, she made a scarf of it, and sought to pass it over the shoulder of the young hero; but he, stepping back a few paces, and bowing at the time in acknowledgment great a favour, untied the same of so little white ribbon with which Mary had bound up his chin, and tied it round his waist, after pressing it to his lips. Then, light as a bird, he leapt from the shelf on the floor, brandishing his sabre all the time.

Immediately did the squeakings and creakings of the mice begin over again; and the king of the mice, as if to reply to the challenge of the Nutcracker, issued from beneath the great table in the middle of the room, followed by the main body of his army. At the same time, the wings, on the right and left, began to appear from beneath the armchair, under which they had taken refuge.

V

THE BATTLE

"TRUMPETS, SOUND THE CHARGE! DRUMS, beat the alarm!" exclaimed the valiant Nutcracker.

And at the same moment the trumpets of Fritz's hussars began to sound, while the drums of his infantry began to beat, and the rumbling of cannon was also heard. At the same time a band of musicians was formed of fat Figaros with their guitars, Swiss peasants with their horns, and Negroes with their triangles. And all these persons, though not called upon by the Nutcracker, did not the less begin to descend from shelf to shelf, playing the beautiful march of the "British Grenadiers."

The music no doubt excited the most peaceably inclined puppets; for, at the same moment, a kind of militia, commanded by the beadle of the parish, was formed, consisting of harlequins, punches, clowns, and pantaloons. Arming themselves with anything that fell in their way, they were soon ready for battle.

All was bustle, even to a man-cook, who, quitting his fire, came down with his spit, on which was a half-roasted turkey, and went and took his place in the ranks. The Nutcracker placed himself at the head of this valiant battalion, which, to the shame of the regular troops, was ready first.

I must tell you everything, or else you might think that I am inclined to be too favourable to that glorious militia; and therefore I must say that if the infantry and cavalry of Master Fritz were not ready so soon as the others, it was because they were all shut up in four boxes. The poor prisoners might therefore well hear the trumpet and drum which called them to battle: they were shut up, and could not get out. Mary heard them stirring in their boxes, like crayfish in a basket; but, in spite of their efforts, they could not free themselves. At length the grenadiers, less tightly fastened in than the others, succeeded in raising the lid of their box, and then helped to liberate the light infantry. In another instant, these were free; and, well knowing how useful cavalry is in a battle, they hastened to release the hussars, who began to canter gaily about, and range themselves four deep upon the flanks.

But if the regular troops were thus somewhat behind hand, in consequence of the excellent discipline in which Fritz maintained them, they speedily, repaired the lost time: for infantry, cavalry, and artillery began to descend with the fury of an avalanche, amidst the plaudits of Miss Rose and Miss Clara, who clapped their hands as they passed, and encouraged them with their voices, as the ladies from whom they were descended most likely were wont to do in the days of ancient chivalry.

Meantime the king of the mice perceived that he had to encounter an entire army.

In fact, the Nutcracker was in the centre with his gallant band of militia; on the left was the regiment of hussars, waiting only the moment to charge; on the right was stationed a formidable battalion of infantry; while, upon a footstool which commanded the entire scene of battle, was a park of ten cannon. In addition to these forces, a powerful reserve, composed of gingerbread men, and warriors made of sugar of different colours, had remained in the cupboard, and already began to bustle about. The king of the mice had, however, gone too far to retreat; and he gave the signal by a squeak, which was repeated by all the forces under his command.

At the same moment the battery on the foot stool replied with a volley of shot amongst the masses of mice.

The regiment of hussars rushed onward to the charge, so that on one side the dust raised by their horses' feet, and on the other the smoke of the cannon, concealed the plain of battle from the eyes of Mary, but in the midst of the roar of the cannon, the shouts of the combatants, and the groans of the dying, she heard the voice of the Nutcracker ever rising above the din.

"Serjeant Harlequin," he cried, "take twenty men, and fall upon the flank of the enemy. Lieutenant Punch, form into a square. Captain Puppet, fire in platoons. Colonel of Hussars, charge in masses, and not four deep, as you are doing. Bravo, good leaden soldiers—bravo! If all my troops behave as well as you, the day is ours!"

But, by these encouraging words even, Mary was at no loss to perceive that the battle was deadly, and that the victory remained doubtful. The mice, thrown back by the hussars—decimated by the fire of the platoons—and shattered by the park of artillery, returned again and again to the charge, biting and tearing all who came in their way. It was like the combats in the days of chivalry—a furious struggle foot to foot and hand to hand, each one bent upon attack or defence, without waiting to think of his neighbour Nutcracker vainly endeavoured to direct the evolutions in a disciplined manner, and form his troops into dense columns. The hussars, assailed by a numerous corps of mice, were scattered, and failed to rally round their colonel; a vast bat talion of the enemy had cut them off from the main body of their army, and had actually advanced up to the militia, which performed prodigies of valour. The beadle of the parish used his battle-axe most gallantly; the man-cook ran whole ranks of mice through with his spit; the leaden soldiers remained firm as a wall; but Harlequin and his twenty men had been driven back, and were forced to retreat under cover of the battery; and Lieutenant Punch's square had been broken up. The remains of his troops fled and threw the militia into disorder; and Captain Puppet, doubtless for want of cartridges, had ceased to fire, and was in full retreat. In consequence of this backward movement throughout the line, the park of cannon was exposed.

The king of the mice, perceiving that the success of the fight depended upon the capture of that battery, ordered his bravest troops to attack it. The foot stool was accordingly stormed in a moment, and the artillery men were cut to pieces by the side of their cannon.

One of them set fire to his powder wagon, and met a heroic death with twenty of his comrades. But all this display was useless against numbers; and in a short time a volley of shot, fired upon them from their own cannon, and which swept the forces commanded by the Nutcracker, convinced him that the battery of the footstool had fallen into the hands of the enemy.

From that moment the battle was lost, and the Nutcracker now thought only of beating an honourable retreat: but, in order to give breathing time to his troops, he summoned the reserve to his aid.

Thereupon the gingerbread men and the corps of sugar warriors descended from the cupboard and took part in the battle. They were certainly fresh, but very inexperienced, troops: the gingerbread men especially were very awkward, and, hitting right and left, did as much injury to friends as to enemies. The sugar warriors stood firm; but they were of such different natures—emperors, knights, Tyrolese peasants, gardeners, cupids, monkeys, lions, and crocodiles—that they could not combine their movements, and were strong only as a mass.

Their arrival, however, produced some good; for scarcely had the mice tasted the gingerbread men and the sugar warriors, when they left the leaden soldiers, whom they found very hard to bite, and turned also from the punches, harlequins, beadles, and cooks, who were only stuffed with bran, to fall upon the unfortunate reserve, which in a moment was surrounded by thousands of mice, and, after an heroic defence, devoured arms and baggage.

Nutcracker attempted to profit by that moment to rally his army; but the terrible spectacle of the destruction of the reserve had struck terror to the bravest hearts. Captain Puppet was as pale as death; Harlequin's clothes were in rags; a mouse had penetrated into Punch's hump, and, like the youthful Spartan's fox, began to devour his entrails; and not only was the colonel of the hussars a prisoner with a large portion of his troops, but the mice had even formed a squadron of cavalry, by means of the horses thus taken.

The unfortunate Nutcracker had no chance of victory left: he could not even retreat with honour; and therefore he determined to die.

He placed himself at the head of a small body of men, resolved like himself to sell their lives dearly.

In the meantime terror reigned among the dolls: Miss Clara and Miss Rose wrung their hands, and gave vent to loud cries.

"Alas!" exclaimed Miss Clara; "Must I die in the flower of my youth—I, the daughter of a king, and born to such brilliant destinies?"

"Alas!" said Miss Rose; "Am I doomed to fall into the hands of the enemy, and be devoured by the filthy mice?"

The other dolls ran about in tears; their cries mingling with those of Miss Clara and Miss Rose.

Meanwhile matters went worse and worse with Nutcracker: he was abandoned by the few friends who had remained faithful to him. The remains of the squadron of hussars took refuge in the cupboard; the leaden soldiers had all fallen into the power of the enemy; the cannoneers had long previously been dispersed; and the militia was cut to pieces, like the three hundred Spartans of Leonidas, without yielding a step. Nutcracker had planted himself against the lower part of the cupboard, which he vainly sought to climb up: he could not do so without the aid of Miss Rose or Miss Clara; and they had found nothing better to do than to faint. Nutcracker made a last effort, collected all his courage, and cried in an agony of despair, "A horse! A horse! My kingdom for a horse!" But, as in the case of Richard III, his voice remained without even an echo—or rather betrayed him to the enemy.

Two of the rifle brigade of the mice seized upon his wooden cloak; and at the same time the king of the mice cried with his seven mouths, "On your heads, take him alive! Remember that I have my mother to avenge! This punishment must serve as an example to all future Nutcrackers!"

And, with these words, the king rushed upon the prisoner.

But Mary could no longer support that horrible spectacle.

"Oh! My poor Nutcracker!" she exclaimed: "I love you with all my heart, and cannot see you die thus!"

At the same moment, by a natural impulse, and without precisely knowing what she was doing, Mary took off one of her shoes, and threw it with all her force in the midst of the combatants. Her aim was so good that the shoe hit the king of the mice, and made him roll over in the dust. A moment afterwards, king and army—conquerors and conquered—all alike disappeared, as if by enchantment. Mary felt a more severe pain than before in her arm. She endeavoured to reach an armchair to sit down; but her strength failed her—and she fainted!

VI

The Illness

Whr Mary awoke from her deep sleep, she found herself lying in her little bed, and the sun penetrated radiant and brilliant through the windows. By her side was seated a gentleman whom she shortly perceived to be a surgeon named Vandelstern, and who said in a low voice, the moment she opened her eyes, "She is awake."

Then the judge's wife advanced towards the bed, and gazed upon her daughter for a long time with an anxious air.

"Ah! My dear mamma," exclaimed little Mary, upon seeing her mother; "are all those horrible mice gone? And is my poor Nutcracker saved?"

"For the love of heaven, my dear Mary, do not repeat all that nonsense," said the lady. "What have mice, I should like to know, to do with the Nutcracker? But you, naughty girl, have frightened us all sadly. And it is always so when children are obstinate and will not obey their parents. You played with your toys very late last night: you most likely fell asleep; and it is probable that a little mouse frightened you. At all events, in your alarm, you thrust your elbow through one of the panes of the cupboard, and cut your arm in such a manner that Mr. Vandlestern, who has just extracted the fragments of glass, declares that you ran a risk of cutting an artery and dying through loss of blood. Heaven be thanked that I awoke—I know not at what o'clock—and that, recollecting how I had left you in the room, I went down to look after you. Poor child! You were stretched upon the floor, near the cupboard; and all round you were strewed the dolls, the puppets, the punches, the leaden soldiers, pieces of the gingerbread men, and Fritz's hussars—all scattered about pell-mell—while in your arms you held the Nutcracker. But how was it that you had taken off one of your shoes, and that it was at some distance from you?"

"Ah! My dear mother," said Mary, shuddering as she thought of what had taken place; "all that you saw was caused by the great battle that took place between the puppets and the mice: but the reason of my terror was that I saw the victorious mice about to seize the poor Nutcracker, who commanded the puppets;—and it was then that I threw my shoe at the king of the mice. After that, I know not what happened."

The surgeon made a sign to the judge's lady, who said in a soft tone to Mary, "Do not think anymore of all that, my dear child. All the mice are gone, and the little Nutcracker is safe and comfortable in the glass cupboard."

The judge then entered the room, and conversed for a long time with the surgeon; but of all that they said Mary could only catch these words—"It is delirium."

Mary saw immediately that her story was not believed, but that it was looked upon as a fable; and she did not say anymore upon the subject, but allowed those around her to have their own way. For she was anxious to get up as soon as possible and pay a visit to the poor Nutcracker. She, however, knew that he had escaped safe and sound from the battle; and that was all she cared about for the present.

Nevertheless Mary was very restless. She could not play, on account of her wounded arm; and when she tried to read or look over her picture books, everything swam so before her eyes, that she was obliged to give up the task. The time hung very heavily upon her hands; and she looked forward with impatience to the evening, because her mamma would then come and sit by her, and tell her pleasant stories.

One evening, the judge's wife had just ended the pretty tale of "Prince Facardin," when the door opened, and Godfather Drosselmayer thrust in his head, saying, "I must see with my own eyes how the little invalid gets on."

But when Mary perceived Godfather Drosselmayer with his glass wig, his black patch, and his drab frock coat, the remembrance of the night when the Nutcracker lost the famous battle against the mice, returned so forcibly to her mind, that she could not prevent herself from crying out, "O Godpapa Drosselmayer, you were really very ugly! I saw you quite plainly, when you were astride upon the clock, and when you covered it with your wings to prevent it from striking, because it would have frightened away the mice. I heard you call the king with the seven heads. Why did you not come to the aid of my poor Nutcracker, naughty Godpapa were the cause of my bed."

The judge's wife listened to all this with a kind of stupor; for she thought that the poor little girl was relapsing into delirium. She therefore said, in a low tone of alarm, "What are you talking about, Mary? Are you taking leave of your senses?"

"Oh no!" answered Mary; "Godpapa Drosselmayer knows I am telling the truth."

But the godfather, without saying a word, made horrible faces, like a man who was sitting upon thorns; then all of a sudden he began to chant these lines in a gloomy and sing-song tone:

"Old Clock-bell, beat
Low, dull, and hoarse—
Advance, retreat,
Thou gallant force!

The bell's lone sound proclaims around
The hour of deep midnight;
And the piercing note from the screech-owl's throat
Puts the king himself to flight.

Old clock-bell, beat
Low, dull, and hoarse:—
Advance, retreat,
Thou gallant force!"

Mary contemplated Godfather Drosselmayer with increasing terror; for he now seemed to her more hideously ugly than usual. She would indeed have been dreadfully afraid of him, if her mother had not been present, and if Fritz had not at that moment entered the room with a loud shout of laughter.

"Do you know, Godpapa Drosselmayer," said Fritz, "that you are uncommonly amusing today: you seem to move about just like my punch that stands behind the store; and, as for the song, it is not common sense."

But the judge's wife looked severe.

"My dear doctor," she said, "your song is indeed very strange, and appears to me to be only calculated to make little Mary worse."

"Nonsense!" cried Godfather Drosselmayer: "Do you not recognise the old chant which I am in the habit of humming when I mend your clocks?"

At the same time he seated himself near Mary's bed, and said to her in a rapid tone, "Do not be angry with me, my dear child, because I did not tear out the fourteen eyes of the king of the mice with my own hands; but I knew what I was about—and now, as I am anxious to make it up with you, I will tell you a story."

"What story?" asked Mary.

"*The History of the Crackatook Nut and Princess Pirlipata.* Do you know it?"

"No, my dear godpapa," replied Mary, whom the offer of a story reconciled to the doctor that moment. "Go on."

"My dear doctor," said the judge's wife, "I hope that your story will not be so melancholy as your song?"

"Oh! No, my dear lady," returned Godfather Drosselmayer. "On the contrary, it is very amusing."

"Tell it to us, then!" cried both the children.

Godfather Drosselmayer accordingly began in the following manner.

The History of the Crackatook Nut
and Princess Pirlipata (An Interlude)

Part I.
How Princess Pirlipata Was Born, and How the
Event Produced the Greatest Joy to Her Parents

THERE WAS LATELY, IN THE neighbourhood of Nuremberg, a little kingdom, which was not Prussia, nor Poland, nor Bavaria, nor the Palatinate, and which was governed by a king.

This king's wife, who was consequently a queen, became the mother of a little girl, who was therefore a princess by birth, and received the sweet name of Pirlipata.

The king was instantly informed of the event, and he hastened out of breath to see the pretty infant in her cradle. The joy which he felt in being the father of so charming a child, carried him to such an extreme that, quite forgetting himself, he uttered loud cries of joy, and began to dance round the room, crying, "Oh! Who has ever seen anything so beautiful as my Pirlipatetta?"

Then, as the king had been followed into the room by his ministers, his generals, the great officers of state, the chief judges, the councillors, and the puisne judges, they all began dancing round the room after the king, singing:

> *"Great monarch, we ne'er*
> *In this world did see*
> *A child so fair*
> *As the one that there*
> *Has been given to thee!*
> *Oh! Ne'er, and Oh! Ne'er,*
> *Was there child so fair!"*

And, indeed—although I may surprise you by saying so—there was not a word of flattery in all this; for, since the creation of the world, a sweeter child than Princess Pirlipata never had been seen. Her little face appeared to be made of the softest silken tissue; like the white and rosy tints of the lily combined. Her eyes were of the purest and brightest blue; and nothing was more charming than to behold the golden thread of her hair, flowing in delicate curls over shoulders as white as alabaster. Moreover, Pirlipata, when born, was already provided with two complete rows of the most pearly teeth, with which—two hours after her birth she bit the finger of the lord chancellor so hard, when, being near sighted, he stooped down to look close at her, that, although he belonged to the sect of stoic philosophers, he cried out according to some, "Oh! The dickens!" whereas others affirm, to the honour of philosophy, that he only said, "Oh! Oh!" However, up to the present day opinions are divided upon this important subject, neither party being willing to yield to the other. Indeed, the only point on which the *Dickensonians* and the *Ohists* are agreed is, that the princess really did bite the finger of the lord high chancellor. The country thereby learnt that there was as much spirit as beauty belonging to the charming Pirlipata.

Everyone was therefore happy in a kingdom so blest by heaven, save the queen herself, who was anxious and uneasy, no person knew why. But what chiefly struck people with surprise, was the care with which the timid mother had the cradle of the infant watched. In fact, besides having all the doors guarded by sentinels, and in addition to the two regular nurses, the queen had six other nurses to sit round the cradle, and who were relieved by half a dozen others at night. But what caused the greatest interest, and which no one could understand, was that each of these six nurses was compelled to hold a cat upon her knees, and to tickle it all night so as to prevent it from sleeping, and keep it purring.

I am certain, my dear children, that you are as curious as the inhabitants of that little kingdom without a name, to know why these extra nurses were forced to hold cats upon their knees, and to tickle them in such a way that they should never cease purring; but, as you would vainly endeavour to find out the secret of that enigma, I shall explain it to you, in order to save you the headache which would not fail to be the result of all your guesswork.

It happened one day that half a dozen great kings took it into their heads to pay a visit to the future father of Princess Pirlipata, for at that time the princess was not born. They were accompanied by the royal princes, the hereditary grand dukes, and the heirs apparent, all most agreeable personages. This arrival was the signal for the king whom they visited, and who was a most hospitable monarch, to make a large drain upon his treasury, and give tournaments, feasts, and dramatic representations. But this was not all. He having learnt from the intendant of the royal kitchens, that the Astronomer-Royal of the court had announced that the moment was favourable for killing pigs, and that the conjunction of the stars foretold that the year would be propitious for sausage making, the king commanded a tremendous slaughter of pigs to take place in the courtyard. Then, ordering his carriage, he went in person to call upon all the kings and princes staying in his capital, and invite them to dine with him; for he was resolved to surprise them by the splendid banquet which he intended to give them. On his return to the palace, he retired to the queen's apartment, and going up to her, said in a coaxing tone, with which he was always accustomed to make her do anything he wished, "My most particular and very dear love, you have not forgotten—have you—how doatingly fond I am of black puddings? You surely have not forgotten that?"

The queen understood by the first word what the king wanted of her. In fact she knew by his cunning address, that she must now proceed, as she had done many times before, to the very useful occupation of making, with her own royal hands, the greatest possible quantity of sausages, polonies, and black puddings. She therefore smiled at that proposal of her husband; for, although filling with dignity the high situation of queen, she was less proud of the compliments paid her upon the manner in which she bore the sceptre and the crown, than of those bestowed on her skill in making a black pudding, or any other dish. She therefore contented herself by curtseying gracefully to her husband, saying that she was quite ready to make him the puddings which he required.

The grand treasurer accordingly received orders to carry the immense enamelled cauldron and the large silver saucepans to the royal kitchens, so that the queen might make the black puddings, the polonies, and the sausages. An enormous fire was made with sandalwood; the queen put on her kitchen apron of white damask, and in a short time delicious odours steamed from the cauldron. Those sweet perfumes spread through the passages, penetrated into all the rooms, and reached the throne room where the king was holding a privy council. The king was very fond of good eating, and the smell made a profound impression upon him. Nevertheless, as he was a wise prince, and was famed for his habits of self-command, he resisted for a long time the feeling which attracted him towards the kitchens: but at last, in spite of the command which he exercised over himself, he was compelled to yield to the inclination that now ruled him.

"My lords and gentlemen," he accordingly said, rising from his throne, "with your permission I will retire for a few moments; pray wait for me."

Then this great king hastened through the passages and corridors to the kitchen, embraced his wife tenderly, stirred the contents of the cauldron with his golden sceptre, and tasted them with the tip of his tongue.

Having thus calmed his mind, he returned to the council, and resumed, though somewhat abstractedly, the subject of discussion. He had left the kitchen just at the important moment when the fat, cut up in small pieces, was about to be broiled upon the silver grid irons. The queen, encouraged by his praises, now commenced that important operation; and the first drops of grease had just dripped upon the live coals, when a squeaking voice was heard to chant the following lines:

> *"Dear sister, pray give to the Queen of the Mice,*
> *A piece of that fat which is grilling so nice;*
> *To me a good dinner is something so rare,*
> *That I hope of the fat you will give me a share."*

The queen immediately recognised the voice that thus spoke; it was the voice of Dame Mousey.

Dame Mousey had lived for many years in the palace. She declared herself to be a relation of the royal family, and was Queen of the kingdom of Mice. She therefore maintained a numerous court beneath the kitchen hearthstone.

The queen was a kind and good-natured woman; and although she would not publicly recognise Dame Mousey as a sister and a sovereign, she nevertheless showed her in private a thousand attentions. Her husband, more particular than herself, had often reproached her for thus lowering herself. But on the present occasion she could not find it in her heart to refuse the request of her little friend; and she accordingly said, "Come, Dame Mousey, without fear, and taste my pork fat as much as you like. I give you full leave so."

Dame Mousey accordingly leapt upon the hearth, quite gay and happy, and took with her little paws the pieces of fat which the queen gave her.

But, behold! The murmurs of joy which escaped the mouth of Dame Mousey, and the delicious smell of the morsels of fat on the grid iron, reached her seven sons, then her relations, and next her friends, all of whom were terribly addicted to gourmandising, and who now fell upon the fat with such fury, that the queen was obliged, hospitable as she was, to remind them that if they continued at that rate only five minutes more, there would not be enough fat left for the black puddings. But, in spite of the justice of this remonstrance, the seven sons of Dame Mousey took no heed of them; and setting a bad example to their relations and friends, rushed upon their aunt's fat, which would have entirely disappeared, had not the cries of the queen brought the man cook and the scullery boys, all armed with brushes and brooms, to drive the mice back again under the hearthstone.

But the victory, although complete, came somewhat too late; for there scarcely remained a quarter enough fat necessary for the polonies, the sausages, and the black puddings. The remnant, however, was scientifically divided by the royal mathematician, who was sent for in all possible haste, between the large cauldron containing the materials for the puddings, and the two saucepans in which the sausages and polonies were cooking.

Half an hour after this event, the cannon fired, the clarions and trumpets sounded, and then came the potentates, the royal princes, the hereditary dukes, and the heirs apparent to the thrones, all dressed in their most splendid clothes, and some riding on gallant chargers. The king received them on the threshold of the palace, in the most courteous manner possible; then, having conducted them to the banqueting room, he took his seat at the head of the table in his quality of sovereignhood, and having the crown upon his head and the sceptre in his hand. The guests all placed themselves at table according to their rank, as crowned kings, royal princes, hereditary dukes, or heirs apparent.

The board was covered with dainties, and everything went well during the soup and first course but when the polonies were placed on table, the king seemed to be agitated; when the sausages were served up, he grew very pale; and when the black puddings were brought in, he raised his eyes to heaven, sighs escaped his breast, and a terrible grief seemed to rend his soul. At length he fell back in his chair, and covered his face with his hands, sobbing and moaning in so lamentable a manner, that all the guests rose from their seats and surrounded him with great anxiety. At length the crisis seemed very serious; the court physician could not feel the beating of the pulse of the unfortunate monarch, who was thus overwhelmed with the weight of the most profound, the most frightful, and the most unheard of calamity. At length, upon the most violent remedies, such as burnt feathers, volatile salts, and cold keys thrust down the back, had been employed, the king seemed to return to himself. He opened his eyes, and said in a scarcely audible tone, "*not enough fat!*"

At these words, the queen grew pale in her turn, she threw herself at his feet, crying in a voice interrupted by sobs, "Oh! My unfortunate,

THE HISTORY OF A NUTCRACKER

unhappy, and royal husband, what grief have I not caused you, by refusing to listen to the advice which you have so often given me! But you behold the guilty one at your feet, and you can punish her as severely as you think fit."

"What is the matter?" demanded the king, "and what has happened that I know not of?"

"Alas! Alas!" answered the queen, to whom her husband had never spoken in so cross a tone; "Alas! Dame Mousey, her seven sons, her nephews, her cousins, and her friends, devoured the fat."

But the queen could not say anymore; her strength failed her, she fell back and fainted.

Then the king rose in a great rage, and cried in a terrible voice, "Let her ladyship the royal housekeeper explain what all this means! Come, speak!"

Then the royal namely, that being housekeeper related all that she knew; alarmed by the queen's cries, she ran and beheld her majesty beset by the entire family of Dame Mousey, and that, having summoned the cooks and scullery boys, the plunderers were compelled to retreat.

The king, perceiving that this was a case of high treason, resumed all his dignity and calmness, and commanded the privy council to meet that minute, the matter being of the utmost importance. The council assembled, the business was explained, and it was decided by a majority of voices, "That Dame Mousey, being accused of having eaten of the fat destined for the sausages, the polonies, and the black puddings of the king, should be tried for the same offence; and that if the said Dame Mousey was found guilty, she and all her race should be banished from the kingdom, and all her goods or possessions, namely, lands, castles, palaces, and royal residences should be confiscated."

Then the king observed to his councillors that while the trial lasted, Dame Mousey and her family would have sufficient time to devour all the fat in the royal kitchens, which would expose him to the same privation as that which he had just endured in the presence of six crowned heads, without reckoning royal princes, hereditary dukes, and heirs apparent. He therefore demanded a discretionary power in respect to Dame Mousey and her family.

The privy council divided, for the form of the thing, but the discretionary power was voted, as you may well suppose, by a large majority.

The king then sent one of his best carriages, preceded by a courier that greater speed might be used, to a very skilful mechanic who lived at Nuremberg, and whose name was Christian Elias Drosselmayer.

This mechanic was requested to proceed that moment to the palace upon urgent business. Christian Elias Drosselmayer immediately obeyed, for he felt convinced that the king required him to make some work of art. Stepping into the vehicle, he travelled day and night, until he arrived in the king's presence. Indeed, such was his haste, that he had not waited to change the drab-coloured coat which he usually wore. But, instead of being angry at that breach of etiquette, the king was much pleased with his haste; for if the famous mechanic had committed a fault, it was in his anxiety to obey the king's commands.

The king took Christian Elias Drosselmayer into his private chamber, and explained to him the position of affairs; namely, that it was decided upon to make a striking example of the race of mice throughout the kingdom; that, attracted by the fame of his skill, the king had fixed upon him to put the decree of justice into execution; and that the said king's only fear was lest the mechanic, skilful though he were, should perceive insurmountable difficulties in the way of appeasing the royal anger.

But Christian Elias Drosselmayer reassured the king, promising that in eight days there should not be a single mouse left in the kingdom.

In a word, that very same day he set to work to make several ingenious little oblong boxes, inside which he placed a morsel of fat at the end of a piece of wire. By seizing upon the fat, the plunderer, whoever he might be, caused the door to shut down behind him, and thus became a prisoner. In less than a week, a hundred of these boxes were made, and placed, not only beneath the hearthstone, but in all the garrets, lofts, and cellars of the palace. Dame Mousey was far too cunning and sagacious not to discover at the first glance the stratagem of Master Drosselmayer. She therefore assembled her seven sons, their nephews, and their cousins, to warn them of the snare that was laid for them. But, after having appeared to listen to her, in consequence of the respect which they had for her, and the veneration which her years commanded, they withdrew, laughing at her terrors; then, attracted by the smell of the fried pork fat, they resolved, in spite of the representations made to them, to profit by the charity that came they knew not whence.

At the expiration of twenty-four hours, the seven sons of Dame Mousey, eighteen of her nephews, fifty of her cousins, and two hundred and thirty-five of her other connexions, without reckoning thousands of her subjects, were caught in the mousetraps and ignominiously executed.

Then did Dame Mousey, with the remnant of her court and the rest of her subjects, resolve upon abandoning, a place covered with the blood of her massacred relatives and friends. The tidings of that resolution became known, and reached the ears of the king. His majesty expressed his satisfaction, and the poets of the court composed sonnets upon his victory, while the courtiers compared him to Sesostris, Alexander, and Cæsar.

The queen was alone anxious and uneasy; she knew Dame Mousey well, and suspected that she would not leave unavenged the death of her relations and friends. And, in fact, at the very moment when the queen, by way of atoning for her previous fault, was preparing with her own hands a liver soup for the king, who doated upon that dish, Dame Mousey suddenly appeared and chanted the following lines:

> "Thine husband, void of pity and of fear,
> Hath slain my cousins, sons, and nephews dear;
> But list, O Queen! To the decrees of fate:
> The child which heaven will shortly give to thee,
> And which the object of thy love will be,
> Shall bear the rage of my vindictive hate.
>
> Thine husband owneth castles, cannon, towers,
> A council's wisdom, and an army's powers,
> Mechanics, ministers, mousetraps, and snares:
> None of all these, alas! To me belong;
> But heaven hath given me teeth, sharp, firm, and strong,
> That I may rend in pieces royal heirs."

Having sung these words she disappeared, and no one saw her afterwards. But the queen, who expected a little baby, was so overcome by the prophecy, that she upset the liver soup into the fire.

Thus, for the second time, was Dame Mousey the cause of depriving the king of one of his favourite dishes, where at he fell into a dreadful rage. He, however, rejoiced more than ever at the step he had taken to rid his country of the mice.

It is scarcely necessary to say that Christian Elias Drosselmayer was sent away well rewarded, and returned in triumph to Nuremberg.

Part II.

How, In Spite of the Precautions Taken By the Queen, Dame Mousey Accomplishes Her Threat in Regard to Princess Pirlipata

AND NOW, MY DEAR CHILDREN, you know as well as I do, wherefore the queen had Princess Pirlipata watched with such wonderful care. She feared the vengeance of Dame Mousey; for, according to what Dame Mousey had said, there could be nothing less in store for the heiress of this little kingdom without a name, than the loss of her life, or at all events her beauty; which last affliction is considered by some people worse for one of her sex. What redoubled the fears of the queen was, that the machines invented by Master Drosselmayer were totally useless against the experience of Dame Mousey. The astronomer of the court, who was also grand prophet and grand astrologer, was fearful lest his office should be suppressed unless he gave his opinion at this important juncture: he accordingly declared that he read in the stars the great fact that the illustrious family of the cat Murr was alone capable of defending the cradle against the approach of Dame Mousey. It was for this reason that each of the six nurses was forced to hold a cat constantly upon her knees. Those cats might be considered as underofficers attached to the court; and the nurses sought to lighten the cares of the duty performed by the cats, by gently rubbing them with their fair hands.

You know, my dear children, that there are certain times when a person watches even while actually dozing; and so it was that, one evening, in spite of all the efforts which the six nurses made to the contrary, as they sate round the cradle of the princess with the cats upon their knees, they felt sleep rapidly gaining upon them.

Now, as each nurse kept her own ideas to herself, and was afraid of revealing them to their companions, hoping all the time that their drowsiness would not be perceived by the others, the result was, that, one after another, they closed their eyes—their hands stopped from stroking the cats—and the cats themselves, being no longer rubbed and scratched, profited by the circumstance to take a nap.

I cannot say how long this strange slumber had lasted, when, towards midnight, one of the nurses awoke with a start. All the others were in a state of profound lethargy: not a sound—not even their very breathing, was heard: the silence of death reigned around, broken only by the slight creak of the worm biting the wood. But how frightened was the nurse when she beheld a large and horrible mouse standing up near her on its hind legs, and, having plunged its head into the cradle, seemed very busy in biting the face of the princess! She rose with a cry of alarm; and at that exclamation, all the other nurses jumped up. But Dame Mousey—for she indeed it was—sprang towards one corner of the room. The cats leapt after her: alas! It was too late Dame Mousey had disappeared by a crevice in the floor.

At the same moment Princess Pirlipata, who was awoke by all that din, began to cry. Those sounds made the nurses leap with joy.

"Thank God!" they said; "Since Princess Pirlipata cries she is not dead."

They then all ran towards the cradle—but their despair was great indeed when they saw what had happened to that delicate and charming creature!

In fact, instead of that face of softly-blended white and red—that little head, with its golden hair—those mild blue eyes, azure as the sky itself—instead of all these charms the nurses beheld an enormous and misshapen head upon a deformed and ugly body. Her two sweet eyes had lost their heavenly hue, and became goggle, fixed, and haggard. Her little mouth had grown from ear to ear; and her chin was covered with a beard like grizzly cotton. All this would have suited old Punch; but seemed very horrible for a young princess.

At that moment the queen entered. The twelve nurses threw themselves with their faces against the ground; while the six cats walked about to discover if there were not some open window by which they might escape upon the tiles.

At the sight of her child the despair of the poor mother was something frightful to behold; and she was carried off in a fainting fit into the royal chamber. But it was chiefly the unhappy father whose sorrow was the most desperate and painful to witness. The courtiers were compelled to put padlocks upon the windows, for fear he should throw himself out; and they were also forced to line the walls with mattresses, lest he should dash out his brains against them. His sword was of course taken away from him; and neither knife nor fork, nor any sharp or pointed instruments were left in his way. This was the more easily effected; inasmuch as he ate nothing for the two or three following days, crying without ceasing, "Oh! Miserable king that I am! Oh! Cruel destiny that thou art!"

Perhaps, instead of accusing destiny, the king should have remembered that, as is generally the case with mankind, he was the author of his own misfortunes; for had he known how to content himself with black puddings containing a little less fat than usual, and had he abandoned his ideas of vengeance, and left Dame Mousey and her family in peace beneath the hearthstone, the affliction which he deplored would not have happened. But we must confess that the ideas of the royal father of Princess Pirlipata did not tend at all in that direction.

On the contrary—believing, as all great men do, that they must necessarily attribute their misfortunes to others he threw all the blame upon the skilful mechanic Christian Elias Drosselmayer. Well convinced, moreover, that if he invited him back to court to be hung or beheaded, he would not accept the invitation, he desired him to come in order to receive a new order of knighthood which had just been created for men of letters, artists, and mechanics. Master Drosselmayer was not exempt from human pride: he thought that a star would look well upon the breast of his drab surtout coat; and accordingly set off for the king's court. But his joy was soon changed into fear; for on the frontiers of the kingdom, guards awaited him. They seized upon him, and conducted him from station to station, until they reached the capital.

The king, who was afraid of being won over to mercy, would not see Master Drosselmayer when the latter arrived at the palace; but he ordered him to be immediately conducted to the cradle of Pirlipata, with the assurance that if the princess were not restored by that day month to her former state of beauty, he would have the mechanic's head cut off.

Master Drosselmayer did not pretend to be bolder than his fellow-men, and had always hoped to die a natural death. He was therefore much frightened at this threat. Nevertheless, trusting, a great deal to his knowledge, which his own modesty had never prevented him from being aware of to its full extent, he acquired courage. Then he set to work to discover whether the evil would yield to any remedy, or whether it were really incurable, as he from the first believed it to be.

With this object in view, he skilfully took off the head of the Princess, and next all her limbs. He likewise dissected the hands and the feet, in order to examine, with more accuracy, not only the joints and the muscles, but also the internal formation. But, alas! The more he worked into the frame of Pirlipata, the more firmly did he become convinced that as the princess grew, the uglier she would become.

He therefore joined Pirlipata together again; and then, seating himself by the side of her cradle, which he was not to quit until she had resumed her former beauty, he gave way to his melancholy thoughts.

The fourth week had already commenced, and Wednesday made its appearance, when, according to custom, the king came in to see if any change had taken place in the exterior of the princess. But when he saw that it was just the same, he shook his sceptre at the mechanic, crying; "Christian Elias Drosselmayer, take care of yourself! You have only three days left to restore me my daughter just as she was wont to be; and if you remain obstinate in refusing to cure her, on Monday next you shall be beheaded."

Master Drosselmayer, who could not cure the princess, not through any obstinacy on his part, but through actual ignorance how to do it, began to weep bitterly, surveying, with tearful eyes, Princess Pirlipata, who was cracking nuts as comfortably as if she were the most beautiful child upon earth. Then, as he beheld that melting spectacle, the mechanic was struck for the first time by that particular taste for nuts which the princess had shown since her birth; and he remembered also the singular fact that she was born with teeth. In fact, immediately after her change from beauty to ugliness she had begun to cry bitterly, until she found a nut near her: she had then cracked it, eaten the kernel, and turned round to sleep quietly. From that moment the nurses had taken good care to fill their pockets with nuts, and give her one or more whenever she made a face.

"Oh! Instinct of nature! Eternal and mysterious sympathy of all created beings!" cried Christian Elias Drosselmayer, "Thou showest me the door which leads to the discovery of thy secrets! I will knock at it, and it will open!"

At these words, which surprised the king, the mechanic turned towards his majesty and requested the favour of being conducted into the presence of the astronomer of the court. The king consented, but on condition that it should be with a guard. Master Drosselmayer would perhaps have been better pleased to take that little walk all alone; but, as under the circumstances he could not help himself, he was obliged to submit to what he could not prevent, and proceed through the streets of the capital escorted like a felon.

On reaching the house of the astrologer, Master Drosselmayer threw himself into his arms; and they embraced each other a midst torrents of tears, for they were acquaintances of long standing, and were much attached to each other. They then retired to a private room, and examined a great number of books which treated upon likings and dislikings, and a host of other matters not a whit less profound. At length night came; and the astrologer ascending to his tower, and aided by Master Drosselmayer, who was himself very skilful in such matters, discovered, in spite of the difficulty of the heavenly circles which crossed each other in all directions, that in order to break the spell which rendered Princess Pirlipata hideous, and to restore her to her former beauty, she must eat the kernel of the Crackatook nut, the shell of which was so hard that the wheel of a forty-eight pounder might pass over it without breaking it. Moreover, it was necessary that this nut should be cracked in the presence of the princess, and by a young man who had never been shaved, and who had always worn boots. Lastly, it was requisite that he should present the nut to the princess with his eyes closed, and in the same way step seven paces backward without stumbling.

Such was the answer of the stars.

Drosselmayer and the astronomer had worked without ceasing for four days and four nights, to clear up this mysterious affair. It was on the Sunday evening,—the king had finished his dinner, and was just beginning on the dessert,—when the mechanic, who was to be beheaded next day, entered the royal dining room, full of joy, and announced that he had discovered the means of restoring Princess Pirlipata to her former beauty. At these news, the king caught him in his arms, with the most touching kindness, and asked him what those means were.

The mechanic thereupon explained to the king the result of his consultation with the astrologer.

"I knew perfectly well, Master Drosselmayer," said the king, "that all your delay was only through obstinacy. It is, however, settled at last; and after dinner we will set to work. Take care, then, dearest mechanic, to have the young man who has never been shaved, and who wears boots, in readiness in ten minutes, together with the nut Crackatook. Let him, moreover, abstain from drinking wine for the next hour, for fear he should stumble while walking backwards like a crab; but when once it is all over, is welcome to my whole cellar, and may chooses."

But, to the great astonishment of the king, Master Drosselmayer seemed quite frightened at these words; and, as he held his tongue, the king insisted upon knowing why he remained silent and motionless instead of hastening to execute the orders of his sovereign.

"Sire," replied the mechanician, throwing himself on his knees before the king, "it is perfectly true that we have found out the means of curing Princess Pilipata, and that those means consist of her eating a Crackatook nut when it shall have been cracked by a young man who has never been

THE HISTORY OF A NUTCRACKER

shaved, and who has always worn boots; but we have not as yet either the young man or the nut—we know not where to find them, and in all probability we shall have the greatest difficulty in discovering both the nut and the Nutcracker."

At these words, the king brandished his sceptre above the head of the mechanician, crying, "Then hasten to the scaffold!"

But the side of the queen, on her side, hastened to kneel by of Master Drosselmayer, and begged her august husband to remember that by cutting off the head of the mechanician he would be losing even that ray of hope which remained to them during his lifetime; that the chances were that he who had discovered the horoscope would also find the nut and the nutcracker; that they ought to believe the more firmly in the present prediction of the astronomer, inasmuch as nothing which he had hitherto prophesied had ever come to pass, but that it was evident his presages must be fulfilled someday or another, inasmuch as the king had named him his grand prophet; and that, as the princess was not yet of an age to marry (she being now only three months old), and would not even be marriageable until she was fifteen, there was consequently a period of fourteen years and nine months during which Master Drosselmayer and the astrologer might search after the Crackatook nut and the young man who was to break it. The queen therefore suggested that a reprieve might be awarded to Christian Elias Drosselmayer, at the expiration of which he should return to surrender himself into the king's power, whether he had found the means of curing the princess, or not; and either to be generously rewarded, or put to death without mercy.

The king, who was a very just man, and who on that day especially had dined splendidly upon his two favourite dishes—namely, liver soup and black puddings—lent a favourable ear to the prayer of his wise and courageous queen.

He therefore decided that the astrologer and the mechanician should that moment set out in search of the nut and the Nutcracker; for which purpose he granted fourteen years and nine months, with the condition that they should return, at the expiration of that reprieve, to place themselves in his power, so that, if they were empty-handed, he might deal with them according to his own royal pleasure.

If, on the contrary, they should make their reappearance with the Crackatook nut which was to restore the princess to all her former beauty, the astrologer would be rewarded with a yearly pension of six hundred pounds and a telescope of honour; and the mechanician would receive a sword set with diamonds, the Order of the Golden Spider (the grand order of the state), and a new frock coat.

As for the young man who was to crack the nut, the king had no doubt of being able to find one suitable for the purpose, by means of advertisements constantly inserted in the national and foreign newspapers.

Touched by this declaration on the part of the king, which relieved them from half the difficulty of their task, Christian Elias Drosselmayer pledged his honour that he would either find the Crackatook nut, or return, like another Regulus, to place himself in the hands of the king.

That same evening the astrologer and the mechanician departed from the capital of the kingdom to commence their researches.

Part III.
How the Mechanician and the Astrologer Wander Over the Four Quarter of the World, and Discovered a Fifth, Without Finding the Crackatook Nut

IT WAS NOW FOURTEEN YEARS and five months since the astrologer and the mechanician first set out on their wanderings through all parts, without discovering a vestige of what they sought. They had first of all travelled through Europe; then they visited America, next Africa, and afterwards Asia: they even discovered a fifth part of the world, which learned men have since called New Holland, because it was discovered by two Germans! But throughout that long series of travels, although they had seen many nuts of different shapes and sizes, they never fell in with the Crackatook nut.

They had, however, in, alas! A vain hope, passed several years at the court of the King of Dates and at that of the Prince of Almonds: they had uselessly consulted the celebrated Academy of Grau Monkeys and the famous Naturalist Society of Squirrels; until at length they arrived, sinking with fatigue, upon the borders of the great forest which touches the feet of the Himalayan Mountains. And now they dolefully said to each other that they had only a hundred and twenty-two days to find what they sought, after an useless search of fourteen years and five months.

If I were to tell you, my dear children, the strange adventures which happened to the two travellers during that long wandering, I should occupy you every evening for an entire month, and should then weary you in the long run. I will therefore only tell you that Christian Elias Drosselmayer, who was the most eager in search after the nut, since his head depended upon finding it, gave himself up to greater dangers than his companion, and lost all his hair by a stroke of the sun received in the tropics. He also lost his right eye by an arrow which a Caribbean Chief aimed at him. Moreover, his drab frock coat, which was not new when he left Germany, had literally fallen into rags and tatters His situation was therefore most deplorable and yet, so much do men cling to life, that, damaged as he was by the various accidents which had be fallen him, he beheld with increasing terror the approach of the moment when he must return to place himself in the power of the king.

Nevertheless, the mechanician was a man of honour: he would not break a promise so sacred as that which he had made. He accordingly resolved, whatever might happen, to set out the very next morning on his return to Germany. And indeed there was no time to lose; fourteen years and five months had passed away, and the two travellers had only a hundred and twenty-two days, as we have already said, to reach the capital of Princess Pirlipata's father.

Christian Elias Drosselmayer accordingly made known his noble intention to his friend the astrologer; and both decided that they would set out on their return next morning.

And, true to this intention, the travellers resumed their journey at daybreak, taking the direction of Bagdad. From Bagdad they proceeded to Alexandria, where they embarked for Venice. From Venice they passed through the Tyrol; and from the Tyrol they entered into the kingdom of Pirlipata's father, both sincerely hoping that he was either dead or in his dotage.

But, alas! It was no such thing! Upon reaching the capital, the unfortunate mechanician learnt that the worthy monarch not only had not lost his intellectual faculties, but was also in better health than ever. There was consequently no chance for him—unless Princess Pirlipata had become cured of her ugliness without any remedy at all, which was not possible; or, that the king's heart had softened, which was not probable—of escaping the dreadful fate which threatened him.

He did not however present himself the less boldly at the gate of the palace, for he was sustained by the idea that he was doing a heroic action; and he accordingly desired to speak to the king.

The king, who was easy of access, and who gave an audience to whomsoever he had business with, ordered the grand master of the ceremonies to bring the strangers into his presence.

The grand master of the ceremonies then stated that the strangers were of a most villainous appearance, and could not possibly be worse dressed. But the king answered that it was wrong to judge the heart by the countenance, and the gown did not make the parson.

Thereupon, the grand master of the ceremonies, having perceived the correctness of these observations, bowed respectfully and proceeded to fetch the mechanician and the astrologer.

The king was the same as ever, and they immediately recognised him; but the travellers were so changed, especially poor Elias Drosselmayer, that they were obliged to declare who they were.

Upon seeing the two travellers return of their own accord, the king gave a sign of joy, for he felt well convinced that they would not have come back if they had not found the Crackatook nut. But he was speedily undeceived; and the mechanician, throwing himself at his feet, confessed that, in spite of the most earnest and constant search, his friend and himself had returned empty-handed.

The king, as we have said, although of a passionate disposition, was an excellent man at bottom; he was touched by the punctuality with which Christian Elias Drosselmayer had kept his word; and he changed the sentence of death, long before pronounced against him, into imprisonment for life. As for the astrologer, he contented himself by banishing that great sage.

But as three days were still remaining of the period of fourteen years and nine months' delay, granted by the king, Master Drosselmayer, who was deeply attached to his country, implored the king's permission to profit by those three days to visit Nuremberg once more.

This request seemed so just to the king, that he granted it without any restriction.

Master Drosselmayer, having only three days left, resolved to profit by that time as much as possible; and, having fortunately found that two places in the mail were not taken, he secured them that moment.

Now, as the astrologer was himself condemned to banishment, and as it was all the same to him which way he went, he took his departure with the mechanician.

Next morning, at about ten o'clock, they were at Nuremberg. As Master Drosselmayer had only one relation in the world, namely, his brother, Christopher Zacharias Drosselmayer, who kept one of the principal toy shops in Nuremberg, it was at his house that he alighted.

Christopher Zacharias Drosselmayer was overjoyed to see his poor brother Christian Elias, whom he had believed to be dead. In the first instance he would not admit that the man with the bald head and the black patch upon the eye was in reality his brother; but the mechanician showed him his famous drab surtout coat, which, all tattered as it was, had retained in certain parts some traces of its original colour; and in support of that first proof he mentioned so many family secrets, unknown to all save to Zacharias and himself, that the toy merchant was compelled to yield to the evidence brought forward.

He then inquired of him what had kept him so long absent from his native city, and in what country he had left his hair, his eye, and the missing pieces of his coat.

Christian Elias Drosselmayer had no motive to keep secret from his brother the events which had occurred. He began by introducing his companion in misfortune; and, this formal usage having been performed, he related his adventures from A to Z, ending them by saying that he had only a few hours to stay with his brother, because, not having found the Crackatook nut, he was on the point of being shut up in a dungeon forever.

While Christian Elias was telling his story, Christopher Zacharias had more than once twiddled his finger and thumb, turned round upon one leg, and made a certain knowing noise with his tongue. Under any other circumstances, the mechanician would have demanded of him what those signs meant; but he was so full of thought, that he saw nothing; and it was only when his brother exclaimed, "Hem! Hem!" twice, and "Oh! Oh! Oh!" three times, that he asked the reason of those expressions.

"The reason is," said Christopher Zacharias, "that it would be strange indeed if—but, no—and yet—"

"What do you mean?" cried the mechanician.

"If" continued the toy merchant.

"If what?" again said Master Drosselmayer.

But instead of giving any answer, Christopher Zacharias, who, during those short questions and answers, had no doubt collected his thoughts, threw his wig up into the air, and began to caper about, crying, "Brother, you are saved! You shall not go to prison; for either I am much mistaken or I myself am in possession of the Crackatook nut."

And, without giving any further explanation to his astonished brother, Christopher Zacharias rushed out of the room, but returned in a moment with a box containing a large gilt filbert, which he presented to the mechanician.

The mechanician, who dared not believe in such good luck, took the nut with hesitation, and turned it round in all directions so as to examine it with the attention which it deserved. He then declared that he was of the same opinion as his brother, and that he should be much astonished if that filbert were not indeed the Crackatook nut. Thus saying, he handed it to the astrologer, and asked his opinion.

The astrologer examined it with as much attention as Master Drosselmayer had done; but shaking his head, he replied, "I should also be of the same opinion as yourself and brother, if the nut were not gilt; but I have not seen anything in the stars showing that the nut which we are in search of ought to be so ornamented. Besides, how came your brother by the Crackatook nut?"

"I will explain the whole thing to you," said Christopher, "and tell you how the nut fell into my hands, and how it came to have that gilding which prevents you from recognising it, and which indeed is not its own naturally."

Then—having made them sit down, for he very wisely thought that after travelling for fourteen years and nine months, they must be tired— he began as follows: —

"The very day on which the king sent for you under pretence of giving you an Order of Knighthood, a stranger arrived at Nuremberg, carrying with him a bag of nuts which he had to sell. But the nut-merchants of this town, being anxious to keep the monopoly to themselves, quarrelled with him just opposite my shop. The stranger, with a view to defend himself more easily, placed his bag of nuts upon the ground, and the fight continued, to the great delight of the little boys and the ticket-porters; when a waggon, heavily laden, passed over the bag of nuts. Upon seeing this accident, which they attributed to the justice of heaven, the merchants considered that they were sufficiently avenged, and left the stranger alone. He picked up his bag, and all his nuts were found to be cracked, save ONE—one only—which he handed to me with a strange kind of smile, requesting me to buy it for a new zwanziger of the year 1720, and declaring that the day would come when I should not repent the bargain, dear as it then might seem. I felt in my pocket, and was much surprised to find a zwanziger of the kind mentioned by this man. The coincidence seemed so strange, that I gave him my zwanziger; he handed me the nut, and took his departure.

"I placed the nut in my window for sale; and although I only asked two kreutzers more than the money I had given for it, it remained in the window for seven or eight years without finding a purchaser. I then had it gilt to increase its value; but for that purpose I uselessly spent two zwanzigers more; for the nut has been here ever since the day I bought it."

At that moment the astronomer, in whose hands the nut had remained, uttered a cry of joy. While Master Drosselmayer was listening to his brother's story, the astrologer had delicately scraped off some of the gilding of the nut; and on the shell he had found the word "CRACKATOOK" engraven in Chinese characters.

All doubts were now cleared up; and the three individuals danced for joy, the real Crackatook nut being actually in their possession.

Part IV.

How, After Having Found the Crackatook Nut, the Mechanician and the Astrologer Find the Young Man Who is to Crack It

CHRISTIAN ELIAS DROSSELMAYER WAS IN such a hurry to announce the good news to the king, that he was anxious to return by the mail that very moment; but Christian Zecharias begged him to stay at least until his son should come in. The mechanician yielded the more easily to this request, because he had not seen his nephew for fifteen years, and because, on recalling the ideas of the past, he remembered that at the time when he quitted Nuremberg, he had left the said nephew a fine fat romping fellow of only three and a half, but of whom he (the uncle) was doatingly fond.

While he was thinking of a handsome young man these things, of between eighteen and nineteen entered the shop of Christopher Zacharias, whom he saluted by the name of "Father."

Then Christopher Zacharias, having embraced him, presented him to Christian Elias, saying to the young man, "And now embrace your uncle."

The young man hesitated; for Uncle Drosselmayer, with his frock coat in rags, his bald head, and the plaster upon his eye, did not seem a very inviting person. But his father observed the hesitation, and as he was fearful that Christian Elias's feelings would be wounded, he pushed his son forward, and thrust him into the arms of the mechanician.

In the meantime the astrologer had kept his eyes fixed upon the young man with a steady attention which seemed so singular that the youth felt ill at his ease in being so stared at, and left the room.

The astrologer then put several questions to Christopher Zecharias concerning his son; and the father answered them with all the enthusiasm of a fond parent.

Young Drosselmayer was, as his appearance indicated, between seventeen and eighteen. From his earliest years he had been so funny and yet so tractable, that his mother had taken a delight in dressing him like some of the puppets which her husband sold: namely, sometimes as a student, sometimes as a postilion, sometimes as a Hungarian, but always in a garb that required boots; because, as he possessed the prettiest little foot in the world, but had a rather small calf, the boots showed off the little foot, and concealed the fault of the calf.

"And so," said the astrologer to Christopher Zecharias, your son has always worn boots?"

Christian Elias now stared in his turn.

"My son has never worn anything but boots," replied the toy man. "At the age of ten," he continued, "I sent him to the University of Tubingen, where he remained till he was eighteen, without contracting any of the bad habits of his companions, such as drinking swearing, and fighting. The only weakness of which I believe him to be guilty, is that he allows the four or five wretched hairs which he has upon his chin to grow, without permitting a barber to touch his countenance."

"And thus," said the astrologer, "your son has never been shaved?"

Christian Elias stared more and more.

"Never," answered Christopher Zecharias.

"And during the holidays," continued the astrologer, "how did he pass his time?"

"Why," replied the father, "he used to remain in the shop, in his becoming student's dress; and, through pure good-nature, he cracked nuts for all the young ladies who came to the shop to buy toys, and who, on that account, called him *Nutcracker*."

"Nutcracker!" cried the mechanician.

"Nutcracker!" repeated the astrologer in his turn.

And then they looked at each other while Christopher Zecharias looked at them both.

"My dear sir," said the astrologer to the toy man," in my opinion your fortune is as good as made."

The toy man, who had not heard this prophecy without a feeling of pleasure, required an explanation, which the astrologer, however, put off until the next morning.

When the mechanician and the astrologer were shown to their apartment, and were alone together, the astrologer embraced his friend, crying, "It is he! We have him!"

"Do you think so?" demanded Christian Elias, in the tone of a man who had his doubts, but who only wished to be convinced.

"Can there be any uncertainty?" exclaimed the astrologer: "he has all the necessary qualifications!"

"Let us sum them up."

"He has never worn anything but boots."

"True!"

"He has never been shaved."

"True, again!"

"And through good nature, he has stood in his father's shop to crack nuts for young persons, who never called him by any other name than *Nutcracker*."

"All this is quite true."

"My dear friend," added the astrologer, "one stroke of good luck never comes alone. But if you still doubt, let us go and consult the stars."

They accordingly ascended to the roof of the house; and, having drawn the young man's horoscope, discovered that he was intended for great things.

This prophecy, which confirmed all the astrologer's hopes, forced the mechanician to adopt his opinion.

"And now," said the astrologer, in a triumphant tone, "there are only two things which we must not neglect."

"What are they?" demanded Christian Elias.

"The first is, that you must fit to the nape of your nephew's neck a large piece of wood, which must be so well connected with the lower jaw that it will increase its power by the fact of pressure."

"Nothing is more easy," answered Christian Elias; "it is the A, B, C of mechanics."

"The second thing," continued the astrologer, "is, that on arriving at the residence of the king, we must carefully conceal the fact that we have brought with us the young man who is destined to crack the Crackatook nut. For my opinion is that the more teeth there are broken, and the more jaws there are dislocated in trying to break the Crackatook nut, the more eager the king will be to offer a great reward to him who shall succeed where so many will have failed."

"My dear friend," answered the mechanician, "you are a man of sound sense. Let us go to bed."

And, with these words, having quitted the top of the house, they descended to their bedroom, where, having drawn their cotton night-caps over their ears, they slept more comfortably than they had done for fourteen years and nine months past.

On the following morning, at an early hour, the two friends went down to the apartment of Christopher Zecharias, and told him all the fine plans they had formed the evening before. Now, as the toy man was not wanting in ambition, and as, in his paternal fondness, he fancied that his son must certainly possess the strongest jaws in all Germany, he gladly assented to the arrangement, which was to take from his shop not only the nut but also the *Nutcracker*.

The young man himself was more difficult to persuade. The wooden counterbalance which it was proposed to fix to the back of his neck, instead of the pretty little tie which kept his hair in such neat folds, particularly vexed him. But his father, his uncle, and the astrologer made him such splendid promises, that he consented. Christian Elias Drosselmayer, therefore, went to work that moment; the wooden balance was soon made; and it was strongly fixed to the nape of the young man now so full of hope. Let me also state, to satisfy your curiosity, that the contrivance worked so well that on the very first the skilful mechanician received brilliant proofs of his success, for the young man was enabled to crack the hardest apricot stones, and the most obstinate peach stones.

These trials having been made, the astrologer, the mechanician, and young Drosselmayer set out immediately for the king's dwelling. Christopher Zecharias was anxious to go with them; but, as he was forced to take care of his shop, that excellent father resigned himself to necessity, and remained behind at Nuremberg.

Part V.
END OF THE HISTORY OF PRINCESS PIRLIPATA

THE MECHANICIAN AND THE ASTROLOGER, on reaching the capital, took good care to leave young Drosselmayer at the inn where they put up. They then proceeded to the palace to announce that having vainly sought the Crackatook nut all over the world, they had at length found it at Nuremberg: But of him who was to crack it, they said not a word, according to the arrangement made between them.

The joy at the palace was very great.

The king sent directly for the privy councillor who had the care of the public mind, and who acted as censor in respect to the newspapers; and this great man, by the king's command, drew up an article to be inserted in the *Royal Gazette*, and which all other newspapers were ordered to copy, to the effect that "*all persons who fancied they had teeth good enough to break the Crackatook nut, were to present themselves at the palace, and if they succeeded, would be liberally rewarded for their trouble.*"

This circumstance was well suited to show how rich the kingdom was in strong jaws. The candidates were so numerous, that the king was forced to form a jury, the foreman of whom was the crown dentist; and their duty was to examine all the competitors, to see if they had all their thirty-two teeth perfect, and whether any were decayed.

Three thousand five hundred candidates were admitted to this first trial, which lasted a week, and which produced only an immense number of broken teeth and jaws put out of place.

It was therefore necessary to make a second appeal; and all the national and foreign newspapers were crammed with advertisements to that purpose. The king offered the post of Perpetual Judge of the Academy, and the order of the Golden Spider to whomsoever should succeed in cracking the Crackatook nut. There was no necessity to have a degree of Doctor of Philosophy, or Master of Arts, to be competent to stand as a candidate.

This second trial produced five thousand candidates. All the learned societies of Europe sent deputies to this important assembly. Several members of the English Royal Society were present; and a great number of critics belonging to the leading London newspapers and literary journals; but they were not able to stand as candidates, because their teeth had all been broken long before in their frequent attempts to tear to pieces the works of their brother authors.

This second trial, which lasted a fortnight, was, alas! As fruitless as the first. The deputies of the learned societies disputed amongst themselves, for the honour of the associations to which they respectively belonged, as to who should break the nut; but they only left their best teeth behind them.

As for the nut itself, its shell did not even bear the marks of the attempts that had been made to crack it.

The king was in despair. He resolved, however, to strike one grand blow; and, as he had no male descendant, he declared, by means of a third article in the *Royal Gazette*, the national newspapers, and the foreign journals, that the hand of Princess Pirlipata and the inheritance of the throne should be given to him who might crack the Crackatook nut. There was one condition to this announcement; namely, that this time the candidates must be from sixteen to twenty-four years of age. The promise of such a reward excited all Germany.

All Competitors poured in from all parts of Europe; and they would even have come from Asia, Africa, and America, and that fifth quarter of the world which had been discovered by Christian Elias Drosselmayer and his friend the astrologer, if there had been sufficient time.

On this occasion the mechanician and the astrologer thought that the moment was now come to produce young Drosselmayer; for it was impossible for the king to offer a higher reward than that just announced. Only, certain of success as they were, and although this time a host of princes and royal and imperial jaws had presented themselves, the mechanician and the astronomer did not appear with their young friend at the register office until just as it was about to close; so that the name of NATHANIEL DROSSELMAYER was numbered the 11,375th, and stood last.

It was on this occasion as on the preceding ones.

The 11,374 rivals of young Drosselmayer were foiled; and on the nineteenth day of the trial, at twenty-five minutes to twelve o'clock, and just as the princess accomplished her fifteenth year, the name of Nathaniel Drosselmayer was called.

The young man presented himself, accompanied by his two guardians, the mechanician and the astrologer. It was the first time that these two illustrious persons had seen the princess since they had beheld her in her cradle; and since that period great changes had taken place in her. But I must inform you, with due candour, that those changes were not to her advantage. When a child, she was shockingly ugly: she was now frightfully so. Her form had lost, with its growth, none of its important features. It is therefore difficult to understand how those skinny legs, those flat hips, and that distorted body, could have supported such a monstrous head. And that head had the same grizzly hair—the same green eyes—the same enormous mouth—and the same cotton beard on the chin, as we have already described; only all these features were just fifteen years older.

Upon perceiving that monster of ugliness, poor Nathaniel shuddered and inquired of the mechanician and the astrologer if they were quite sure that the kernel of the Crackatook nut would restore the princess to her beauty: because, if she were to remain in that state, he was quite willing to make the trial in a matter where all the others had failed; but he should leave the honour of the marriage and the profit of the heir ship of the throne to anyone who might be inclined to accept them. It is hardly necessary to state that both the mechanician and the astrologer reassured their young friend, promising that, the nut once broken, and the kernel once eaten, Pirlipata would become that very moment the most beautiful princess on the face of the earth.

But if the sight of Princess Pirlipata had struck poor Nathaniel with dismay, I must tell you, in honour of the young man, that *his* presence had produced a very different effect upon the sensitive heart of the heiress of the crown; and she could not prevent herself from exclaiming, when she saw him, "Oh! How glad I should be if he were to break the nut!"

Thereupon the chief governess of the princess replied, "I think I have often observed to your highness, that it is not customary for a young and beautiful princess like yourself to express her opinion aloud relative to such matters."

Nathaniel was indeed calculated to turn the heads of all the princesses in the world. He wore a little military frock coat, of a violet colour, all braided, and with golden buttons, and which his uncle had had made for this solemn occasion.

His breeches were of the same stuff; and his boots were so well blacked, and sat in such an admirable manner, that they seemed as if they were painted. The only thing which somewhat spoilt his appearance was the ugly piece of wood fitted to the nape of his neck; but Uncle Drosselmayer had so contrived that it seemed like a little bag attached to his wig, and might at a stretch have passed as an eccentricity of the toilet, or else as a new fashion which Nathaniel's tailor was trying to push into vogue at the court.

Thus it was, that when this charming young man entered the great hall, what the princess had had the imprudence to say aloud, the other ladies present said to themselves; and there was not a person, not even excepting the king and the queen, who did not desire at the bottom of his heart that Nathaniel might prove triumphant in the adventure which he had undertaken.

On his side, young Drosselmayer approached with a confidence which encouraged the hopes that were placed in him. Having reached the steps leading to the throne, he bowed to the king and queen, then to Princess Pirlipata, and then to the spectators; after which he received the Crackatook nut from the grand master of the ceremonies, took it delicately between his forefinger and thumb, placed it in his mouth, and gave a violent pull at the wooden balance hanging behind him.

Crack! Crack!—And the shell was broken in several pieces.

He then skilfully detached the kernel from the fibres hanging to it, and presented it to the princess, bowing gracefully but respectfully at the same time; after which he closed his eyes, and began to walk backwards. At the same moment the princess swallowed the kernel; and, O! Wonder! Her horrible ugliness disappeared, and she became a young lady of angelic beauty. Her face seemed to have borrowed the hues of the rose and the lily: her eyes were of sparkling azure; and thick tresses, resembling masses of golden thread, flowed over her alabaster shoulders.

The trumpets and the cymbals sounded enough to make one deaf; and the shouts of the people responded to the noise of the instruments. The king, the ministers, the councillors of state, and the judges began to dance, as they had done at the birth of Pirlipata; and eau-de-cologne was obliged to be thrown in the face of the queen, who had fainted for joy.

This great tumult proved very annoying to young Nathaniel Drosselmayer, who, as you must remember, had yet to step seven paces backwards. He, however, behaved with a coolness which gave the highest hopes relative to the period when he should be called upon to reign in his turn; and he was just stretching out his leg to take the seventh step, when the queen of the mice suddenly appeared through a crevice in the floor. With horrible squeaks she ran between his legs; so that just at the very moment when the future Prince Royal placed his foot upon the ground, his heel came so fully on the body of the mouse that he stumbled in such a manner as nearly to fall.

O sorrow! At that same instant the handsome young man became as ugly as the princess was before him: his legs shrivelled up; his shrunken form could hardly support his enormous head; his eyes became green, haggard, and goggle; his mouth split from ear to ear; and his delicate little sprouting beard changed into a white and soft substance, which was afterwards found to be cotton.

But the cause of this event was punished at the same moment that she produced it. Dame Mousey was weltering in her own blood upon the floor. Her wickedness did not therefore go without its punishment. In fact, young Drosselmayer had trampled so hard upon her with his heel, that she was crushed beyond all hope of recovery. But, while still writhing on the floor, Dame Mousey squeaked forth the following words, with all the strength of her agonizing voice:

> *"Crackatook! Crackatook! Fatal nut that thou art,*
> *Through thee has Death reached me, at length, with his dart!*
> *Heigho! Heigho!*
>
> *But the Queen of the Mice has thousands to back her,*
> *And my son will yet punish that wretched Nutcracker,*
> *I know! I know!*
>
> *Sweet life, adieu!*
> *Too soon snatch'd away!*
> *And thou heaven of blue,*
> *And thou world so gay,*
> *Adieu! Adieu!"*

The verses of Dame Mousey might have been better; but one cannot be very correct, as you will all agree, when breathing the last sigh!

And when that last sigh was rendered, a great officer of the court took up Dame Mousey by the tail, and carried her away for the purpose of interring her remains in the hole where so many of her family had been buried fifteen years and some months beforehand.

As, in the middle of all this, no one had troubled themselves about Nathaniel Drosselmayer except the mechanician and the astrologer, the princess, who was unaware of the accident which had happened, ordered the young hero to be brought into her presence; for, in spite of the lesson read her by the governess, she was in haste to thank him. But scarcely had she perceived the unfortunate Nathaniel, than she hid her face in her hands; and, forgetting the service which he had rendered her, cried, "Turn out the horrible Nutcracker! Turn him out! Turn him out!"

The grand marshal of the palace accordingly took poor Nathaniel by the shoulders and pushed him downstairs.

The king, who was very angry at having a nutcracker proposed to him as his son-in-law, attacked the astrologer and the mechanician; and, instead of the income of six hundred pounds a year and the telescope of honour which he had promised the first,—instead, also, of the sword set with diamonds, the Order of the Golden Spider, and the drab frock coat, which he ought to have given to the latter,—he banished them both from his kingdom, granting them only twenty-four hours to cross the frontiers.

Obedience was necessary. The mechanician, the astrologer, and young Drosselmayer (now become a Nutcracker), left the capital and quitted the country. But when night came, the two learned men consulted the stars once more, and read in them that, all deformed though he were, Nathaniel would not the less become a prince and king, unless indeed he chose to remain a private individual, which was left to his own choice. This was to happen when his deformity should disappear; and that deformity would disappear when he should have commanded an army in battle,— when he should have killed the seven headed king of the mice, who was born after Dame Mousey's seven first sons had been put to death,— and, lastly, when a beautiful lady should fall in love with him.

But while awaiting these brilliant destinies, Nathaniel Drosselmayer, who had left the paternal shop as the only son and heir, now returned to it in the form of a nutcracker!

I need scarcely tell you that his father did not recognise him; and that, when Christopher Zacharias inquired of the mechanician and his friend the astrologer, what had become of his dearly beloved son, those two illustrious persons replied, with the seriousness of learned men, that the king and the queen would not allow the saviour of the princess to leave them, and that young Nathaniel remained at court covered with honour and glory.

As for the unfortunate nutcracker, who felt how deeply painful was his situation, he uttered not a word, but resolved to await patiently the change which must someday or another take place in him.

Nevertheless, I must candidly admit, that in spite of the good nature of his disposition, he was desperately vexed with Uncle Drosselmayer, who, coming at a moment he was so little expected, and having enticed him away by so many fine promises, was the sole and only cause of the frightful misfortune that had occurred to him.

Such, my dear children, is the History of the Crackatook, Nut, just as Godfather Drosselmayer told it to little Mary and Fritz; and you can now understand why people often say, when speaking of anything difficult to do, "That is a hard nut to crack."

The History of a Nutcracker (Resumed)

VII

The Uncle And The Nephew

I F ANYONE OF MY YOUNG friends now around me has ever cut himself with glass, which he has most likely done in the days of his disobedience, he must know by experience that it is a particularly disagreeable kind of cut, because it is so long in healing Mary was, therefore, forced to stay a whole week in bed; for she always felt giddy whenever she tried to get up. But at last she got well altogether, and was able to skip about the room as she was wont to do.

You would not do my little heroine the injustice to suppose that her first visit was to any other place than the glass cupboard, which now seemed quite charming to look at. A new pane had been put in; and all the windows had been so well cleaned by Miss Trudchen, that all the trees, houses, dolls, and other toys of the Christmas Eve seemed quite new, gay, and polished. But in the midst of all the treasures of her little kingdom, and before all other things, Mary perceived her Nutcracker smiling upon her from the second shelf where he was placed, and with his teeth all in as good order as ever they were. While thus joyfully examining her favourite, an idea which had more than once presented itself to the mind of Mary touched her to the quick. She was persuaded that all Godfather Drosselmayer had told her was not a mere fable, but the true history of the disagreement between the Nutcracker on one side, and the late queen of the mice and her son, the reigning king, on the other side. She, therefore, knew that the Nutcracker could be neither more nor less than Nathaniel Drosselmayer, of Nuremberg, the amiable but enchanted nephew of her godfather; for that the skilful mechanician who had figured at the court of Pirlipata's father, was Doctor Drosselmayer, she had never doubted from the moment when he introduced his drab frock coat into his tale. This belief was strengthened when she found him losing first his hair by a sunstroke, and then his eye by an arrow, events which had rendered necessary the invention of the ugly black patch, and of the ingenious glass wig, of which I have already spoken.

"But why did not your uncle help you, poor Nutcracker?" said Mary, as she stood at the glass cupboard, gazing up at her favourite; for she remembered that on the success of the battle depended the disenchantment of the poor little man and his elevation to the rank of king of the kingdom of toys. Then she thought that all the dolls, puppets, and little men must be well prepared to receive him as their king;—for did they not obey the Nutcracker as soldiers obey a general? That indifference on the part of Godfather Drosselmayer was so much the more annoying to little Mary, because she was certain that those dolls and puppets to which, in her imagination, she gave life and motion, really did live and move.

Nevertheless, there was now no appearance of either life or motion in the cupboard, where everything was still and quiet. But Mary, rather than give up her sincere belief, thought that all this was occasioned by the sorcery of the late queen of the mice and her son; and so firm was she in this belief, that, while she gazed up at the Nutcracker, she continued to say aloud what she had only begun to say to herself.

"And yet," she resumed, "although you are unable to move, and are prevented by enchantment from saying a single word to me, I am very sure, my dear Mr. Drosselmayer, that you understand me perfectly, and that you are well aware of my good intentions with regard to you. Reckon, then, upon my support when you require it; and in the meantime, do not vex yourself. I will go straight to your uncle, and beg him to assist you; and if he only loves you a little, he is so clever that I am sure he can help you."

In spite of the eloquence of this speech, the Nutcracker did not move an inch; but it seemed to Mary that a sigh came from behind the glass, the panes of which began to sound very low, but wonderfully soft and pleasing; while it appeared to Mary that a sweet voice, like a small silver bell, said, "Dear little Mary, thou art my guardian angel! I will be thine, and Mary shall be mine!" And at these words, so mysteriously heard, Mary felt a singular sensation of happiness, in spite of the shudder which passed through her entire frame.

Twilight had now arrived; and the judge returned home, accompanied by Doctor Drosselmayer. In a few moments Miss Trudchen got tea ready, and all the family were gathered round the table, talking gaily. As for Mary, she had been to fetch her little armchair, and had seated herself in silence at the feet of Godfather Drosselmayer. Taking advantage of a moment when no one was speaking, she raised her large blue eyes towards the doctor, and, looking earnestly at him, said, "I now know, dear godpapa, that my Nutcracker is your nephew, young Drosselmayer, of Nuremberg. He has become a prince, and also king of the kingdom of toys, as your friend the astrologer prophesied. But you know that he is at open war with the king of the mice. Come, dear godpapa, tell me why you did not help him when you were sitting astride upon the clock? And why do you now desert him?"

And, with these words, Mary again related, amidst the laughter of her father, her mother, and Miss Trudchen, the events of that famous battle which she had seen. Fritz and Godfather Drosselmayer alone did not enjoy the whole scene.

"Where," said the godfather, "does that little girl get all those foolish ideas which enter her head?"

"She has a very lively imagination," replied Mary's mother; "and, after all, these are only dreams and visions occasioned by fever."

"And I can prove *that*," shouted Fritz; "for she says that my red hussars took to flight, which cannot possibly be true—unless indeed they are abominable cowards, in which case they would not get the better of me, for I would flog them all soundly."

Then, with a singular smile, Godfather Drosselmayer took Mary upon his knees, and said with more kindness than before, "My dear child, you do not know what course you are pursuing in espousing so warmly the cause of your Nutcracker. You will have to suffer much if you persist in taking the part of one who is in disgrace; for the king of the mice, who considers him to be the murderer of his mother, will persecute him in all ways. But, in any case, remember that it is not I—but you alone—who can save him. Be firm and faithful—and all will go well."

Neither Mary nor anyone else understood the words of Godfather Drosselmayer: on the contrary, those words seemed so strange to the judge, that he took the doctor's hand, felt his pulse for some moments in silence, and then said, "My dear friend, you are very feverish, and I should advise you to go home to bed."

VIII

The Duel

D URING THE NIGHT WHICH FOLLOWED the scene just related, and while the moon, shining in all its splendour, cast its bright rays through the openings in the curtains, Mary, who now slept with her mother, was awakened by a noise that seemed to come from the corner of the room, and was mingled with sharp screeches and squeakings.

"Alas!" cried Mary, who remembered to have heard the same noise on the occasion of the famous battle; "Alas! The mice are coming again! Mamma, mamma, mamma!"

But her voice was stifled in her throat, in spite of all her efforts: she endeavoured to get up to run out of the room, but seemed to be nailed to her bed, unable to move her limbs. At length, turning her affrighted eyes towards the corner of the room, whence the noise came, she beheld the king of the mice scraping for himself a way through the wall, and thrusting in first one of his heads, then another, then a third, and so on until the whole seven, each with a crown, made their appearance. Having entered the room, he walked several times round it like a victor who takes possession of his conquest: he then leapt with one bound upon a table that was standing near the bed. Gazing upon her with his fourteen eyes, all as bright as carbuncles, and with a gnashing of his teeth and a horrible squeaking noise, he said, "Fe, fa, fum! You must give me all your sugar plums and your sweet cakes, little girl, and if not, I will eat up your friend the Nutcracker."

Then, having uttered this threat, he fled from the room by the same hole as he had entered by.

Mary was so frightened by this terrible apparition, that she awoke in the morning very pale and almost broken-hearted, the more so that she dared not mention what had taken place during the night, for fear of being laughed at. Twenty, times was she on the point of telling all, either to her mother, or to Fritz; but she stopped, still thinking that neither the one nor the other would believe her. It was, however, pretty clear that she must sacrifice her sugar plums and her sweet cakes to the safety of the poor Nutcracker. She accordingly placed them all on the ledge of the cupboard that very evening.

Next morning, the judge's wife said, "I really do not know whence come all the mice that have suddenly invaded the house; but those naughty creatures have actually eaten up all my poor little Mary's sugar plums."

The lady was not quite right; the sugar plums and cakes were only *spoilt*, not *eaten up*; for the gluttonous king of the mice, not finding the sweet cakes as good as he had expected, messed them about so that they were forced to be thrown away.

But as it was not sugar plums that Mary liked best, she did not feel much regret at the sacrifice which the king of the mice had extorted from her; and, thinking that he would be contented with the first contribution with which he had taxed her, she was much pleased at the idea of having saved Nutcracker upon such good terms.

Unfortunately her satisfaction was not of long duration; for the following night she was again awoke: by hearing squeaking and whining close by her ears.

Alas! It was the king of the mice again, his eyes shining more horribly than on the preceding night; and, in a voice interrupted by frequent whines and squeaks, he said, "You must give me your little sugar dolls and figures made of biscuit, little girl; if not, I will eat up your friend the Nutcracker."

Thereupon the king of the mice went skipping away, and disappeared by the hole in the wall.

Next morning, Mary, now deeply afflicted, went straight to the glass cupboard, and threw a mournful look upon her figures of sugar and biscuit; and her grief was very natural, for never were such nice-looking sweet things seen before.

"Alas!" she said, as she turned towards the Nutcracker, "what would I not do for you, my dear Mr. Drosselmayer? But you must admit all the same that what I am required to do is very hard."

At these words the Nutcracker assumed so piteous an air, that Mary, who fancied that she was forever beholding the jaws of the king of the mice opening to devour him, resolved to make this second sacrifice to save the unfortunate young man. That very evening, therefore, she placed her sugar figures and her biscuits upon the ledge of the cupboard, where the night before she had put her sugar plums and sweet cakes. Kissing them, however, one after another, as a token of farewell, she yielded up her shepherds, her shepherdesses, and her sheep, concealing behind the flock at the same time a little sugar baby with fat round cheeks, and which she loved above all the other things.

"Now really this is too bad!" cried the judge's wife next morning: "It is very clear that these odious mice have taken up their dwelling in the glass cupboard; for all poor Mary's sugar figures are eaten up."

At these words large tears started from Mary's eyes; but she dried them up almost directly, and even smiled sweetly as she thought to herself, "What matter my shepherds, shepherdesses, and sheep, since the Nutcracker is saved!"

"Mamma," cried Fritz, who was present at the time, "I must remind you that our baker has an excellent grey cat, which we might send for, and which would soon put an end to all this by snapping up the mice one after another, and even Dame Mousey herself afterwards, as well as her son the king."

"Yes," replied the judge's wife; "but that same cat would jump upon the tables and shelves, and break my glasses and cups to pieces."

"Oh! There is no fear of *that!*" cried Fritz. "The baker's cat is too polite to do any such thing; and I wish I could walk along the pipes and the roofs of houses as skilfully as he can."

"No cats here, if you please!" cried the judge's wife, who could not bear those domestic animals.

"But, after all," said the judge, who overheard what was going on, "some good may follow from the remarks of Fritz: if you will not have a cat, get a mousetrap."

"Capital!" cried Fritz: "That idea is very happy, since Godpapa Drosselmayer invented mousetraps."

Everyone now laughed; and as, after a strict search, no such thing as a mousetrap was found in the house, the servant went to Godfather Drosselmayer, who sent back a famous one, which was baited with a bit of bacon, and placed in the spot where the mice had made such.

Mary went to bed with the hope that morning would find the king of the mice a prisoner in the box, to which his gluttony was almost certain to lead him. But o'clock, and while she was in her first sleep, by something cold and velvety that leapt arms and face; and, at the same moment, the whining and squeaking which she knew so well, rang in her ears. The horrible king of the mice was there seated on her pillow, with his eyes shooting red flames and his seven mouths wide open, as if he were about to eat poor Mary up.

"I laugh at the trap—I laugh at the trap," said the king of the mice: "I shall not go into the little house, and the bacon will not tempt me. I shall not be taken: I laugh at the trap! But you must give me your picture books and your little silk frock; if not, I will eat up your friend the Nutcracker."

You can very well understand that after such a demand as this, Mary awoke in the morning with her heart full of sorrow and her eyes full of tears. Her mother, moreover, told her nothing new when she said that the trap had remained empty, and that the king of the mice had suspected the snare. Then, as the judge's wife left the room to see after the breakfast, Mary entered her papa's room, and going up to the cupboard, said, "Alas, my dear good Mr. Drosselmayer, where will all this end? When I have given my picture books to the king of the mice to tear, and my pretty little silk frock, which my guardian angel sent me, to rend into pieces, he will not be content, but will every day be asking me for more. And when I have nothing else left to give him, he will perhaps eat me up in your place. Alas! What can a poor little girl like me do for you, dear good Mr. Drosselmayer? What can I do?"

While Mary was weeping and lamenting in this manner, she observed that the Nutcracker had a drop of blood upon his neck. From the day when she had discovered that her favourite was the son of the toy man and the nephew of the Doctor, she had left off carrying him in her arms, and had neither kissed nor caressed him. Indeed, so great was her timidity in this respect, that she had not even dared to touch him with the tip of her finger. But at this moment, seeing that he was hurt, and fearing lest his wound might be dangerous, she took him gently out of the cupboard, and began to wipe away with her handkerchief the drop of blood which was upon his neck. But how great was her astonishment, when she suddenly felt the Nutcracker moving about in her hands! She replaced him quickly upon the shelf: his lips quivered from ear to ear, which made his mouth seem larger still; and, by dint of trying to speak, he concluded by uttering the following words: "Ah, dear Miss Silberhaus—excellent friend—what do I not owe you? And how much gratitude have I to express to you? Do not sacrifice for me your picture books and your silk frock; but get me a sword—a good sword—and I will take care of the rest!"

The Nutcracker would have said more; but his words became unintelligible—his voice sank altogether—and his eyes, for a moment animated by an expression of the softest melancholy, grew motionless and vacant. Mary felt no alarm: on the contrary, she leapt for joy, for she was very happy at the idea of being able to save the Nutcracker, without being compelled to give up her picture books or her silk frock. One thing alone vexed her—and that was, where could she find the good sword that the little man required? Mary resolved to explain her difficulty to Fritz, who, in spite of his blustering manners, she knew to be a good-natured boy. She accordingly took him close up to the glass cupboard, told him all that had happened between Nutcracker and the king of the mice, and ended by explaining the nature of the service she required of him. The only thing which made a great impression upon Fritz was the idea that his hussars had really acted in a cowardly manner in the thickest of the battle: he therefore asked Mary if the accusation were really true; and as he knew that she never told a story, he believed her words.

Then, rushing up to the cupboard, he made a speech to his soldiers, who seemed quite ashamed of themselves. But this was not all: in order to punish the whole regiment in the person of its officers, he degraded them one after the other, and expressly ordered the band not to play the *Hussar's March* during parade.

The turning to Mary, he said, "As for the Nutcracker, to be a brave little fellow, I think I can manage his business; for, as I put a veteran major of horse guards upon half pay yesterday, he having finished his time in the service, I should think he cannot want his sword any longer. It is an excellent blade, I can assure you!"

It now remained to find the major. A search was commenced, and he was found living on his half pay in a little tavern which stood in a dark corner of the third shelf in the cupboard. As Fritz had imagined, he offered no objection to give up his sword, which had become useless to him, and which was that instant fastened to the Nutcracker's neck.

The fear which Mary now felt prevented her from sleeping all the next night; and she was so wide awake that she heard the clock strike twelve in the room where the cupboard was. Scarcely had the hum of the last stroke ceased, when strange noises came from the direction of the cupboard; and then there was a great clashing of swords, as if two enemies were fighting in mortal combat. Suddenly one of the duellists gave a squeak!

"The king of the mice!" cried Mary, full of joy and terror at the same time.

There was then a dead silence; but presently someone knocked gently— very gently at the door; and a pretty little voice said, "Dearest Miss Silberhaus, I have glorious news for you: open the door, I beseech you!"

Mary recognised the voice of young Drosselmayer. She hastily put on her little frock, and opened the door. The Nutcracker was there, holding the blood-stained sword in his right hand and a candle in his left. The moment he saw Mary he knelt down, and said,

"It is you alone, O dearest lady! Who have nerved me with the chivalrous courage which I have just shown, and who gave me strength to fight that insolent wretch who dared to threaten you. The vile king of the mice is bathed in his blood. Will you, O lady! Deign to accept the trophies of the victory—trophies that are offered by the hand of a knight who is devoted to you until death?"

With these words the Nutcracker drew from his left arm the seven golden crowns of the king of the mice, which he had placed there as if they were bracelets, and which he now offered to Mary, who received them with joy.

The Nutcracker, encouraged by this amiability on her part, then rose and spoke thus: "Oh! Dear Miss Silberhaus, now that I have conquered my enemy, what beautiful things can I show you, if you would have the condescension to go with me only a few places hence! Oh! Do not refuse me—do not refuse me, dear lady I implore you!"

Mary did not hesitate a moment to follow the Nutcracker, knowing how great were her claims upon his gratitude, and being quite certain that he had no evil intention towards her.

"I will follow you," she said, "my dear Mr. Drosselmayer; but you must not take me very far, nor keep me long away, because I have not yet slept a wink."

"I will choose the shortest, although the most difficult, path," said the Nutcracker; and, thus speaking, he led the way, Mary following him.

IX

The Kingdom of Toys

They both reached, in a short time, a large old cupboard standing in a passage near the door, and which was used as a clothes press. There the Nutcracker stopped; and Mary observed, to her great astonishment, that the folding doors of the cupboard, which were nearly always kept shut, were now wide open, so that she could see plainly her father's travelling cloak lined with fox-skin, which was hanging over the other clothes. The Nutcracker climbed very skilfully along the border of the cloak; and, clinging to the braiding, he reached the large cape, which, fastened by a piece of lace, fell over the back of the cloak. From beneath this

"Now, dear young lady," said the Nutcracker, "have the goodness to give me your hand and ascend with me."

Mary complied; and scarcely had she glanced up the sleeve, when a brilliant light burst upon her view, and she suddenly found herself transported into the midst of a fragrant meadow, which glittered as if it were strewed with precious stones!

"Oh! How charming!" cried Mary, dazzled by the sight. "Where are we?"

"We are in the Field of Sugar Candy, Miss; but we will not remain here, unless you wish to do so. Let us pass through this door."

Then Mary observed a beautiful gate through which they left the field. The gate seemed to be made of white marble, red marble, and blue marble; but when Mary drew near it she saw that it was made only of preserves, candied orange peel, burnt almonds, and sugared raisins. This was the reason, as she learnt from the Nutcracker, why that gate was called the Gate of Burnt Almonds.

The gate opened into a long gallery, the roof of which was supported by pillars of barley-sugar. In the gallery there were five monkeys, all dressed in red, and playing music, which, if it were not the most melodious in the world, was at least the most original. Mary made so much haste to see more, that she did not even perceive that she was walking upon a pavement of pistachio nuts and macaroons, which she took for marble. At length she reached the end of the gallery, and scarcely was she in the open air, when she found herself surrounded by the most delicious perfumes, which came from a charming little forest that opened before her. This forest, which would have been dark were it not for the quantity of lamps that it contained, was lighted up in so brilliant a manner that it was easy to distinguish the golden and silver fruits, which were suspended to branches ornamented with white ribands and nosegays, resembling marriage favours.

"Oh! My dear Mr. Drosselmayer," cried Mary, "what is the name of this charming place, I beseech you?"

"We are now in the Forest of Christmas, Miss," answered the Nutcracker; "and it is here that people come to fetch the trees to which the presents sent by the guardian angels are fastened."

"Oh!" continued Mary, "May I not remain here one moment? Everything is so nice here, and smells so sweet!"

The Nutcracker clapped his hands together; and several shepherds and shepherdesses, hunters and huntresses, came out of the forest, all so delicate and white that they seemed made of refined sugar. They carried on their shoulders an armchair, made of chocolate, incrusted with angelica, in which they placed a cushion of jujube, inviting Mary most politely to sit down. Scarcely had she done so when, as at operas, the shepherds and shepherdesses, the hunters and huntresses, took their places and began to dance a charming ballet to an accompaniment of horns and bugles, which the hunters blew with such good will that their faces became flushed just as if they were made of conserve of roses. Then, the dance being finished, they all disappeared in a grove.

"Pardon me, dear Miss Silberhaus," said the Nutcracker, holding out his hand towards Mary,—"pardon me for having exhibited to you so poor a ballet; but those simpletons can do nothing better than repeat, over and over again, the same step. As for the hunters, they blew their bugles as if they were afraid of them; and I can promise you that I shall not let it pass so quietly. But let us leave those creatures for the present, and continue our walk, if you please."

"I really found it all very delightful," said Mary, accepting the invitation of the Nutcracker; "and it seems to me, my dear Mr. Drosselmayer, that you are harsh towards the little dancers."

The Nutcracker made a face, as much as to say, "We shall see; but your plea in their favour shall be considered."

They then continued their journey, and reached a river which seemed to send forth all the sweet scents that perfumed the air.

"This," said the Nutcracker, without even waiting to be questioned by Mary, "is the River of Orange Juice. It is one of the smallest in the kingdom; for, save in respect to its sweet odour, it cannot be compared to the River of Lemonade, which falls into the southern sea, or the Sea of Punch. The Lake of Sweet Whey is also finer: it joins the northern sea, which is called the Sea of Milk of Almonds."

At a short distance was a little village, in which the houses, the church, and the parsonage were all brown; the roofs however were gilt, and the walls were resplendent with incrustations of red, blue, and white sugarplums.

"This is the Village of Sweet Cake," said the Nutcracker; "it is a pretty little place, as you perceive, and is situate on the Streamlet of Honey. The inhabitants are very agreeable to look upon; but they are always in a bad humour, because they are constantly troubled with the toothache. But, my dear Miss Silberhaus," continued the Nutcracker, "do not let us stop at all the villages and little towns of the kingdom. To the capital! To the capital!"

The Nutcracker advanced, still holding Mary's hand, but walking more confidently than he had hitherto done; for Mary, who was full of curiosity, kept by his side, light as a bird. At length, after the expiration of some minutes, the odour of roses was spread through the air, and everything around them now seemed to be of a rose tint. Mary remarked that this was the perfume and the reflection of a River of Essence of Roses, which flowed along, its waves rippling melodiously. Upon the sweet-scented waters, silver swans, with collars of gold round their necks, swam gently along, warbling the most delicious songs, so that this harmony, with which they were apparently much pleased, made the diamond fishes leap up around them.

"Ah!" cried Mary, "This is the pretty river which Godpapa Drosselmayer made me at Christmas; and I am the girl who played with the swans!"

X

The Journey

THE NUTCRACKER CLAPPED HIS HANDS together once more; and, at that moment, the River of Essence of Roses began to rise visibly; and from its swelling waves came forth a chariot made of shells, and covered with precious stones that glittered in the sun. It was drawn by golden dolphins; and four charming little Moors, with caps made of the scales of goldfish and clothes of hummingbirds' feathers, leapt upon the bank. They first carried Mary, and then the Nutcracker, very gently down to the chariot, which instantly began to advance upon the stream.

You must confess that it was a ravishing spectacle, and one which might even be compared to the voyage of Cleopatra upon the Cydnus, which you read of in Roman History, to behold little Mary in the chariot of shells, surrounded by perfume, and floating on the waves of essence of roses. The golden dolphins that drew the chariot, tossed up their heads, and threw into the air the glittering jets of rosy crystal, which fell in variegated showers of all the colours of the rainbow. Moreover, that pleasure might penetrate every sense, a soft music began to echo round; and sweet silvery voices were heard singing in the following manner:

> *"Who art thou, thus floating where essence of rose*
> *In a stream of sweet perfume deliciously flows?*
> *Art thou the Fairies' Queen?*
>
> *Say, dear little fishes that gleam in the tide;*
> *Or answer, ye cygnets that gracefully glide*
> *Upon that flood serene!"*

And all this time the little Moors, who stood behind the seat on the chariot of shells, shook two parasols, hung with bells, in such a manner that those sounds formed an accompaniment to the vocal melody. And Mary, beneath the shade of the parasols, leant over the waters, each wave of which as it passed reflected her smiling countenance.

In this manner she traversed the River of Essence of Roses, and reached the bank on the opposite side. Then, when they were within an oar's length of the shore, the little Moors leapt, some into the water, others on the bank, the whole forming a chain so as to convey Mary and the Nutcracker ashore upon a carpet made of angelica, all covered with mint drops.

The Nutcracker now conducted Mary through a little grove, which was perhaps even prettier than the Christmas Forest, so brilliantly did each tree shine, and so sweetly did they all smell with their own peculiar essence. But what was most remarkable was the quantity of fruits hanging to the branches, those fruits being not only of singular colour and transparency—some yellow as the topaz, others red like the ruby—but also of a wondrous perfume.

"We are now in the Wood of Preserved Fruits," said the Nutcracker, "and beyond that boundary is the capital." And, as Mary thrust aside the last branches, she was stupified at beholding the extent, the magnificence, and the novel appearance of the city which rose before her upon a mound of flowers. Not only did the walls and steeples glitter with the most splendid colours, but, in respect to the shape of the buildings, it was impossible to see any so beautiful upon the earth. The fortifications and the gates were built of candied fruits, which shone in the sun with their own gay colours, all rendered more brilliant still by the crystallised sugar that covered them. At the principal gate, which was the one by which they entered, silver soldiers presented arms to them, and a little man, clad in a dressing gown of gold brocade, threw himself into the Nutcracker's arms, crying, "Oh! Dear prince, have you come at length? Welcome—welcome to the City of Candied Fruits!"

Mary was somewhat astonished at the great title given to the Nutcracker; but she was soon drawn from her surprise by the noise of an immense quantity of voices all chattering at the same time; so that she asked the Nutcracker if there were some disturbance or some festival in the Kingdom of Toys?

"There is nothing of all that, dear Miss Silberhaus," answered the Nutcracker; "but the City of Candied Fruits is so happy a place, and all its people are so joyful, that they are constantly talking and laughing. And this is always the same as you see it now. But come with me; let us proceed, I implore of you."

Mary, urged by her own curiosity and by the polite invitation of the Nutcracker, hastened her steps, and soon found herself in a large marketplace, which had the most magnificent aspects that could possibly be seen. All the houses around were of sugar, open with fretwork, and having balcony over balcony; and in the middle of the marketplace was an enormous cake, from the inside of which flowed four fountains, namely, lemonade, orangade, sweet milk, and goose berry syrup. The basins around were filled with whip syllabub, so delicious in appearance, that several well-dressed persons publicly ate of it by means of spoons. But the most agreeable and amusing part of the whole scene, was the crowd of little people who walked about, arm-in-arm, by thousands and tens of thousands, all laughing, singing, and chattering, at the tops of their voices, so that Mary could now account for the joyous din which she had heard. Besides the inhabitants of the capital, there were men of all countries— Armenians, Jews, Greeks, Tyrolese, officers, soldiers, clergymen, monks, shepherds, punches, and all kinds of funny people, such as one meets with in the world.

Presently the tumult redoubled at the entrance of a street looking upon the great square; and the people stood aside to allow the cavalcade to pass. It was the Great Mogul, who was carried upon a palanquin, attended by ninety-three lords of his kingdom and seven hundred slaves: but, at the same time, it happened that from the opposite street the Grand Sultan appeared on horseback, followed by three hundred janissaries. The two sovereigns had always been rivals, and therefore enemies; and this feeling made it impossible for their attendants to meet each other without quarrelling. It was even much worse, as you may well suppose, when those two powerful monarchs found themselves face to face: in the first place there was a great confusion, from the midst of which the citizens sought to save themselves; but cries of fury and despair were soon heard, for a gardener, in the act of running away, had knocked off the head of a Brahmin, greatly respected by his own class; and the Grand Sultan's horse had knocked down a frightened punch, who endeavoured to creep between the animal's legs to get away from the riot. The din was increasing, when the gentleman in the gold brocade dressing gown, who had saluted the Nutcracker by the title of Prince at the gate of the city, leapt to the top of the huge cake with a single bound; and having rung a silvery sweet-toned bell three times, cried out three times, "Confectioner! Confectioner! Confectioner!"

That instant did the tumult subside and the combatants separate. The Grand Sultan was brushed, for he was covered with dust; the Brahmin's head was fixed on, with the injunction that he must not sneeze for three days, for fear it should fall off again; and order was restored. The pleasant sports began again, and everyone hastened to quench his thirst with the lemonade, the orangade, the sweet milk, or the gooseberry syrup, and to regale himself with the whip-syllabub.

"My dear Mr. Drosselmayer," said Mary," what is the cause of the influence exercised upon those little folks by the word *confectioner* repeated thrice?"

"I must tell you, Miss," said the Nutcracker, "that the people of the City of Candied Fruits believe, by experience, in the transmigration of souls, and are in the power of a superior principle, called *confectioner*, which principle can bestow on each individual what form he likes by merely baking him, for a shorter or longer period, as the case may be. Now, as everyone believes his own existing shape to be the best, he does not like to change it. Hence the magic influence of the word *confectioner* upon the people of the City of Candied Fruits, when pronounced by the chief magistrate. It is sufficient, as you perceive, to appease all that tumult; everyone, in an instant, forget earthly things, broken ribs, and bumps upon the head; and, restored to himself says, '*What is man? And what may he not become?*'"

While they were thus talking, they reached the entrance of the palace, which shed around a rosy lustre, and was surmounted by a hundred light and elegant towers. The walls were strewed with nosegays, of violets, narcissi, tulips, and jasmine, which set off with their various hues the rose-coloured ground from which they stood forth. The great dome in the centre was covered with thousands of gold and silver stars.

"O, heavens!" exclaimed Mary. "What is that wonderful building?"

"The Palace of Sweet Cake," answered the Nutcracker; "and it is one of the most famous monuments in the capital of the Kingdom of Toys."

Nevertheless, lost in wonder as she was, Mary could not help observing that the roof of one of the great towers was totally wanting, and that little gingerbread men, mounted on a scaffold of cinnamon, were occupied in repairing it. She was about to question the Nutcracker relative to this accident, when he said, "Alas! It is only a short time ago that this palace was threatened by a great disgrace, if not with absolute ruin. The giant Glutton ate up the top of that tower; and he was already on the point of biting the dome, when the people hastened to give him as a tribute the quarter of the city called Almond and Honeycake District, together with a large portion of the Forest of Angelica, in consideration of which he agreed to take himself off without making any worse ravages than those which you see."

At that moment a soft and delicious music was heard.

The gates of the palace opened by themselves, and twelve little pages came forth, carrying in their hands branches of aromatic herbs, lighted like torches. Their heads were made of pearl, six of them had bodies made of rubies, and the six others of emeralds, wherewith they trotted joyously along upon two little feet of gold, sculptured with all the taste and care of Benvenuto Cellini.

They were followed by four ladies, about the same size as Miss Clara, Mary's new doll; but all so splendidly dressed and so richly adorned, that Mary was not at a loss to perceive in them the royal princesses of the City of Preserved Fruits. They all four, upon perceiving the Nutcracker, hastened to embrace him with the utmost tenderness, exclaiming at the same time, and as it were with one voice,

"Oh! Prince—dear prince! Dear—dear brother!" The Nutcracker seemed much moved; he wiped away the tears which flowed from his eyes, and, taking Mary by the hand, said, in a feeling tone, to the four princesses, "My dear sisters, this is Miss Silberhaus whom I now introduce to you: She is the daughter of Chief Justice Silberhaus, of Nuremberg, a gentleman of the highest respectability. It is this young lady who saved my life; for, if at the moment when I lost the battle she had not thrown her shoe at the king of the mice—and, again, if she had not afterwards lent me the sword of a major whom her brother had placed on the half-pay list—I should even now be sleeping in my tomb, or what is worse, be devoured by the king of the mice."

"Ah! My dear Miss Silberhaus," cried the Nutcracker, with an enthusiasm which he could not control, "Pirlipata, although the daughter of a king, was not worthy to unloose the latchet of your pretty little shoes."

"Oh! No—no; certainly not!" repeated the four princesses in chorus; and, throwing their arms round Mary's neck, they cried, "Oh! Noble liberatrix of our dear and much-loved prince and brother! Oh! Excellent Miss Silberhaus!"

And, with these exclamations, which their heartfelt joy cut short, the four princesses conducted the Nutcracker and Mary into the palace, made them sit down upon beautiful little sofas of cedarwood, covered with golden flowers, and then insisted upon preparing a banquet with their own hands. With this object, they hastened to fetch a number of little vases and bowls made of the finest Japan porcelain, and silver knives, forks, spoons, and other articles of the table. They then brought in the finest fruits and most delicious sugar plums that Mary had ever seen, and began to bustle about so nimbly that Mary was at no loss to perceive how well they understood everything connected with cooking. Now, as Mary herself was well acquainted with such matters, she wished inwardly to take a share in all that was going on; and, as if she understood Mary's wishes, the most beautiful of the Nutcracker's four sisters, handed her a little golden mortar, saying, "Dear liberatrix of my brother, pound me some sugar candy, if you please."

Mary hastened to do as she was asked; and while she was pounding the sugar candy in the mortar, whence a delicious music came forth, the Nutcracker began to relate all his adventures: but, strange as it was, it seemed to Mary, during that recital, as if the words of young Drosselmayer and the noise of the pestle came gradually more and more indistinct to her ears. In a short time she seemed to be surrounded by a light vapour; then the vapour turned into a silvery mist, which spread more and more densely around her, so that it presently concealed the Nutcracker and the princesses from her sight. Strange songs, which reminded her of those she had heard on the River of Essence of Roses, met her ears, commingled with the increasing murmur of waters; and then Mary thought that the waves flowed beneath her, raising her up with their swell. She felt as if she were rising high up—higher—and higher; when, suddenly, down she fell from a precipice that she could not measure.

CONCLUSION

O NE DOES NOT FALL SEVERAL thousand feet without awaking: thus was it that Mary awoke; and, on awaking, she found herself in her little bed. It was broad daylight, and her mother, who was standing by her, said, "Is it possible to be so lazy as you are? Come, get up, and dress yourself, dear little Mary, for breakfast is waiting."

"Oh! My dear mamma," said Mary, opening her eyes wide with astonishment, "whither did young Mr. Drosselmayer take me last night? And what splendid things did he show me?"

Then Mary related all that I have just told you; and when she had done her mother said, "You have had a very long and charming dream, dear little Mary; but now that you are awake, you must forget it all, and come and have your breakfast."

But Mary, while she dressed herself, persisted in maintaining that she had really seen all she spoke of. Her mother accordingly went to the cupboard and took out the Nutcracker, who, according to custom, was upon the third shelf.

Bringing it to her daughter, she said, "How can you suppose, silly child, that this puppet, which is made of wood and cloth, can be alive, or move, or think?"

"But, my dear mamma," said Mary, perpetually, "I am well aware that the Nutcracker is none other than young

At that moment Mary heard a loud shout of laughter behind her.

It was the judge, Fritz, and Miss Trudchen, who made themselves merry at her expense.

"Ah!" cried Mary, "How can you laugh at me, dear papa, and at my poor Nutcracker? He spoke very respectfully of you, nevertheless, when we went into the Palace of Sweet Cake, and he introduced me to his sisters."

The shouts of laughter redoubled to such an extent that Mary began to see the necessity of giving some proof of the truth of what she said, for fear of being treated as a simpleton. She therefore went into the adjoining room and brought back a little box in which she had carefully placed the seven crowns of the king of the mice.

"Here, mamma," she said, "are the seven heads of the king of the mice, which the Nutcracker gave me last night as a proof of his victory."

The judge's wife, full of surprise, took the seven little crowns, which were made of an unknown but very brilliant metal, and were carved with a delicacy of which human hands were incapable. The judge himself could not take his eyes off them, and considered them to be so precious, that, in spite of the prayers of Fritz, he would not let him touch one of them. The judge and his wife then pressed Mary to tell them whence came those little crowns; but she could only persist in what she had said already: and when her father, annoyed at what he heard and at what he considered obstinacy on her part, called her a little "storyteller," she burst into tears, exclaiming, "Alas! Unfortunate child that I am! What would you have me tell you?"

At that moment the door opened, and the doctor made his appearance.

"What is the matter?" he said, "And what have they done to my little goddaughter, that she cries and sobs like this? What is it? What is it all?"

The judge acquainted Doctor Drosselmayer with all that had occurred; and, when the story was ended, he showed him the seven crowns. But scarcely had the doctor seen them, when he burst out laughing, and said, "Well! Really this is too good! These are the seven crowns that I used to wear to my watch-chain some years ago, and which I gave to my goddaughter on the occasion of her second birthday. Do you not remember, my dear friend?"

But the judge and his wife could not recollect anything about the present stated to have been given. Nevertheless, believing what the godfather said, their countenances became more calm. Mary, upon seeing this, ran up to Doctor Drosselmayer, saying, "But you know all, godpapa! Confess that the Nutcracker is your nephew, and that it was he who gave me the seven crowns."

But Godfather Drosselmayer did not at all seem to like these words; and his face became so gloomy, that the judge called little Mary to him, and taking her upon his knees, said, "Listen to me, my dear child, for I wish to speak to you very seriously. Do me the pleasure, once for all, to put an end to these silly ideas; because, if you should again assert that this ugly and deformed Nutcracker is the nephew of our friend the doctor, I give you due warning that I will throw, not only the Nutcracker, but all the other toys, Miss Clara amongst them, out of the window."

Poor Mary was therefore unable to speak anymore of all the fine things with which her imagination was filled; but you can well understand that when a person has once travelled in such a fine place as the Kingdom of Toys, and seen such a delicious town as the City of Preserved Fruits, were it only for an hour, it is not easy to forget such sights.

Mary therefore endeavoured to speak to her brother of the whole business; but she had lost all his confidence since the moment when she had said that his hussars had taken to flight. Convinced, therefore, that Mary was a storyteller, as her father had said so, he restored his officers to the rank from which he had reduced them, and allowed the band to play as usual the *Hussar's March*—a step which did not prevent Mary from entertaining her own opinion relative to their courage.

Mary dared not therefore speak further of her adventures. Nevertheless, the remembrance of the Kingdom of Toys followed her without ceasing; and when she thought of all that, she looked upon it as if she were still in the Christmas Forest, or on the River of Essence of Roses, or in the City of Preserved Fruits; so that, instead of playing with her toys as she had been wont to do, she remained silent and pensive, occupied only with her own thoughts, while everyone called her "the little dreamer."

But one day, when the doctor, with his wig laid upon the ground, his tongue thrust into one corner of his mouth, and the sleeves of his yellow coat turned up, was mending a clock by the aid of a long pointed instrument, it happened that Mary, who was seated near the glass cupboard contemplating the Nutcracker, and buried in her own thoughts, suddenly said, quite forgetful that both the doctor and her mamma were close by, "Ah! My dear Mr. Drosselmayer, if you were not a little man made of wood, as my papa declares, and, if you really were alive, I would not do as Princess Pirlipata did, and desert you because, in serving me, you had ceased to be a handsome young man; for I love you sincerely!"

But scarcely had she uttered these words, when there was such a noise in the room, that Mary fell off her chair in a fainting fit.

When she came to herself, she found that she was in the arms of her mother, who said, "How is it possible that a great little girl like you, is so foolish as to fall ask off can your chair—and just at the moment, too, when young Mr. Drosselmayer, who has finished his travels, arrives at Nuremberg? Come, wipe your eyes, and be a good girl."

Indeed, as Mary wiped her Godpapa Drosselmayer, with his hat under his arm, and back, entered the room. He eyes, the door opened, and his glass wig upon his head, his drab frock coat upon his wore a smiling countenance, and held by the hand a young man, who, although very little, was very handsome. This young man wore a superb frock coat of red velvet embroidered with gold, white silk stockings, and shoes brilliantly polished.

He had a charming nosegay on the bosom of his shirt, and was very dandified with his curls and hair-powder; moreover, long tresses, neatly braided, hung behind his back. The little sword that he wore by his side was brilliant with precious stones; and the hat which he carried under his arm was of the finest silk.

The amiable manners of this young man showed who he was directly; for scarcely had he entered the room, when he placed at Mary's feet a quantity of magnificent toys and nice confectionery—chiefly sweet cake and sugar plum, the finest she had ever tasted, save in the Kingdom of Toys. As for Fritz, the doctor's nephew seemed to have guessed his martial taste, for he brought him a sword with a blade of the finest Damascus steel. At table, and when the dessert was placed upon it, the amiable youth cracked nuts for all the company: the hardest could not resist his teeth for a moment. He placed them in his mouth with his right hand; with the left he pulled his hair behind; and, crack! The shell was broken.

Mary had become very red when she first saw that pretty little gentleman; but she blushed deeper still, when, after the dessert, he invited her to go with him into the room where the glass cupboard was.

"Yes, go, my dear children, and amuse yourselves together," said Godpapa Drosselmayer: "I do not want that room anymore today, since all the clocks of my friend the judge now go well."

The two young people proceeded to the room; but scarcely was young Drosselmayer alone with Mary, when he fell upon one knee, and spoke thus:

"My dear Miss Silberhaus, you see at your feet the happy Nathaniel Drosselmayer, whose life you saved on this very spot. You also said that you would not have repulsed me, as Princess Pirlipata did, if, in serving *you*, I had become hideous. Now, as the spell which the queen of the mice threw upon me was destined to lose all its power on that day when, in spite of my ugly face, I should be beloved by a young and beautiful girl, I at that moment ceased to be a vile Nutcracker and resumed my proper shape, which is not disagreeable, as you may see. Therefore, my dear young lady, if you still possess the same sentiments in respect to myself, do me the favour to bestow your much-loved hand upon me, share my throne and my crown, and reign with me over the Kingdom of Toys, of which I have ere now become the king."

Then Mary raised young Drosselmayer gently, and said, "You are an amiable and a good king, sir; and as you have moreover a charming kingdom, adorned with magnificent palaces, and possessing a very happy people, I receive you as my future husband, provided my parents give their consent."

Thereupon, as the door of the room had opened very gently without the two young folks having heard it, so occupied were they with their own sentiments, the judge, his wife, and Godpapa Drosselmayer came forward, crying "Bravo!" with all their might; which made Mary as red as a cherry. But the young man was not abashed; and, advancing towards the judge and his wife, he bowed gracefully to them, paid them a handsome compliment, and ended by soliciting the hand of Mary in marriage. The request was immediately granted.

That same day Mary was engaged to Nathaniel Drosselmayer, on condition that the marriage should not take place for a year.

At the expiration of the year, the bridegroom came to fetch the bride in a little carriage of mother of pearl in crusted with gold and silver, and drawn by ponies of the size of sheep, but which were of countless worth, because there were none others like them in the world. The young king took his bride to the Palace of Sweet Cake, where they were married by the chaplain. Twenty-two thousand little people, all covered with pearls, diamonds, and brilliant stones, danced at the bridal.

Even at the present day, Mary is still queen of that beautiful country, where may be seen brilliant forests of Christmas; rivers of orangade, sweet milk, and essence of roses; transparent palaces of sugar whiter than snow and clearer than ice; in a word, all kinds of wonderful and extraordinary things may there be seen by those who have eyes sharp enough to discover them.

The Nutcracker

CHARACTERS:

MOTHER. A happy, busy young woman

FATHER. A dignified, kindly man

GRANDPA. A rosy-faced, jovial child-lover

TOMMY. Thirteen and awkward

JOHNNY. Ten years old and wild

BABY. Five years old and inquisitive

LITTLE MARIE. A dainty, petted girl of eight; wears large pink bow on her curls

CANDY-FAIRY. An animated peppermint stick. White slippers; stockings red and white striped, like peppermint candy; short red and white ballet skirt; high, pointed cap of white with red stripes spiraling around it. She carries a large peppermint candy cane as wand

CHINESE BOY. Typical Chinese boy with long, loose pantaloons, loose coat to hips, little pill box hat, long cue

WIND-FAIRY. A lithe figure draped in gauzes of various blues and greens

MOUSE-KING. The largest mouse. He wears a golden crown

THE NUTCRACKER. A loose-jointed wooden figure of a man, about twenty inches long, costumed as a cavalier. Brimmed hat painted white, with blue feather. Blue cape, white suit, with silver trimmings on coat, vest, and short trousers. Stockings and shoes painted white, buckles silver

PRINCE CHARMING. An animated Nutcracker: a young man dressed exactly as Nutcracker is painted

BIG MARIE. A young lady dressed in long-trained gown of material the same as that of Little Marie's dress. Her hair, the same color as the child's, is massed on top of her head as tho' a child had quickly pinned up its curls. A pink bow is prominent on head. The whole figure suggests a child masquerading as a grown up, and represents Marie's idea of herself as a young lady

TIN SOLDIERS. As seen in any toy-shop

GINGERBREADS. Fat, clumsy figures of men of brown gingerbread; red candy buttons on coats, and brown skull-caps

MOUSE BRIGADE. A band of little grey mice with long tails

THE REEDS. Dressed in straight, long gown of dark green and brown; the sleeves much longer than tips of fingers, so that, at flexing of elbows and swaying of arms, they appear to be the long leaves of the reeds. Over the head and neck and shoulders is draped a lighter brown scarf, like the cap or head of the reed

THE FLOWERS. All kinds and colors, expressed in costumes *ad libitum*

❄

TIME, Christmas Eve.

PLACE, a comfortable home.

ARGUMENT

The Christmas tree hangs full of things; but Grandpa adds to them his gift to little Marie, a Nutcracker shaped like a handsome young prince. Yet when the gifts are distributed, Johnny tries to snatch the Nutcracker from Marie and—his (the Nutcracker's) leg is torn off. But Grandpa promises to get him "fixed," and the children go to bed.

Marie puts the Nutcracker in her doll-crib, and starting to sing him to sleep, falls asleep herself. Then things begin to happen, for the Nutcracker is a *Magic* Nutcracker.

The Christmas things turn life-size and come alive; Gingerbread Children, Tin Soldiers, Candy-Fairy, Chinese Boy, Reed Flute Children, etc., and the Candy-Fairy dance and sing.

And next, the Reed Flute Children dance, while the Wind-Fairy sings.

Then the Mouse-King, followed by the savage Mouse Brigade, enters. They at once begin to battle with the Gingerbread Children. But the Tin Soldiers hurry to help their Gingerbread friends, the Nutcracker Prince, a crutch under one arm, and a sword in his other, leading them. As he falls on his knee and is about to be killed, however, Marie, coming in (as a Young Lady), hurls her slipper at the Mouse-King, he falls dead.

The Nutcracker is now a real Prince Charming, for the Mouse-King was a wizard who had enchanted him until such time as a maiden should "love him more than she fears a mouse." And Marie has broken the spell by killing the Mouse-King with her slipper. Now as his people, the Flowers, gather around them, he thanks her for her rescue, and promises to take her to his wonderland.

Scene I

A comfortably furnished sitting room. Door right front. Right rear, a huge Christmas tree reaching to ceiling, laden with toys, tinsel, fruit, candy, etc. Centre left, a table.

Underneath tree at left, a big box of gingerbreads in forms of men. Some have fallen out of box, which lies tipped over. Others are half out of the box.

Left front, a fully outfitted doll's bed.

Centre rear, a large box of tin soldiers stand on floor, upright, so that the soldiers are seen standing in rows.

Hanging in conspicuous places on lower branches of tree are seen toys about twenty inches long, painted and dressed exactly like the peppermint Candy-Fairy; a Chinese Doll, flutes, and also some mechanical mice.

Mother and Father are busily arranging tree, untying packages, etc.

MOTHER: (*folding a blanket on doll's bed.*) So!—There!

FATHER: (*hanging flutes on tree.*) So!—There!

> *(The door bangs open. Grandpa comes stumbling in, every pocket of overcoat bulging with packages, both arms full of packages, hat on back of head, his face wreathed in smiles.)*

GRANDPA: Well! Here I am!

MOTHER: (*laughing out.*) Father!

FATHER: Why Dad! Did you leave any toys in the shops and booths?

(Mother and Father help Grandpa take dolls and toys out of his pockets. Then they help him take off his coat; all amidst joyful exclamations of approval. Grandpa is delighted, and now he takes a package which he begins to unfold with special cure.)

GRANDPA: *(chuckling with glee.)* And this—*this* is the most wondrous gift of all! In the marketplace, among the vendors of toys, there sat an old woman. She held this up to me *(Grandpa holds up the Nutcracker)*, saying, "Buy! Buy!"

FATHER *and* MOTHER: What is it?

GRANDPA: A Nutcracker!

FATHER *and* MOTHER: A Nutcracker?

GRANDPA: Yes! A Nutcracker! As I was about to pass the old woman, for I really had *so* many bundles already, she called aloud to me once more, holding this fellow up before me. "Buy! Buy! Buy this magic Nutcracker, Sir! See, he's a very *prince* of a fellow, and besides, he will surely bring good luck to whoever owns him! Buy the magic Nutcracker! Buy! Good Sir!" And so *(almost shamefacedly)* I bought him too! Isn't he a comical fellow? Ah! But see what a grand prince he is! Well, well, my little Marie shall have him, and if there's any good luck attached to him, may it be heres!—*(Warmly)* My little Marie!

(All burst into laughter at Grandpa's words. Music of Miniature Overture begins.)

Miniature Overture

Words adapted by Jane Kerley
to
Music by Tschaikowsky

Grandpa (*busily untying parcel*)

Hush! Hush, and hur - ry now. This work must soon, must

soon be done. The gin-ger-bread, where is it?

My poor head! What a vis-it, what a vis-it! There is the gin-ger-bread,

Father (*pointing to large*

box of gingerbread on the floor)

Put it on the chair. No! it were bet - ter to leave it there!

Ped. *

Mother (*arranging a group of toys*)   **Father** (*the same*)

Tom-my's things right here!   Ba-by's things right here!   John-ny's things right here!

Grandpa (*the same*)   **Father**   **Grandpa**   **Mother**   **All**

Ma-rie's things right here!   There!   There!   There!   There!

Mother (*viewing all with*

Now   let   the

evident satisfaction)

chil - dren come,   Now   joy   shall   know   no   mea - sure!

Now let the chil-dren come, That we may share their

plea - sure! Oh dear me! Where is the ma-gic Nut-crack-er? The

Grandpa (*suddenly puts one hand on forehead as he searches, with oth-*)

Nut-crack-er! Ah, the ma - gic Nut-crack-er Prince!

er, for Nutcracker)   (*holds up Nutcracker for inspection, and in serio-comic fashion bur-*)

dolce cantabile

Gaze up - on_ his_ ma-gic_ face, Ob - serve his prince-ly_

lesques homage to the toy, to the delight of Mother and Father, who gayly mimic Grandpa's

p con grazia

gestures, and bow ceremoniously to the Nutcracker)

grace!   Ah!

Yes, the ma - gic Nut - crack - er -

Prince!   Gaze up - on his hand - some face!

Ah! Yes, you shall go to dear Ma - rie, And

all your ma - gic hers shall be, yes, all your ma - gic

hers shall be, yes, all your ma - gic hers shall

bel!   Read-y!

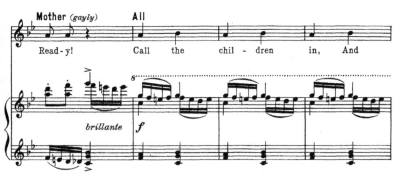

Read-y!   Call   the   chil - dren   in,   And

let the fun be - gin,   the fun be - gin.

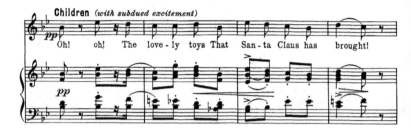

Children *(with subdued excitement)*

Oh! oh! The love-ly toys That San-ta Claus has brought!

Oh! oh! the love-ly toys! They're fin-er than I thought!

Oh! oh! the love-ly toys, That San-ta Claus has

brought.____ Oh! oh! the love-ly toys! They're

fin - er than I thought!____

Tommy *(discovering the gingerbread)*   Johnny   Tom-

Gin-ger-bread so dan - dy!   Su-gar-plums! And the choc'-late-can-dy!   A

my   Baby   Marie

re-gi-ment of sol-diers!   See the dan-cing mouse!   The dol-ly's bed!

Tommy   Baby *(to Mother)*   Johnny *(to Father)*

And the dol-ly's house!   What a lot of fun!   Make the mous-ie run!   What

Father

kind of flutes are these? You'll play them soon with ease!

Tommy
(holds up toy peppermint fairy)

I must taste this fair-y—

(takes a bite) *(patting his stomach)*

Bite off one toe air-y!   M m m m   m m m m!

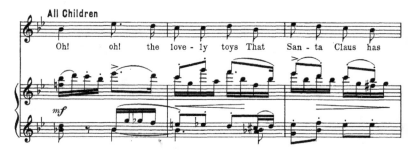

All Children

Oh! oh! the love-ly toys That San-ta Claus has

brought!___ Oh! oh! the love-ly toys, They're

THE NUTCRACKER

Marie *(holding up Nutcracker)* **Grandpa**

fin - er than I thought! What is this? Oh, that, my child, is

Marie *(enthusiastically)*

just a ma - gic Nut-crack - er! Oh, you love - ly

Nut - crack - er prince!___ Ah, you have a___ hand - some

face, And such a___ win - ning grace!___

Ah! Yes,____ I love you best, You hand-some Nut-crack-er prince!

Johnny
(trying

I shall keep you for my own, I'll give you up to_ none! Ma-

to take Nutcracker from Marie) **Marie** *(guarding Nutcracker)*

rie, now let_ me see! No, he be-longs to_ me! No, go a-way! He's

(Johnny tries to take Nutcracker)

mine, I say! He's mine, I say! now go a-way! You shall not touch him

THE NUTCRACKER

Johnny *(fighting to obtain possession of Nutcracker)*

while I'm near! You self-ish girl, now give him here! Give him to me!

Marie — No, Sir! Johnny — Give him to me! Marie — No, Sir! Johnny — Self - ish

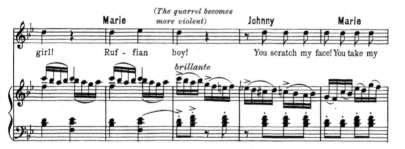

Marie — girl! Ruf - fian boy! *(The quarrel becomes more violent)* Johnny — You scratch my face! Marie — You take my

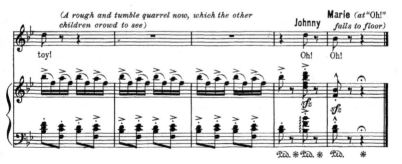

(A rough and tumble quarrel now, which the other children crowd to see) Johnny — Marie *(at "Oh!" falls to floor)*

toy! Oh! Oh!

Marie sits on floor, holding aloft in one hand the Nutcracker, minus one leg, in the other his broken-off leg, and bursts out crying. Her screams are loud and her brothers turn from her in disgust. Mother, Father, and Grandpa come forward to learn cause of confusion.

MOTHER: (*bending over Marie.*) What is it, dear? Oh!—What a noise! (*to boys*) Shame on you, boys, to make your sister cry.

MARIE: (*holds up Nutcracker and broken leg, to convince parents of the tragedy, and sobs.*) Oh! Oh! Oh! My *lovely* Nutcracker,—he was *so* fine! Now look at him! He's all broken! Grandpa gave him to *me!* Grandpa gave him to *me!* My lovely Nutcracker! (*sobbing still more*) Mother! Mother! They've *broken* my Nutcracker!

MOTHER: (*takes Marie in her arms.*) There, there, there! Nevermind, my dear, he can be fixed again. Grandpa will surely have him all fixed for you tomorrow—won't you, Grandpa?

GRANDPA: (*petting Marie.*) Of course I will! Of course I will! There, don't cry anymore. Tomorrow we'll have him fixed as good as new!

FATHER: (*holding out watch on palm of his hand.*) Come now, it's bedtime! Enough for tonight! Tomorrow is another day. Off to bed with you all! (*Boys go off skylarking with Father.*)

MARIE: Ah Mother, before I go to bed, let me put my Nutcracker to bed. He shall have my doll's bed tonight, because he's been so badly hurt.

(*Mother smiles indulgently while Marie, still sobbing quietly, takes doll out of bed and puts Nutcracker in, tucking him up carefully.*)

MARIE: There, my *dear, dear* Nutcracker, try to go to sleep. Tomorrow we'll take you to the doctor, won't we, Grandpa?

GRANDPA: (*reassuringly.*) Yes, yes, of course!

(*Mother and Marie, hand in hand, walk to door. Marie wistfully looks at her Mother.*)

MARIE: Mother, he'll be as good as new?

(They go out. Grandpa smiles after them tenderly. He goes about turning out lights. At last only one remains lit. He goes to door, rubbing hands cheerfully.)

GRANDPA: The children *were* pleased! Yes! And that little Marie (*he shakes his head and chuckles*), how she loves that fool Nutcracker! (*He pushes the electric light button near door. — All lights out. Exit.*)

A half-hour is supposed to elapse before next scene.

SCENE II

Door opens. Marie enters, dressed in slippers and nightgown. She pushes button near door; one light up; room in dim light. She hurries across to doll's bed, drops on knees beside it, bends tenderly over it, whispering.

MARIE: Nutcracker! Are you all right? I couldn't sleep for worrying about you! (*She takes Nutcracker out of bed, wraps him in doll's blanket, settles herself into comfortable position on floor beside bed, and holds Nutcracker on lap.*) Come, I'll rock you to sleep, I'll sing you the Arab cradle—song that Nurse used to sing to me. Come! Come!

Arab Lullaby

Des - ert wind, now be my boy's char - ger, Gal - lop

molto espressivo e cantabile

slow, Gen - tly, gen - tly

dolcissimo

gal - lop with ba - by, Where sweet wa - ters, where sweet wa - ters

(scoldingly)

flow. Ba - by, close your eyes and go to sleep,

(resuming rocking)

Rid - ing comes the Sheik ____ On his

mare so sleek; ____

He will call out, "Who is that rid - ing, ____

____ rid - ing fast - er ____ than I please?"

(with utmost tenderness)

And I'll an - swer, "Sheik, it is ba - by,

(smiles down at Nutcracker)

Ba - by rid - ing on the breeze!"

(softly)

Ah! Then the

Sheik will say, "Ba - by shall

rule some day."

(Scolding, when she observes Nutcracker not yet asleep.)

Cam-el, come and take this bad boy,

who will not sleep! Take him far a - way,

dolce

(menacingly)

where the black dogs their watch keep.

THE NUTCRACKER

(very sweetly)

Ah!

(this time she smiles as she scolds)

Where the black dogs their watch keep.

(sweetly)

Ah! Cam - el, go a - way! Ah!

Marie, as song ends, has drooped across doll's bed, head on pillow, fast asleep. All lights slowly out, as curtain slowly falls.

Scene III

Slow lights disclose scene of enlarged proportions: All toys have assumed human stature. Marie, the doll's bed, the table, chairs, have disappeared. The box of gingerbread on floor is now seen to be the size of a large case; the gingerbread cakes, now children in gingerbread costume, lie in the same positions as the cakes did. The box of tin soldiers is as large as the case of cakes, and children, dressed like soldiers, stand ranged as were the toys. Only the lowest branches of the Christmas tree are seen; projecting from a wing, they are above the tops of cases. From the branches hangs the Candy-Fairy, now a child, with one foot on floor; also the Chinese boy, now a child, stands on floor, but cue tied to branch gives impression that he is suspended from tree. Reed flutes, now children, seem to be hanging from low branches. Some large candies and inanimate toys may be hung on lower branches of tree to add to illusion of changed proportions of scene. Spotlight on Candy-Fairy, who wiggles herself loose from tree and comes hobbling forward at first notes of Candy-Fairy dance. Spot follows Fairy; rest of stage dim.

THE CANDY-FAIRY

Andante ma non troppo

(The Candy-Fairy hobbles forward painfully, but strictly in step with music.)

pp leggero

Candy-Fairy *(petulantly)*

Oh, my poor toe! Oh dear! How it hurts! How it hurts! How it hurts!

mf

(clenching little fists)

(Emphatically,

Oh, that hor-rid boy! My one toe he bit off. Yes he did!

as tho' someone had denied it)   *(limps a step)*

Yes, he did! Yes, he did! How that does an-noy!   Oh, my poor toe!

(almost weeping)

Oh dear! Let me try,   let me try, let me try! Try if I can dance!

(very gingerly points toe)   *(encouraged)*   *(quite airily, yet incredulously)*

Let me see now,   Step quite free now,   Can it be now?

(overjoyed, she pirouettes)   *(she dances freely)*

I can dance!

(delighted with herself)

I dance!   I prance!

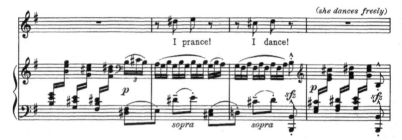

(she dances freely)

I prance!   I dance!

(with the utmost

quasi arpa

aplomb and self-satisfaction she gracefully postures and dances)

am   a   Can - dy -

Fair - y sweet, And

dance on one or

both my feet!

(she stubs her foot)

decresc.

p

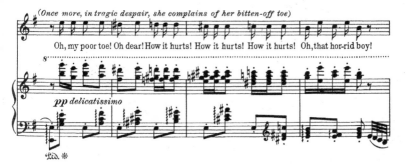

(Once more, in tragic despair, she complains of her bitten-off toe)

Oh, my poor toe! Oh dear! How it hurts! How it hurts! How it hurts! Oh, that hor-rid boy!

pp delicatissimo

Spotlight out. Fairy disappears.—

Scene IV

The Chinese Boy

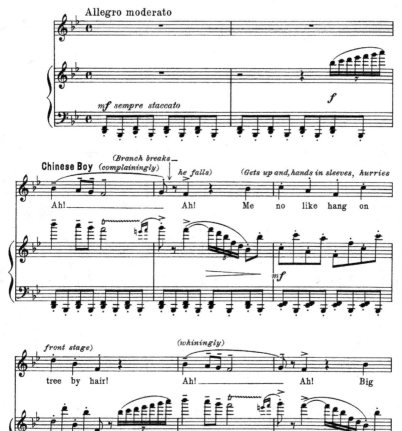

('Mel - 'can) man, he tie me there. *(very decidedly)* Me no like! Me no

Fa - ther

like! *(complainingly)* Small Chi - nee have no fun at all.

(very decidedly) Me no like! Me no like! *(rubbing back of trousers)* Small Chi - nee boy have

(almost crying)

great big fall!   Ah!_____   Ah!   Me

no   want   see   big   ('Mel - 'can)   man!
                       Fa - ther

Ah!_____   Ah!   Me

(with short shuffling steps he hurries about stage, as tho' deciding which way to run)

run a - way so fast I can! Me no want see big

f

'Mel - 'can man! Me run a - way so

cresc.

(Lights out suddenly).

Curtain

fast I can! Me run a - way so fast I can!

ff

Scene V

On dark stage there appears slowly a blue-green light. As it grows brighter a river bank is disclosed. From right to left of stage a baseboard is stretched, painted to represent water. Back of this stand children, dressed as reeds, closely grouped and motionless as reeds in water on a windless night. In center, a flat-topped rock. At first note of dance of Reed-Flutes, there comes swiftly, from dim rear, the Wind-Fairy. She leaps on the rock and sings. As soon as she appears, the reeds move, swaying and bending as her words indicate throughout. A better picture is produced by having large and small children intermingled.

THE REED-FLUTES

Moderato assai

Wind-Fairy *(with graceful swayings and bend-*

p leggero

I'm the Wind that comes a - blow - ing

ings)

O'er the reeds by the wa - ters grow - ing; Now I bend them this way,

mf

p

Now I bend them that way, I can make them twist and turn ac - cord-ing to my blow-ing.

mp

When my mu-sic soft and clear ___ Thrills the reeds all, far or near,___

Then in cho-rus sweet, All their voi-ces meet, Then their slen-der forms so free, They

sway, and sing in ec-sta-sy.___ Wind, come sing for us, we

Chorus of Reeds

pray, That we may dance all day.

Wind-Fairy
Reeds *(in echo)*

Ah!_____ Ah!_____

Wind-Fairy *(gracefully swaying)*

I'm the Wind that comes a - flow - ing O'er the reeds by the wa-ters

delicato

sempre staccato

grow - ing; Now I bend them this way, Now I bend them that way,

I can make them twist and turn ac - cord-ing to my blow-ing.

* If found too difficult, the effect of sighing wind may be accomplished by a downward inflection.

When my mu-sic soft and clear _____ Thrills the reeds all, far or

near, _____ Then in cho-rus sweet All their voi-ces meet,

Sway - ing so fleet. Mm _____

Reeds *(swaying and twist-*

leggero e staccato

ing gently, while the Wind-Fairy, with graceful gestures, seems to direct their music)

Wind-Fairy

I'm the Wind that comes a - flow - ing O'er the reeds by the wa - ters grow - ing; Now I bend them this way, Now I bend them that way, I can make them twist and turn ac - cord - ing to my blow - ing.

sempre staccato

When my mu - sic soft and clear

Thrills the reeds all, far or near,___ Then in cho - rus sweet

(Lights out!)

All their voi - ces meet, Sway - ing so fleet.

THE NUTCRACKER

SCENE VI

Light shows that the Reeds and Wind-Fairy have disappeared, leaving plainly visible the huge boxes of living Soldiers and Gingerbreads, with a spotlight on them.

MARCH

Mice *(suiting actions to words, by quick dashes at Gingerbreads)* **Gingerbreads**

Nib-ble nib-ble Mice un - til they're dead! For-ward now, the

Mice *(briskly flying around)*   *(some Gingerbreads fall)*

Gin - ger-bread! All the mice run quick-ly round, While Gin-ger-breads fall to the ground,

For-ward, march! The re - gi - ment! For-ward, march! On pil - lage bent! We

are the sav - age mouse - bri - gade, The Gin - ger - breads we come to raid; They

quail with fear As we draw near, We're brave from tail to ear!

Switch
of tail

cresc.

(A great battle ensues between Mice and Gingerbreads; the latter are evidently being van-

p   *mf*   *p*   *mf*   *p*

quished, tho' some Mice must also succumb with squeals of anguish. But the Gingerbreads

cresc.

are getting the worst of it)

f ———— *sfz*

Tin Soldiers *(marching forward in formation, but stiff-jointedly)*

For-ward, sol - diers made of tin, For-ward thro' the bat-tle's din,

staccato e leggero

mf

Forward, soldiers true and brave, For your friends the Gingerbreads to save;

mp *f*

(They advance upon Mice and seem able to force

Forward! we must surely win, Gingerbreads and soldiers of tin!

mf

them back)

We shall save the Gingerbread, And leave all the mice here dead!

mp *f*

Mice (*once more attacking furiously*)

For-ward, march! The re - gi - ment! For-ward, march! On

pil - lage bent! We are the sav - age mouse - bri - gade, The

Gin - ger-breads we've come to raid; They quail with fear As we draw near, We're

brave from tail to ear!

Switch of tail

(General battle; dead soldiers lie here and there,

with dead Gingerbreads and a few Mice. One mouse's tail, stepped on, comes off; he picks

it up and belabors Gingerbreads with it.)

Gingerbreads *(rallying to attack)*

Switch Cour - age, cour - age, Gin - ger - bread!

staccato

Mice *(busily biting legs and clawing)*

Nib - ble nib - ble Mice un - til they're dead!

Mice *(redoubling efforts to win, they wildly rush*

put you all to shame! For-ward, march! The re - gi - ment!

about among the Gingerbreads, Soldiers and Prince Charming. They have almost won, when Marie,

For-ward, march! on pil - lage bent!

who enters now as a young lady, views the battle and realizes that the Prince is about to be killed, as he has already fallen on his knee; she takes off her slipper and hurls it at the Mouse King, who falls dead)

Lights out!

Scene VII

Lights up, disclosing stage clear but for figures of Prince Charming and Big Marie, who stands with hands clasped on breasts, gazing at Prince.

THE PRINCE: Unending e'er shall be my thanks to you, O maid, who with one stroke did kill the vicious Mouse-King. Know, that your courage and devotion have put an end to a dreadful curse 'neath which I lived for years. The Mouse-King was no other than the wizard black, who wove a spell around me and condemned me to be a Nutcracker until a maiden's love should release me, yea, until a maiden should prove that she loved me more than she feared—a mouse! When my death seemed sure, fair maid, you came to my aid. You loved me, and you came; oh, let my gratitude be worthy of your love! (*Prince rises.*) I am a prince; the sweetest, purest realm is mine, full of white magic and brimming with love. See, Marie, I call my people to me here; come, let me show you my wonderland! (*He takes Marie's hand, and leads her centre.*)

The Waltz of the Flowers

Tempo di Valzer

(Prince Charming beckons right and left, kindly, yet with authority, and as

he holds out his hand, flower after flower comes running to him happily.   Throughout

this introductory music, he takes the flowers by the hand, singly or by twos, and ceremo-

niously presents them to the grown-up Marie, standing spellbound. She acknowledges their

Cadenza

bows with frank amazement and delight. After each flower is presented, it takes its place

in background groupings, among the mass of flowers assembled from all directions. They

stand ready in place until the singing begins, when they perform a ballet which continues

until lights dim at end.) (The scene should now dis-

close Marie and Prince Charming standing surrounded by a mass of many-colored flowers, to which the Prince points with pride.)

(perturbed; bashfully)

'Neath the ma - gic of the spell! You must be Prince Charm-ing:-

sfz *f cantando*

(with sudden conviction) *(with frank,*

Oh, you are Prince Charm - ing! No more

f

Ped. *

girlish simplicity)

fears a - larm - ing: You are he, I know you

sfz

(with bewitching, spontaneous confidence)

well! Here and there, Ev-'ry - where, Oh, my Prince, I sought you e'er,-

dolce *mf* *cantabile*

p

wait - ed   for__ a maid - en,__   A maid   my free-dom must bring!

Great - er   far   than your fear__   of the Mouse-King   Was your

love,__   your dear love,__   Yes, your love   my free-dom   did bring!__   Oh, Ma-

(he kneels and
kisses her hand)

Marie

rie,__   Stay with me,__   It was   you who set   me free!__   Here and

there,   Ev-'ry - where,   O my Prince, I sought you   e'er!___

Prince Charming (leading

Ma-rie, come dance___ with

her thro' a few steps of a stately dance)

me!___   No sweet-er flow-er I   see,   In this gar-den fair,

No flow'r more rare;   Oh hear   me   swear, I___ love you!

Ma-rie, come be___ my bride,___ Stay ev-er here at my

side. In this won - der-land, Where now we stand,

You com-mand!

Marie

Ma - gic so en-tran - cing, Flow - ers, flow - ers dan - cing,

Prince Charming

Ma - gic so en-tran - cing, Flow - ers, flow - ers dan - cing,

You are he I know so well!

You are she I know so well!

(Prince Charming takes Marie's hand and leads her slowly off stage, pointing ahead

as tho' to indicate their path. — Stage dark; change of scene while the music proceeds

Scene VIII

Same as Scene II. Little Marie is fast asleep on floor, head on doll's bed. Enter Grandpa in dressing gown and slippers. He discovers Marie and hurries towards her.

GRANDPA: There, just as I thought! She had to come back to her Nutcracker! What a child, what a child! (*He bends over her and is about to pick her up in his arms.*) Come, come to Grandpa. (*He sees Nutcracker in her arms and tries to take it, Marie holds it fast.*)

GRANDPA: Well, well! Come on, then, I'll take the Nutcracker too. (*He takes up child, blanket and Nutcracker in his arms, Marie's had over his shoulder, and walks to door.*)

MARIE: (*half asleep.*) Grandpa dear, my Nutcracker is a wonderful Prince—oh, a wonderful Prince! Can you surely have him fixed for me, my Prince?

GRANDPA: Yes, yes, tomorrow, of course. (*Almost at door; very piano the music of Prince Charming is repeated.*)

GRANDPA: (*at door.*) Drat that Nutcracker! (*Exit.*)

CURTAIN

Princess Pirlipantine

and

the Nutcracker

How the Princess Pirlipatine was born, and how the King, her father, decided to celebrate her birth

ONCE UPON A TIME, NOT far from the town of Berylia, there was a little kingdom which was neither Polish nor Austrian nor Hungarian nor Italian nor Swiss, and it was governed by a King.

Now the wife of this King (who consequently was a Queen) had a baby daughter; and this daughter, being a Princess by birth, received the pleasant and distinguished name of Pirlipatine.

When the Princess arrived, the King was immediately informed of this happy event. He ran breathlessly to the Queen's chamber, and, seeing this pretty little girl lying in her cradle, was completely carried away with delight at being the father of so charming a babe. At first he could only utter cries of joy, then he began to dance round the cradle, then hopping about on one leg he kept repeating:

"Goodness gracious! Have you ever seen anything so beautiful as my Pirlipatine?"

Behind the King came the ministers, the generals, the great officers of state, the privy councillors, and the judges; and all of them, seeing the King hopping about on one leg, began to imitate him, crying:

"No, no, never, Sire, never, never in all the world has there ever been anything so beautiful as your Pirlipatine."

And indeed, although you may be surprised to hear it, there was really no flattery in these words; for in fact never since the creation of the world had such a beautiful Princess been born as Princess Pirlipatine. Her little body seemed to be made of a delicate silken tissue, pink as a rose and white as a lily. Her eyes were of the deepest azure, intensely bright, and nothing could be more charming than her golden locks, falling in delightful little curls about her snowy shoulders. Added to this, she had already two small rows of teeth, more like pearls than teeth, with which, two hours after her arrival, she bit the finger of the Grand Chancellor (who, being short-sighted, had stooped to look at her more closely) so vigorously that although a taciturn and philosophical man, he is said to have cried out:

"Oh the blazes!"

Others, however, having regard for his philosophical nature, aver that he said only: "Oh! Oh! Oh!"

Even today opinion is divided upon this important point; neither side being willing to give way. And the only thing upon which the "blazers" and the "ohers" are agreed, the only fact which is incontestable, is that the Princess Pirlipatine bit the Grand Chancellor's finger. Thenceforth the whole country knew that there was as much spirit as beauty in the pretty little body of Pirlipatine.

Everybody, then, was happy in this favoured kingdom. I say everybody, but the Queen herself was troubled and anxious without anyone knowing why. All were struck by the extraordinary care with which she caused her child's cradle to be guarded. Not only were all the doorways filled with detachments of the Life-Guard, but besides the two Chief-Nurses-Extraordinary who watched continually over the Princess, there were six Nurses-in-Ordinary who sat round her cradle, and these were changed every night. But the fact which excited everyone's curiosity more than anything else, and what nobody could make head or tail of, was why each of these six nurses was obliged to hold a cat in her lap and to stroke it all night long so that it never stopped purring.

I am quite sure that you are as curious as the inhabitants of this nameless little kingdom to know why these six nurses were obliged to hold cats in their laps and to stroke them without stopping so that they never ceased purring for a moment. But as you could not possibly guess the answer to this riddle, I will tell you so that you will be spared the headache which you would assuredly get if you were to puzzle over it for too long. It was like this.

It happened one day that half-a-dozen of quite the best Kings and Queens in that part of the country agreed to pay a visit to the future father of the Princess; for at that time the Princess was not yet born. They were accompanied by the Royal Princes, by the hereditary Grand Dukes, and by all the most agreeable Pretenders.

It was an event of such importance for the King whom they were visiting (who was one of the most magnificent monarchs) that he felt obliged to make a heavy inroad upon his treasury, and to hold tournaments, pageants, and plays in their honour. But that was not all. Having learnt from the Superintendent of the Royal Kitchens that the Astronomer-Royal had announced that the time for killing pigs was at hand, and that the conjunction of the stars indicated that it would be a favourable year for making bacon, he ordered that there should be a great slaying of pigs in all the royal piggeries. Then, getting into his coach, he went in person to each of the Kings and each of the Princes and each of the Grand Dukes and each of the Pretenders who were staying at that moment in his capital, and invited them all to dinner with him; for he wanted to enjoy their surprise at beholding the magnificent banquet which he intended giving. Then, as soon as ever he reached home, he went straight to the Queen's apartments, and going up to her said in the wheedling tone which he always used when he wanted anything:

"My dear, you haven't forgotten how fond I am of black pudding, have you? Tell me you haven't forgotten."

At the very first word the Queen understood what the King wanted. In fact Her Majesty plainly understood by these insidious words that she would have to make (as she had already made many times before) with her own royal hands, the largest possible quantity of sausages, chitterlings, and black puddings. Then she smiled at her husband's suggestion, for although she carried out her duties as a Queen very honourably and creditably, yet she was less sensible to compliments paid her regarding the dignity with which she bore the sceptre and the crown than she was to compliments on her skill in making puddings or sweetmeats. Therefore she made a graceful curtsey to her husband, saying that it was as much her part to make black puddings for the King as it was for her to do anything else.

The Grand Treasurer was at once ordered to deliver up to the Royal Kitchen the huge cauldron of silver gilt and the great silver stew pans which were always used for making black puddings and sausages. An enormous fire of sandalwood was lit. The Queen put on her cooking apron of white damask, and soon the most delicious odour was coming from the cauldron. This delightful smell spread rapidly down all the corridors, penetrated into all the rooms of the palace, and finally reached the Throne Room, where the King was holding a council.

Now the King was a great epicure, and this smell gave him a lively pleasure. Nevertheless, seeing that he was a serious Prince and had a reputation for coolness in all emergencies, he withstood for some time the attraction which urged him towards the kitchen. But at last, in spite of his control over his emotions, he was forced to yield to the irresistible perfume which assailed his nostrils.

"Gentlemen," he said, getting up, "with your permission I must retire for a moment. I shall be back in a minute. Wait till I come."

And, crossing the rooms and the corridors, he made his way hastily towards the kitchen.

Pushing open the door, he folded the Queen in his arms; then he stirred the contents of the cauldron with his sceptre, then licked the top of the sceptre thoughtfully with the tip of his tongue. Having thus regained his composure, he returned to the council and took up (though a trifle preoccupied) the discussion at the point where he had dropped it.

II

OF THE ROYAL BANQUET,
AND WHAT BEFEL THEREAT

THE KING HAD LEFT THE kitchen just at the important moment when the bacon, cut up in morsels, was about to be roasted on the silver gridiron. The Queen, encouraged by his praises, was herself attending to this important operation, and the first drops of fat were already beginning to fall hissing upon the fire, when a little trembling voice was heard saying:

> *"My sister, gave me a morsel to eat,*
> *Though I'm also a Queen t'will be a treat*
> *So spare me a piece of your roasted fat*
> *For I rarely taste anything quite like that."*

The Queen recognised the voice immediately: it was that of the Lady Mousekin.

Dame Mousekin had lived in the palace for many years. She professed to be related to the Royal Family, and called herself Queen of the Mouse Tribe. For she held a very considerable court beneath the kitchen hearth.

The Queen was a kind and generous woman, and although she refused openly to recognise the Lady Mousekin as a Queen and sister, yet secretly she had a tender regard for her, and was so indulgent towards her that her husband often reproached her for acting thus beneath her dignity. Therefore, as you will readily understand, upon this important occasion the Queen had not the heart to refuse her small friend. So she said:

"Come along, Dame Mousekin, you can come out boldly. I give you my permission to taste the bacon as much as you please."

In an instant Dame Mousekin appeared, gay and frisky, and, jumping upon the fender, deftly seized with her small paws the morsels of bacon which the Queen handed to her one after the other.

But all at once, attracted by the shrill cries of pleasure which their Queen was uttering, and especially by the toothsome smell which arose from the grilled bacon, the seven sons of Dame Mousekin, their wives and their relations, rushed up frisking and dancing just like her. They were mischievous rascals, dreadfully quick with their little mouths, and they threw themselves upon the bacon in such a way that the Queen was obliged, hospitable as she was, to remark that if they continued in this fashion there would be no bacon left for the puddings. But in spite of the justice of this remark, the seven sons of Dame Mousekin paid not the slightest attention. Setting a disgraceful example to their wives and relations, and in spite of the protests of their mother and queen, they threw themselves upon the bacon, which would have disappeared in a trice had not the cries of the Queen, who was unable to chase away all her importunate guests, brought up the Superintendent-of-the-Kitchens at a run. The Superintendent called the Head Cook, the Head Cook called the Head Scullion, and the Head Scullion called the Head Turnspit. Dashing up armed with brooms, ladles and rolling pins, they succeeded in driving all the mice under the hearth.

But the victory, although it was a complete one, was very nearly too late; hardly a quarter of the bacon necessary for making chitterlings, Sausages, and puddings remained. This remainder was divided scientifically (according to the calculations of the King's Mathematician, who had been sent for in haste) between the great cauldron in which the puddings were boiling and the two great stew pans containing the chitterlings and sausages.

Half an hour after this event cannons suddenly roared, and clarions and trumpets sounded. All the Kings and Queens and all the Royal Princes and all the hereditary Grand Dukes and all the Pretenders who were in the capital began to arrive. They were dressed in their most magnificent clothes; some rode in crystal coaches, others came on their review horses. The King received them at the steps of the palace, and greeted them with the most charming courtesy and graceful cordiality. Then, when they had left their cloaks and umbrellas in the hall, he led them into the dining room and took up his seat at the head of the table, for he was their suzerain or overlord, being head of all the Kings in those parts. The other Kings and Queens and Royal Princes and hereditary Grand Dukes and agreeable Pretenders sat down at the table in strict order of precedence.

The table was sumptuously laid, and all went well between the soup and the entrée. But when the chitterlings came on everyone noticed that the King seemed agitated; when the sausages arrived he turned pale; and the black pudding was hardly placed before him when he cast up his eyes and uttered a heartbroken sigh. Then some terrible anguish seemed to take possession of him: he fell over the back of his chair, covered his face with his hands, and wept in a most heart-rending way. The guests sprang up from their seats and gathered round him in the greatest alarm. The crisis seemed grave indeed; the Court Physician felt for his pulse in vain; the King was apparently afflicted by a most serious, a most alarming, and a most unheard of malady.

Finally, after the most violent remedies had been tried (such as holding burning feathers and smelling salts under his nose, dropping door keys down his back, and pouring hot soup in his boots) the King appeared to recover Somewhat. He opened his eyes, and, in a voice so feeble that it could scarcely be heard, whispered:

"NOT ENOUGH BACON."

At these words it was the Queen's turn to grow pale. She threw herself on her knees, and cried in a voice stifled with sobs:

"Oh my unhappy, unfortunate, and royal spouse! What distress have I caused you by not listening to the advice which you have given me so often? Behold the culprit at your knees, punish her as severely as she deserves."

"What's that?" said the King; "what on earth have you been doing that you haven't told me about?"

"Alas! Alas!" replied the Queen, to whom her husband had never spoken so rudely or ungrammatically before; "Alas! It was Dame Mousekin with her seven sons, their wives, their cousins, and their relations, who devoured all the bacon!"

But the Queen could say no more. Her grief overcame her; she fell on the carpet and fainted.

Then the King got up, furious, and cried out in a terrible voice:

"MADAME SUPERINTENDENT, WHAT IS THE MEANING OF THIS?"

Then the Superintendent came forward trembling, and related all that she knew, namely, how, attracted by the cries of the Queen, she had seen Her Majesty battling with the whole family of Dame Mousekin, and how she in her turn had called out to the Head Cook, who, assisted by the Scullions (who were assisted by the Turnspits), had forced all the robbers to retreat under the hearth.

Immediately the King, seeing at once that it was a case of high treason, recovered his dignity and his calm, and ordered that, in view of the enormity of the crime, his Privy Council should assemble forthwith and that the matter should be placed before the wisest of his Councillors.

Forthwith the council assembled, and after some hours of discussion, it was decided, by a majority, that as Dame Mousekin was accused of having eaten the bacon destined for the King's sausages, the King's black puddings, and the King's chitterlings, the King's writ should be served upon her, and that if she were found guilty she should be condemned to perpetual banishment, *nolens volens*, from the kingdom, together with all her tribe, and that whatsoever goods and chattels she possessed, both in lands, castles, fortresses, royal residences, and hereditaments, should be forfeited to the King.

The King, however, took occasion to point out to his Privy Council that during all time this action was being tried, the Lady Mousekin and her family would have plenty of time to eat up all his bacon; and this would expose him to other affronts similar to the one which he had just experienced in the presence of six crowned heads, not to mention the Princes of royal blood, the hereditary Grand Dukes and the Pretenders. He demanded, therefore, that a discretionary power should be granted him with regard to Dame Mousekin and her family.

The Council immediately agreed to this proposal. It was carried unanimously, and the King was formally accorded the discretionary power for which he had asked.

III

EHU DAPPLEBLOCK APPEARS

THE KING TOOK ACTION IMMEDIATELY. He sent one of his best carriages, preceded by an out rider (in order to hurry things up), to a certain very skilful craftsman who lived in the town of Berylia and was called Ehu Dappleblock, inviting him to come to the palace at once on a very urgent affair. Ehu Dappleblock obeyed immediately; for, besides being a well disciplined man, he was a shrewd fellow, and knew well that so famous a King would not send for him unless he wished him to contrive some masterpiece. So, getting into the carriage, he travelled night and day until he arrived at the palace. In fact he had hurried so much that he had not even had time to put any clothes into his portmanteau, and he came into the King's presence in the old yellow over coat which he usually wore. But instead of being annoyed at this breach of etiquette, the King thanked Ehu for coming, for, if he had committed a fault, the distinguished craftsman (being a well-disciplined man) had at least committed it unwittingly by obeying the King's commands so promptly.

The King took Dappleblock into his study and explained the situation to him. His Majesty was determined to set an example by purging the whole kingdom of the Mouse tribe, and having heard of Dappleblock's skill, he had decided to make Ehu the instrument which should execute his justice. One thing only he feared: that the craftsman, clever as he was, should consider the difficulties of the project insurmountable.

But Ehu Dappleblock reassured the King, and promised him that in eight days there should not be a single mouse left in all the kingdom.

The same day Ehu caused some curious little oblong boxes to be made, and in each of these he placed a morsel of bacon on the end of a piece of wire. In nibbling the bacon, the thief, whoever he might be, would cause a little trapdoor to shut behind him and so make him a prisoner. In less than a week a hundred of these boxes had been made and placed—not only under the hearth, but in all the granaries and cellars of the palace.

Dame Mousekin was far too wise and too far-seeing not to discover Master Dappleblock's ruse at the very first glance. She summoned her seven sons, their wives, their nephews and their cousins, to warn them of the plot which had been contrived against them. But, after listening with the respect which they owed to her rank and age, they retired laughing at her fears, and, attracted by the smell of the roasted bacon (which had more effect upon them than all the arguments of their mother), they resolved to profit by this sudden windfall which had come to them from goodness knows where.

At the end of twenty-four hours the seven sons of Dame Mousekin, their seven wives, eighteen nephews, fifty cousins, and two hundred and thirty five of their relations in varying degrees (without counting some thousands of Dame Mousekin's other subjects) had been caught in the mousetraps and ignominiously put to death. Then Dame Mousekin, with the remnant of her Court and the remainder of her people, resolved to abandon the haunts thus stained with the blood of her subjects.

The report of this resolution soon came to the King's ears. His Majesty was transported with joy, the Court Poets wrote eloquent son nets on his victory, whilst the ladies of the Court likened him to Sesostris, Alexander, and Caesar.

The Queen alone was sad and troubled. She knew Dame Mousekin only too well, and was aware that the Mouse-Queen would never allow the death of her sons and relations to pass unavenged. Indeed at the very moment when the Queen was preparing for the King, with her own hands, a purée of liver (of which he was particularly fond) in order to make him forget her offence, Dame Mousekin suddenly appeared before her. Shaking her paw at the trembling Queen, Dame Mousekin uttered these ominous words:

> "Though murder of my sons assuage
> Your husband's unrelenting rage,
> Yet tremble, royal Queen.
>
> The child which you will shortly see,
> The object of your love, shall be
> The object of my spleen.
>
> The King has wise men by the score,
> Soldiers and cannons, forts galore,
> And lots of mousetraps, too.
>
> I lack these things, but I've a charm
> Which to your babe shall bring much harm,
> And quickly make you rue."

Thereupon she disappeared, and from that moment nobody had seen her again. But the Queen, who had been told by the Astronomer-Royal a few days before that she was going to have a baby, was so terrified by this prediction that she allowed all the purée to fall into the fire.

Thus for the second time Dame Mousekin deprived the King of one of his favourite dishes. This made him more angry than ever, and he congratulated himself on the coup d'etat which he had so happily brought about.

Needless to say Ehu Dappleblock was presented with a magnificent reward, and he returned in triumph to Berylia.

IV

OF THE LAMENTABLE FATE
OF THE PRINCESS PIRLIPATINE

S O NOW YOU WILL UNDERSTAND why it was that the Queen took such elaborate precautions to guard the wonderful little Princess Pirlipatine. She dreaded the vengeance of Dame Mousekin; for, after what that lady had said, the Queen knew that her malice would be directed not only against the Princess as heir to the throne of this happy little nameless kingdom, but against Pirlipatine's very life—or even against her beauty, which is of even more importance to a Princess.

The poor Queen's fear increased when it was found that all the contrivances of Ehu Dappleblock were powerless against the wisdom of the Lady Mousekin. The Astronomer-Royal alone was able to afford her consolation. Being a great prophet and wizard, and fearing lest the King should suppress his office as useless unless he had something to say about the affair, he pretended to have read in the stars, in no uncertain way, that the family of the royal and illustrious Cat Murr alone was capable of preventing Dame Mousekin from approaching the royal cradle. It was for this reason that each of the six nurses was obliged continually to hold one of the tomcats of this distinguished family on her knees. Mistress Murr and her family were attached to the Court as Lap-Warmers-in-Ordinary, and, by a course of delicate and prolonged stroking, had become so proficient in their duties that they could enable the most crusty diplomatists to smooth out the most intricate affairs of state in a few minutes.

But one evening (there are days, as you are doubtless aware, when one gets up, dresses, and goes about one's business in a dream, being really asleep all the time); one evening, I say, the six Nurses-in-Ordinary sitting round the room, each with a cat on her knees, and the two Chief-Nurses-Extraordinary, who were sitting beside the Princess' pillow, felt sleep overcoming them one by one in spite of all their efforts to keep awake. As each one perceived this sensation coming over her, she took care not to let her companion see it, hoping that her lack of vigilance would pass unnoticed, and that her fellow Nurses-in-Ordinary would keep watch for her whilst she slept. The result was that their eyes closed one after the other; the hands which were stroking the cats stopped; and the cats, feeling this, took advantage of the circumstance to doze.

How long this strange sleep lasted I am unable to say; but about midnight one of the Chief-Nurses-Extraordinary woke up with a start. All the nurses round her seemed to be sunk in a deep slumber; not a snore could be heard; even their breathing seemed to have stopped; in fact complete silence reigned. And in the midst of this strange silence she heard a curious noise.

It was like somebody whispering in a high-pitched voice.

Imagine her fright then on beholding, close to her, standing on its hind paws at the foot of the cradle—a mouse!

The Chief-Nurse-Extraordinary uttered a cry of terror. At the sound everyone awoke; but Dame Mousekin (for it was she) flew towards a corner of the room. The Lap-Warmers-in-Ordinary dashed after her; but alas! Too late; Dame Mousekin had disappeared through a chink in the floor. At the same moment the Princess Pirlipatine, awakened by the uproar, began to cry.

At the sound of her voice the Nurses-in-Ordinary and Chief-Nurses-Extraordinary uttered exclamations of joy.

"Heaven be praised," said they; "so long as the Princess Pirlipatine cries she can't be dead."

Then they all rushed to the cradle, but their exclamations of joy gave place to cries of dismay when they saw what had happened to the delicate and charming little Pirlipatine.

In place of her pink and rosy face, in place of her little head covered with golden curls, in place of her azure eyes, blue as the sky, were two sharp little brown eyes and a little pointed snout with whiskers! The Princess Pirlipatine had turned into a mouse—at least so far as her head was concerned.

At this moment the Queen came into the room. The six Nurses-in-Ordinary and the two Chief-Nurses-Extraordinary threw themselves face downwards on the floor, whilst the six Lap-Warmers-in-Ordinary looked anxiously about to see whether anybody had by chance left a window open by which they could gain the roof.

The grief of the poor Queen was piteous to behold. She was carried fainting from the room. But the distress of the unfortunate father was even more lamentable—it was simply heartbreaking. They were obliged to put padlocks on the windows of his room lest he should throw himself out, and to pad the walls for fear that he should break his head against them. Needless to say his sword was taken from him at once, and all knives and forks were removed from his sight as well as everything sharp or pointed.

For the first two or three days he refused to eat anything, to the dismay of the royal attendants, and kept repeating:

"O unhappy monarch that I am! O cruel, cruel fate!"

Instead of accusing Fate, however, the King should have remembered that, like all other people, he had brought about his own misfortune himself. If he had only been content to eat the black puddings with a little less bacon than usual, and if, instead of seeking vengeance, he had left Dame Mousekin and her family alone under the hearth, the misfortune which he now bewailed would never have happened at all. But I regret to say that the royal father of Pirlipatine never once looked at the matter in this philosophical light. On the contrary, just as those in authority always throw the blame for their misfortunes upon somebody else, so the King threw the whole blame on Ehu Dappleblock. But knowing quite well that if he commanded Ehu to return to the Court immediately to be hanged or have his head cut off, Ehu would be particularly careful to refuse the invitation, the King invited him to come and receive a new Order of Knighthood which His Majesty had just created for men-of-letters, artists, and craftsmen.

Dappleblock was not free from pride. He thought that a ribbon would look well on his yellow coat, and he set out immediately for the palace. But his joy soon changed to sadness, for at the frontier of the kingdom guards were waiting for him. He was arrested and brought in chains to the capital.

The King, who doubtless feared lest Ehu's tears should move him to pity, refused to see Dappleblock when he arrived at the palace, but ordered that he should be led immediately before the Princess Pirlipatine's cradle, and that he should be informed that if, in one month from today, the Princess' head had not resumed its normal shape, his own head should be cut off without mercy.

Ehu did not pretend to be a hero, and he had never anticipated dying in any but a perfectly natural way. It had always seemed to him so foolish to die in one's boots when one could remove them and pass away comfortably in bed. So he was distinctly put out by this threat. Nevertheless, relying upon his great knowledge (the extent of which his modesty had never prevented him from appreciating), he plucked up heart and immediately set about the first and most useful thing he could think of doing—which was to see whether the calamity would yield to some sort of remedy or whether it was quite incurable, as he had feared at the first glance.

To this end he deftly took the Princess to pieces. First he removed her head, then her limbs in turn, then he took off her feet and hands in order that he might examine at his leisure not only her joints and springs but also her whole internal machinery. But alas! The more he probed into these mysteries of the Princess Pirlipatine's organism, the more pronounced her likeness to a mouse became. Sorrowfully he put her together again, and, not knowing what else to do or which way to turn, he sat down beside the cradle which he would never be allowed to leave until the Princess had resumed her normal appearance, and burst into tears.

V

EHU SETS OUT TO FIND THE KRAKATUK

THE FOURTH WEEK HAD ALREADY begun, and it was now Wednesday, when, according to his custom, the King came into the room to see whether any change had yet taken place in the Princess' appearance. He peered anxiously into the cradle, and seeing that the Princess still retained her mouse-like shape, he flew into a violent rage. Shaking his sceptre at the craftsman, he cried out:

"Ehu Dappleblock! Look to yourself! You have only three days left in which to restore my daughter to me as she was before. If you persist in refusing to cure her, your head shall be struck off on Sunday before breakfast."

It was inability not obstinacy which prevented Master Dappleblock from curing the Princess. He began to weep bitterly, gazing, with his eyes swimming with tears, at the Princess Pirlipatine, who was cracking a nut with her sharp little teeth as happily as though she were the prettiest little girl in the world.

At this affecting sight Ehu was suddenly struck with the peculiar taste which the Princess had manifested ever since her birth for nuts, and with the singular fact that she had been born with teeth. In fact the moment she had been transformed she had begun to cry out and had continued to cry out until, finding a filbert in her bed, she had cracked it with her teeth, nibbled the kernel, and had gone quietly to sleep. Ever since then the two Chief-Nurses-Extraordinary had been obliged to stuff their pockets with nuts and to give her one or more whenever she made a grimace.

"O marvellous instinct of nature! O eternal and inscrutable affinity between all created beings!" cried Ehu Dappleblock. "You have shown me the door which leads to the discovery of thy mysteries! I will knock upon it and it shall open unto me."

At these strange words, which startled the King considerably, Dappleblock turned round and demanded the favour of being taken forth with to the Astronomer-Royal. The King consented, but only on condition that he went under a strong escort. Ehu would doubtless have preferred to have gone alone; but since he had very little say in the matter he was obliged to put up with what he couldn't help, and was forced to cross the streets of the capital guarded like a prisoner.

Arrived at the house of the Astronomer-Royal Dappleblock threw himself into the wizard's arms, and the two embraced each other with torrents of tears, for they were old acquaintances and were really very fond of each other. Then they retired to a secluded room and consulted a large number of books which dealt with instinct, affinities, antipathies, and a host of other things no less mysterious. Finally, night having overtaken them at their labours, the Astronomer mounted his tower and assisted by Ehu (who himself was well practised in these things) discovered that, in spite of the maze of correlatives, reciprocals, and counterparts which crossed the Princess' horoscope again and again, in order to break the spell which made Pirlipatine mouse-like, and in order to restore her to her former beauty, there was only one thing to be done.

She would have to eat the kernel of the nut Krakatuk.

Now the nut Krakatuk has a very hard shell, so hard that you can wheel a cannon of the largest size over it without breaking it. Yet the stars clearly showed that it was essential that the shell should be broken, in the presence of the Princess, by the teeth of a young man who had never yet been shaved and had never worn anything except top-boots. Lastly, the kernel would have to be handed by him to the Princess with his eyes shut, and, with his eyes still shut, he would then have to take seven steps backwards without stumbling. Such was the verdict of the stars.

Dappleblock and the wizard had worked without stopping for three days and three nights in clearing up this mystery. The escort was quite impatient when at last he appeared. Together they returned to the palace.

It was now Saturday evening, and the King had already dined and was starting on the dessert, when Ehu (who was going to be beheaded at dawn the next day) entered the royal dining room. He was full of joy and was Smiling broadly. Walking jauntily up to the King he announced joyfully that he had at last discovered a way to restore her beauty to the Princess Pirlipatine.

At this news the King folded him to his breast with the most touching cordiality, and asked what the remedy was.

Dappleblock informed the King of the result of his conference with the Astronomer-Royal.

"My dear Ehu," said the King, "I was quite certain all the time that it was only your pride which prevented you from doing all this long ago. However, better late than never: for my part I shouldn't for a moment have allowed *my* pride to interfere with the little arrangement we had made for tomorrow morning. Immediately after dinner, then, we will put your theory into practice. See to it, therefore, good Dappleblock, that in ten minutes' time the unshaven youth, dressed in boots, shall be here with the nut Krakatuk in his hand. But be particularly careful that no one gives him any wine to drink, otherwise he might stumble when he makes his seven steps backwards like a crayfish. Afterwards—well you can tell him that if he does his task successfully the royal cellars will be at his disposal."

To the King's astonishment, however, Ehu appeared to be thunderstruck at these words; and, as he stood there twiddling his thumbs in silence, the King asked him what was the matter, and why he didn't dash off at once to execute his sovereign's orders. But Ehu threw himself on his knees before the King, and bursting into tears, cried out:

"Oh Sire! It is true indeed that we—I mean I—have discovered the means of curing the Princess, and that the remedy consists of making her eat the kernel of the nut Krakatuk, provided it has been cracked by a young man who has never been shaved and who has worn top-boots ever since his birth; but there isn't a young man like this anywhere in the palace or the capital—much less a nut. We haven't the slightest idea where to find either the one or the other, and in all probability it will be a hard and long search to find them."

At these words the King became furious. Brandishing his sceptre over the head of the craftsman, he cried in a terrible voice:

"VERY WELL, THEN, PREPARE FOR DEATH!"

At these words the Queen, who was sitting close to him, came and knelt beside Dappleblock and observed to her royal spouse that if he cut off Ehu's head, they would lose even this ray of hope. The only chance of curing Pirlipatine appeared to be by keeping him alive. It was quite probable, she said, that one who had been so clever as to discover this horoscope would also be able to discover the nut and the nutcracker. Moreover, she argued, it was more reasonable to believe this latest prediction of the Astronomer since none of his predictions had ever come true yet, and one of them was bound to come true some day or other, seeing that the King, whom it was impossible to deceive, had appointed him Astronomer-Royal. Furthermore, the Princess Pirlipatine, being scarcely three months old, was not yet old enough to marry, and in all likelihood would not be old enough to marry until she was fifteen; therefore Master Dappleblock and his friend the Astronomer had four teen years and nine months before them in which to find the nut Krakatuk and the young man who was to crack it. Lastly, she suggested that a respite should be granted to Ehu Dappleblock, provided that he would promise to return at the end of it and place himself in the King's hands once more, whether or not he was in possession of the remedy which could cure the Princess. If he came back empty-handed he should be beheaded without mercy, but if he succeeded, he should be magnificently rewarded.

The King, who was a very conscientious man (and he had just dined off two of his most favourite dishes, namely, a black pudding and a purée of liver) lent a kindly ear to the prayer of his sensible and magnanimous spouse. He decided, therefore, that Ehu and the Astronomer should set out that very instant in search of the nut and the nutcracker, and that fourteen years and nine months should be allowed them for the search. But he stipulated that at the expiration of this respite, both should return and place themselves in his power again, so that, in the event of their failure, he might accord them their proper deserts.

If, on the contrary, however, they brought back the nut Krakatuk and restored the Princess Pirlipatine to her former beauty, they should be superbly rewarded. The Astronomer should receive a life pension of a thousand rose-nobles and a pair of gold-rimmed spectacles, and the craftsman a sword studded with diamonds, the Order of the Golden Mushroom (which was the highest Order of the State) and a new overcoat. As for the young man who was going to crack the nut, the King didn't trouble very much about him. One could always procure the means, he said, of having his name inserted repeatedly in the home and foreign press.

Touched by this generosity, which did away with half the difficulty of his task, Ehu gave his word that either he would find the nut Krakatuk or would return, like another Regulus, and replace himself in the King's hands.

So the same evening the Craftsman and the Astronomer quitted the capital and began their search.

VI

How Ehu Dappleblock and the Astronomer searched the four corners of the globe and discovered a fifth, but without finding the nut Krakatuk

I T WAS NOW FOURTEEN YEARS and five months since the Astrologer and the Craftsman had taken to the road, and as yet they had not found a single trace of what they sought. They had visited Europe first, then America, then Africa, then Asia; they had even discovered a fifth continent, which the geographers have since called Australia, because the Austrians had failed to discover it. But in all their wanderings, although they had come across plenty of nuts of every conceivable shape and size, they had not found the nut Krakatuk. In a vain hope of success they had passed some years at the Court of the King of Dates—they had even spent some time with the Prince of Almonds; they consulted, fruitlessly, the famous Academy of Green Monkeys, and the celebrated Society of Squirrels. At last, worn out with fatigue, they reached the borders of the great forest which clothes the foot of the Himalayas. Sitting down under a large tree which was covered with golden fruit, they reminded one another that they had only one hundred and twenty-two days left in which to find what they had sought in vain for fourteen years and five months.

If I were to tell you all the marvellous adventures which befell the two travellers during their long peregrination, it would take me at least a month and would certainly tire you out. So I will only say that Ehu Dappleblock, being the more determined of the two since his head depended upon their success or failure, had exposed himself to greater hard ships and dangers than his companion, and had lost all his hair, as the result of a sunstroke when they were crossing the Equator, and also his right eye, the result of the arrow of a Caribbean chief. Moreover, his yellow over coat, which he had insisted upon wearing all the time, had certainly not improved in appearance since he left Berylia, and it was now literally in rags. Thus you will readily understand that his appearance was really deplorable. Yet so strong is the instinct of self-preservation in man, that, worn out as he was by the adventures and the hardships which he had suffered, he saw with increasing fright the approach of that fateful time when he would have to return to civilization. For it meant that he would be obliged to place himself once more in the King's hands.

Nevertheless, Dappleblock was a man of honour. There was no hesitating in the face of a promise as solemn as that which he had made. He resolved accordingly, cost him what it might, to set out on his return to Berylia the following day. Indeed there was no time to lose; fourteen years and five months had passed, and the two travellers had now only one hundred and twenty-two days in which to regain the capital of the Princess Pirlipatine's father.

Ehu Dappleblock communicated his generous resolve to his friend the Astronomer, and they decided to begin their return journey on the following morning.

Next day, at dawn, the travellers set out, shaping a course for Baghdad. From Baghdad they reached Alexandria; at Alexandria they embarked for Venice; from Venice they gained Tyrol; and from Tyrol they descended into the kingdom of Pirlipatine's father, secretly hoping that the King would be dead or at least in his second childhood.

But alas! Nothing of the sort had happened. When they arrived at the capital the unfortunate Craftsman learnt that the worthy King was not only in full possession of all his faculties, but that he was in excellent health and rather more testy than usual. There seemed to be no hope for Dappleblock— unless by chance the Princess had been cured of her infirmity, which was very improbable, or that the King's heart had softened, which was still more improbable—to escape the awful fate which threatened him.

However, he presented himself boldly at the gate of the palace— fortified by the thought that he was performing a really heroic action —and demanded an audience of the King. The King, who was always accessible to his subjects and made a point of interviewing personally everyone who came to see him upon business, commanded the Grand Usher to lead the two travellers before him.

The Grand Usher took occasion to observe to His Majesty that the two strangers didn't look very respectable and were wearing really the most appalling clothes. But the King replied that one should not judge the heart by the face, and that the hood did not make the monk.

So the Grand Usher, recognising the truth of these maxims, bowed respectfully and went to fetch the Craftsman and the Astronomer.

The King had not altered in the least. The travellers recognised his voice talking to the cook long before they saw him; and when he appeared they knew him at once. But they themselves were so changed, especially poor Ehu, that they were obliged to mention their names. On learning who they were the King uttered a cry of joy, for he had made up his mind long ago that they would never come back unless they had found the nut Krakatuk. But he was soon disillusioned, for the Craftsman, throwing himself at the King's feet, confessed that in spite of the most conscientious and assiduous search, he and his friend the Astronomer had returned with empty hands.

The King, although rather a hasty man, was really very kind at heart. He was touched with the scrupulousness with which Dappleblock had kept his word, and he instantly commuted his death sentence to that of penal servitude for life. As for the Astronomer, the King was content to exile him forever.

There were still three days left, however, out of the fourteen years and nine months' respite granted to them, so Ehu, who was exceedingly fond of his own country, asked the King's permission to pay a farewell visit to his home at Berylia. The request seemed a just one to the King, so he granted it without any restrictions.

Ehu Dappleblock, with only three days left to himself, resolved to profit by the time, and being lucky enough to find a vacant corner seat in the mail-coach, set out immediately. At the last minute the Astronomer, who, since he was to be exiled, might just as well go to Berylia as anywhere else, squeezed in beside him.

VII

Ehu discovers the nut Krakatuk

O N THE FOLLOWING DAY, ABOUT ten o'clock in the morning, Dappleblock and his companion arrived at Berylia. Ehu's only relation was a brother named Ezra Dappleblock, who was one of the most important toymakers in Berylia. Accordingly they made their way to his house.

Ezra Dappleblock was delighted to see poor Ehu again, for he had long given him up for dead. At first the toymaker did not recognise him, owing to Ehu's bald head and the green patch over his right eye; but Ehu showed him his yellow overcoat which, tattered though it was, still preserved its original colour in places, and, in addition to this positive proof, he told Ezra certain family secrets which could not possibly have been known by anybody else. So the toymaker was obliged to acknowledge Ehu as his brother. Then, in his turn, he asked Ehu why he had been away from his native town for so long, and where he had left his hair, his eye, and the rest of his overcoat.

Ehu had no object in concealing his adventures from his brother. So he began by introducing the Astronomer to him. Then, when this had been successfully accomplished, he related all his misfortunes, from A to Z, and finished by saying that he had less than forty-eight hours to spend with his brother, seeing that owing to his failure to find the Krakatuk, he was going into prison on the following day.

During this recital Ezra behaved in a very extraordinary manner. He cracked his fingers, spun round on his heel, and clicked his tongue more than once. On any other occasion Ehu would doubtless have asked him what he meant by these contortions; but he was so preoccupied that he did not notice anything unusual in his brother's behaviour. It was only when Ezra said "Hum hum!" twice, and "Oh! Oh! Oh!" three times, that Ehu asked him what he meant by these expressions.

"I mean, ho! Ho!" said Ezra, "That if it's all wrong it may be all right, ho! Ho! If it won't be it will, ho! Ho! Ho!"

"What will be all right?" asked Ehu.

"Unless...," continued the toymaker.

"Unless what?" said Ehu.

But instead of replying, Ezra, who had evidently been racking his brains to remember something all the time he was making these absurd remarks, suddenly threw his wig in the air and began to dance about, crying:

"Ehu! You are saved, ho! Ho! Ehu! You needn't go to prison after all, ho! Ho! Ehu! Unless I'm very much mistaken, I've got a Krakatuk here in the house all the time, ho! Ho! Ho!"

And upon this, without giving any other explanation to his bewildered brother, Ezra flew upstairs and came back a moment later carrying a curious little box, which he handed to Ehu.

Ehu opened it slowly, his fingers trembling with excitement.

Inside it was a large golden nut.

The Craftsman had never even dared to hope for such a welcome surprise, much less had he expected it. He took the nut between his finger and thumb gingerly, and turned it this way and that, examining it with the greatest attention. Then, after a lengthy scrutiny, he declared that he entirely concurred with his brother's opinion, and that, in fact, he would be very much surprised indeed if the nut did not turn out to be a genuine Krakatuk. Then he handed it to the Astronomer and asked him his opinion.

Dappleblock's friend examined the nut as carefully as Ehu had done, and then, shaking his head, he remarked:

"I should have agreed with you and your brother if the nut hadn't been golden; but the stars never said anything about it being of that colour. Moreover, how did your brother come by a genuine Krakatuk?"

"I will tell you all about it," said Ezra, "and how it came into my hands and how it acquired that golden coat which puzzles you so much and which certainly isn't natural to it."

Then, bidding them sit down and make themselves comfortable (for he very wisely thought that after travelling continuously for fourteen years and nine months the travellers must be rather tired) he began as follows:

"On the very day that the King sent for you under the pretext of decorating you with a cross, a stranger arrived at Berylia carrying a bag of nuts which he had for sale. But the nut-sellers of the town, who naturally wished to retain among themselves the privilege of selling nuts in Berylia, picked a quarrel with him right in front of the door of my shop. Thereupon the stranger, in order to defend himself more easily, put down his bag of nuts and began to retaliate vigorously, to the great delight of the small boys and commissionaires who had collected, when suddenly a heavily laden wagon came along and passed right over the bag of nuts. On seeing this accident the nut-sellers, who looked upon it as the judgment of heaven, considered themselves sufficiently revenged; so they ceased molesting the stranger and went away. The stranger picked up his bag and found that all the nuts had been broken except one, which he presented to me with a curious smile.

"You can have it," said he, "for a new penny dated 1820."

"And," he continued, "a day would come when I should not regret my purchase, though it seemed to be a poor bargain at the moment.

"So I rummaged in my pockets to see if I had got a coin that was something like the one he demanded, and was surprised to find, in the top pocket of my waistcoat, a new penny of the exact date which he mentioned. How it came there I haven't the least idea; but it seemed to me such an extraordinary coincidence that I handed it to him at once. He gave me the nut in exchange, and disappeared.

"I put the nut in my shop window, but although I asked for it only the price which it had cost me, plus ten shillings, it remained there for seven or eight years without anyone showing the slightest inclination to buy it. So then I gave it a coat of gold paint, to make it look more valuable; but this only cost me twopence more, for the nut is still without a purchaser."

At this moment the Astronomer, who had been holding the nut in his hands all the time Ezra was speaking, uttered a cry of joy. Whilst Ehu Dappleblock had been listening to his brother's story, the Astronomer, with the aid of a pocket-knife, had carefully scratched the gilding on the nut, and, at one end of it he had discovered, engraved in Chinese letters, the word

KRAKATUK

At this all uncertainty vanished, and the identity of the nut was established beyond doubt.

VIII

How, having discovered the nut Krakatuk, Dappleblock and the Astronomer found the young man who could crack it

E HU DAPPLEBLOCK WAS SO ANXIOUS to announce the good news to the King that he wanted to take the mail-coach and return to the capital at once; but Ezra pressed him to wait until his son Nikky came in. Ehu yielded the more willingly to this request as he had not seen his nephew for nearly fifteen years. He remembered that when he left Berylia the lad had been a jolly little fellow three and a half years of age, whom Ezra loved with all his heart.

At this moment a handsome young man of eighteen or nineteen entered the shop and approached Ezra, addressing him as "father."

Ezra embraced him fondly; then pointing to Ehu he said:

"Now go and kiss your Uncle."

The young man hesitated. Uncle Ehu, with his tattered overcoat, his bald head, and his eye-patch, was not a particularly attractive person. But seeing his hesitation, and fearing that Ehu might be offended, his father gave him a shove so that he was forced to embrace Ehu willy-nilly.

During this scene the Astronomer never took his eyes off the young man, and his stare seemed so rude and peculiar that the youth took the earliest pretext to go out; for he thought it was very ill-mannered of the Astronomer to stare at him like this.

As soon as Nikky had gone the Astronomer questioned Ezra about his son, asking him about a good many family matters. To Ehu's annoyance Ezra insisted upon answering every question at great length, going into the most intimate family details. Ehu thought this was quite unnecessary. He cleared his throat several times and once or twice nudged the Astronomer in the ribs with his elbow; but his friend was so interested that he paid not the slightest attention to these demonstrations.

Presently the talk took a turn which showed Ehu that his friend's interest was due to something more than mere idle curiosity. Nikky was, they learnt (as, indeed, his figure indicated) eighteen years of age. When he was quite a child he was such a jolly and pretty little fellow that his mother used to delight in dressing him up like the dolls in the shop window. Sometimes she would clothe him like a student, sometimes as a postillion, sometimes like a Hungarian. But one part of his dress was always the same, for his mother took care to choose only those costumes that required top-boots. For although Nikky possessed the prettiest little feet in the world, his calves were very thin, and top-boots not only hid this defect but suited his slim figure.

"And so," said the Astronomer, "your son has never worn anything but top-boots?"

(Ehu's eyes began to bulge.)

"That is so," said the toymaker; "Nikky has never worn anything but top-boots." Then he continued: "When he was ten I sent him to the University at Padua, where he remained until he was eighteen without contracting any of the evil habits of his fellow students: he was never greedy, he always shut the door after him, and he never bit his nails. The only weakness which he has ever had is that he will persist in allowing those four or five straggling hairs to grow on his chin; for he would never allow a barber to touch his face."

"And so," said the Astronomer, "your son has never been shaved?"

(Ehu's eyes opened wider and wider.)

"Never," replied Ezra.

"And during the vacations," continued the Astronomer, "how did he pass his time?"

"He remained in the shop, wearing his pretty little student costume," said the father; "and, from pure lightness of heart, he used to amuse himself by cracking nuts for the girls and boys who came to buy toys. In fact everyone called him 'The Nutcracker.'"

"The Nutcracker?" cried Ehu.

"The Nutcracker?" cried the Astronomer. Then they stared at one another, and Ezra stared at them.

"My dear sir," said the Astronomer to Ezra, "I have an idea that your fortune is made."

The toymaker naturally was not unmoved by this prognostication; but he wanted to know more. The Astronomer, however, saying that they were both very tired, insisted upon putting off the explanation until the following day.

As soon as Ehu and the Astronomer reached their bedroom the stargazer threw himself upon his companion's neck.

"It is he," he cried. "We have him at last."

"Do you really think so?" asked Dappleblock, in the tone of a man who doubts but really wants to be convinced.

"Do I really think so!" echoed the Astronomer. "Why, he possesses all the necessary qualifications, doesn't he?"

"Let's go over them again," said Ehu.

"Right," said the Astronomer. "To begin with, he has always worn top-boots."

"That's so."

"He has never been shaved."

"True."

"Lastly, from sheer love of the thing, he stays in his father's shop to crack nuts for little girls, who all call him 'The Nutcracker.'"

"That is certainly so."

"My dear Ehu, good fortunes never come singly. But if you are still in doubt, let us consult the stars."

They went up to the top of the house, opened the box-room door, and climbed through the trapdoor on to the roof. Then, having cast the young man's horoscope, they saw that he was destined to a great fortune. This prediction, which confirmed all the Astronomer's hopes, removed Ehu's remaining doubts.

"And now," said the Astronomer, triumphantly, "there are only two things which we must not forget to do."

"What are they?" asked Ehu.

"First of all, you must make a strong wooden contrivance which will fit round your nephew's neck and enable him to double the pressure of his jaws."

"Nothing easier," replied Dappleblock; "it is the A. B. C. of hydrodynamics."

"Secondly," continued the Astronomer, "when we arrive at the palace we must carefully conceal the fact that we have brought the Krakatuk and the Nutcracker with us. For I have an idea that the more teeth that are broken and the more jaws that are dislocated in the attempt to crack the Krakatuk, the greater will be the reward which the King will offer to whoever shall succeed where others have failed."

"My dear fellow," said Ehu, "your foresight is little short of marvellous. Now let's go to bed."

So saying, they came down from the roof, and having regained their room, the travellers went to bed. Pulling their night-caps over their ears, they slept more soundly than they had done for fourteen years and nine months.

But before he got into bed Ehu quietly went out on to the landing and removed the young man's boots from the mat in front of his door.

IX

What happened at Court when the King tried to find a nutcracker

NEXT MORNING AT BREAKFAST THE two friends told Ezra the plans they had formed the night before. Ezra was not lacking in ambition, and in spite of his natural doubt in his son's capabilities, he flattered himself that Nikky possessed the strongest jaws in the country. So he welcomed with enthusiasm the proposal which would rid his shop both of the nut and the nutcracker.

Nikky, however, was not so easily persuaded. The contrivance which Ehu wanted to fit round his neck in place of his handsome lace collar made him feel very uneasy. However, the Astronomer, his uncle, and his father, all made him such magnificent promises that he yielded at last.

Accordingly Ehu set to work at once. The appliance was soon finished and was screwed firmly to the Nutcracker's neck. Lest you should have any doubts concerning the wisdom of this proceeding, I may say at once that the ingenious contrivance succeeded perfectly. From the very first day the most brilliant results were obtained, the young man cracking the very hardest apricot stones and toughest possible peach stones with hardly any effort at all.

These experiments completed, the Astronomer, the Craftsman, and the Nutcracker set out immediately for the palace. Ezra wanted to accompany them; but as someone had to stay behind to look after the shop, he was obliged to forego the pleasure and remained at Berylia.

The first care of Ehu and the Astronomer when they reached the capital was to leave Nikky at their hotel and go and announce their arrival at the palace. They intended to inform the King that they had at last found the nut which they had sought in vain for so many years in all the five quarters of the globe. But about the Nutcracker they were determined not to say a word.

Their news spread joy throughout the palace. The King sent at once for the Reader of the Public Thoughts. This official, who was one of his most intimate counsellors, had control of all the newspapers, and the King commanded him to draw up in a few words an official notice for the *Gazette*. This announcement, which the editors of all the other papers would be obliged to copy under pain of being suppressed immediately, declared that any man who believed his teeth were strong enough to crack the nut Krakatuk had only to present himself at the palace, when, if successful, he would be handsomely rewarded.

It is only cases like this which reveal the strength of a nation's teeth. The competitors were so numerous that it was found necessary to set up a jury, presided over by the Royal Dentist, to examine them, in order to see if they all possessed their complete set of thirty-two teeth, and if any of their teeth had been stopped.

Three thousand five hundred candidates presented themselves for this preliminary examination, which lasted eight days. The only result was that many hundreds of teeth were shed and a number of jaws dislocated. The Royal Dentist made copious notes, and took a large number of names and addresses.

A second appeal was therefore necessary. The provincial and foreign newspapers printed it with big headlines. The King even offered the post of Perpetual President of the Academy and the Grand Cross of the Order of the Mushroom to whoever should produce a pair of jaws strong enough to break the Krakatuk. Even uneducated people were allowed to compete.

This second trial furnished five thousand and two competitors. All the learned societies of Europe sent their representatives to this important congress. There were several members of the Royal Society, including the perpetual secretary of that august body. But he himself was unable to compete, as he had no teeth left, having broken them all in attempting to digest the works of his fellow members.

The second trial lasted fifteen days, and was, unfortunately, even more disastrous than the first. The delegates of the learned societies insisted, for the honour of their associations, in attempting to crack the nut; but they only succeeded in leaving their best teeth behind them. The Royal Dentist filled up a large number of address books, and made numerous appointments.

As for the nut, its shell bore not the slightest sign of the efforts that had been made to crack it.

The King was in despair. He determined to make a last desperate attempt; and as he had no male heir, he ordered a third announcement to be made in all the newspapers at home and abroad, promising the hand of the Princess Pirlipatine and the succession to the throne to whoever should succeed in cracking the nut Krakatuk. The only condition was that this time the competitors should be between sixteen and twenty-four years of age.

This magnificent offer quickly spread throughout all Europe. Competitors began to arrive from the most remote parts. Many started to come even from

Asia, Africa, and America, as well as from that fifth quarter of the globe which had been discovered by Dappleblock and the Astronomer. But they realised sooner or later that the competition would have started, or even finished by the time that the advertisement reached them, so they turned back and went home again.

Ehu and the Astronomer agreed that the moment had now come for them to produce the Nutcracker. It was impossible for the King to offer a richer reward, and it was a good deal more than he had ever offered any body before. And so, confident of success, although a host of Princes with regal and even imperial jaws were presenting themselves as candidates, Ehu took his place at the end of the queue outside the ticket office. Thus the name of Ehu Dappleblock was absolutely the last on the list: his ticket bore the number 11,375.

This final competition proceeded just like the former ones; Ehu's 11,374 predecessors were all put hors de combat one after the other. And on the nineteenth day of the con test, at precisely half past eleven o'clock in the morning, just in fact as the Princess attained her fifteenth year, Ehu Dappleblock's name was called out.

The Nutcracker stepped forward between Ehu and the Astronomer.

X

HOW NIKKY CRACKED THE NUT,
AND WHAT HAPPENED TO HIM IN DOING IT

IT WAS THE FIRST TIME that the two friends had seen the Princess since she had left her cradle, and she had changed a good deal. But it was certainly not for the better. When they had last seen her she was rather alarming, but now her likeness to a mouse was really extraordinary. In fact the Murr family (who, you will remember, were really responsible for the whole trouble) became quite uneasy whenever she entered the room. She had grown much larger, and her diet of bacon-fat and nuts had made her quite stout. Also she never went anywhere without filling her pockets with nuts, and she nibbled one whenever she was not talking or sleeping. In fact she always put a nut in her hand last thing at night before she went to sleep, so that she could begin to nibble as soon as ever she woke up. She was passionately devoted to cheese, and preferred it toasted. Meat she had never tasted.

At the sight of Pirlipatine the poor Nutcracker nearly fainted. He turned anxiously to his uncle and asked him if he were quite sure that the Krakatuk would make her beautiful again. It was all very well for Ehu and the Astronomer, he said, but if the Princess were to remain as she was at present, although he would certainly make an honest attempt to crack the nut if only for the glory of succeeding where so many had failed, he would be quite willing to forego the honour of marrying her. In fact he would be quite content to resign her father's throne to whoever would like it.

Needless to say Ehu and the Astronomer reassured him vigorously, telling him that when once the nut had been cracked and the kernel eaten, Pirlipatine would instantly become the most beautiful girl in the world.

But if the sight of Pirlipatine had chilled the heart of the poor Nutcracker, his appearance had caused a very different sensation in the breast of the Princess. As soon as ever she saw him, she cried out impulsively:

"Oh, I do hope he'll be able to crack the nut."

At this the Princess' governess immediately replied:

"I must point out to your highness that it is neither usual nor becoming for a young lady in your station in life to voice her opinion upon such matters aloud."

As a matter of fact Nikky really was enough to turn the head of any Princess. He had a little short cloak of purple velvet trimmed with golden fur, and under this a tight-fitting coat of orange brocade, with green enamelled buttons, and knickerbockers to match. His little top-boots were the daintiest you ever saw, and they were so highly polished that you could see your face in them. The only thing that tended to spoil his appearance was the wooden contrivance that Ehu had made to assist his jaws in their task. But his father had taken the precaution to give him a high stiff lace collar, which came up to his cheeks and completely hid the apparatus. In fact this collar attracted quite a lot of attention; and many of the discomfited Princes adopted it on the spot to hide the swollen faces which their dislocated jaws occasioned.

And so when this handsome young man stepped forward, there was not one of the servants or dentist's assistants who did not echo the Princess' wish in his heart, and remark to himself that there was no one in the whole kingdom, not even the King and Queen, whom they would rather see accomplish the task of cracking the nut.

As for the Nutcracker, he stepped forward with an air of confidence which redoubled the hopes that all reposed in him. As soon as he reached the royal platform he bowed to the King and Queen, then to the Princess, then to the dentist's assistants. Then he turned to the Master of the Ceremonies, who advanced and offered him the nut Krakatuk. Nikky took it delicately between his finger and thumb like a conjurer, placed it between his teeth, gave the wooden contrivance under his chin a sharp blow with his fist, and

CRICK-CRACK!

the nutshell was broken in several pieces.

Quickly tearing off the husk, he presented the kernel to the Princess, making her a bow that was both graceful and respectful. Then, remembering Ehu's instructions, he shut his eyes and began to step backwards.

At the same instant the Princess swallowed the kernel. Then

WONDER OF WONDERS!

Her head began to shrink, her whiskers shrivelled up, her ears became smaller and rounder, her nose went back and back, the hair disappeared from her face, her eyes changed from brown to blue, and in almost less time than it takes to tell you, the Princess Pirlipatine had become a young girl of exquisite beauty.

Her skin was now soft as a rose petal and smooth as the finest velvet, her eyelashes were silken and dark, her eyes blue as the sky on a summer's day, her golden ringlets fell in thick clusters about her shoulders, her little mouth was small and cherry red, her nose straight and exquisitely chiselled. She was the most beautiful Princess that had ever been seen.

For an instant there was silence, then everybody began to talk at once at the top of their voices. Trumpets sounded, cymbals and drums were banged as loudly as possible, shouts of joy were heard throughout the whole city, mingled with a hubbub of bell-ringing and cheering. The brass band which was stationed close to the palace in case anyone succeeded in cracking the nut, came hurriedly out of the inn and started playing several tunes at once. The King, the Ministers, the Councillors and the Judges began to dance about on one leg, just as they had done when Pirlipatine was born. The Queen fainted with joy, and they were obliged to sponge her face freely with Eau de Cologne before she came to.

The Nutcracker was rather upset by all this noise. He had not yet completed his task, for he still had to perform his seven steps backwards. Nevertheless he began with a self-possession which augured well for the time when he would assume the crown.

He had already poised his leg carefully for the seventh step, when, all of a sudden, Dame Mousekin appeared through a crack in the floor Squeaking dreadfully she darted forward between Nikky's legs. The future heir to the throne was just putting his foot to the ground, in fact the seventh step was almost accomplished, when he trod heavily upon her.

In an instant he stumbled so that he almost fell.

O cruel fate! In less time than it takes to relate the handsome young man had assumed the very deformity from which he had just helped the Princess to recover! His legs grew suddenly thin, his body became fatter and fatter, his nose got longer and longer, and in a moment he was like a mouse!

XI

WHAT HAPPENED AT THE COURT AFTERWARDS

T HE CAUSE OF THIS DISASTER did not escape scot-free. Dame Mousekin lay writhing in pain on the floor. Her wickedness had not gone unpunished. The Nutcracker had trodden upon her so firmly with the heel of his boot that she was mortally wounded. In her pain the mouse-queen now cried out with all her might:

> *"Krakatuk Krakatuk Nut so hard,*
> *Why have you brought me this fate ill starred?*
> *Only my son can avenge me now;*
> *Nutcracker, thee with my shape I endow!*
> *Hi! Hi! Hi!*
> *Pi! Pi! Pi!*
> *Goodbye life,*
> *Full of strife!*
> *Farewell sky,*
> *Blue and high.*
> *Adieu the earth,*
> *With its mirth.*
> *Oh! I die*
> *Hi! Hi! Hi!*
> *Ah!!!"*

When it was obvious to all that Dame Mousekin had breathed her last, the Lord Great Scavenger was sent for. He took up Dame Mousekin gingerly by the tail and carried her out, promising to bury her beside the remains of her family, who, fifteen years and some months previously, had been interred in a common grave.

In the midst of all the noise and rejoicings that were going on, no one except Ehu and the Astronomer paid the slightest attention to poor Nikky. The Princess, unaware of what had happened, commanded that the young hero should be led before her; for, in spite of the reprimand of her governess, she was anxious to thank him at once. But she no sooner caught sight of Nikky than she buried her face in her hands, and, forgetting the great service which he had rendered her, cried out:

"Go away, go away, horrible Nutcracker! Take him away, take him away, take him away!"

Instantly the Grand Usher of the palace stepped forward. Seizing poor Nikky by the shoulders he pushed him hastily towards the staircase.

Ehu was standing petrified at what had happened, but the Astronomer never lost his head for an instant. Seizing Ehu by the arm he hurried him towards the door. But the King, furious that they had dared to propose a Nutcracker as his son-in-law, ordered them to be seized immediately. The guards surrounded them in an instant; escape was impossible. They were led before the royal platform.

At first the King was minded to behead them there and then. But the Queen tactfully pressed a box of his favourite sweetmeats into his hand, and urged him not to do anything in a hurry as it always gave him indigestion. Quickly regaining his normal calm, he proceeded to pass sentence upon them. In place of the pension of ten thousand rose-nobles and the gold-rimmed spectacles which he had promised to the one, and in place of the sword studded with diamonds, the Grand Cross of the Order of the Golden Mushroom, and the new yellow overcoat which he had promised to the other, he exiled them forthwith from the kingdom. In fact he gave them only twenty-four hours in which to cross the frontier.

There was nothing more to be said. Ehu, the Astronomer, and Nikky, left the capital immediately after lunch and had crossed the frontier by tea time. But as soon as night had come, the two wise men stopped the cab, and climbing on to the roof of it, consulted the stars once more. There they read that, in spite of his transformation, the Nutcracker was destined to become a Prince and a King (provided he did not prefer to remain an ordinary private person, for it was left entirely to his choice) and that this would come to pass as soon as his deformity had disappeared. Moreover, the stars clearly showed that his deformity would disappear only when he had defeated, in single combat, the Prince who, after the death of Dame Mousekin and her first seven sons, had ascended the throne as King of the Mice. Lastly, the two diametrically synchronizing correlatives of the horoscope clearly indicated that in order to overcome the Prince he would have to take three bites of the fruit that grows upon the Bangalu tree.

Full of hope for the accomplishment of this brilliant destiny, the three drove on to Berylia. Here they took the precaution to change the Nutcracker's clothes, and Nikky, who had left his father's shop as an only son, entered it again as a Nutcracker.

Needless to say Ezra Dappleblock did not recognise his son, and when he asked his brother Ehu and the Astronomer what had become of Nikky, those two distinguished individuals replied, with the readiness and strict regard for truth which always characterise learned men, that the King and Queen had not wished to part with the Princess' deliverer.

Nikky felt that his position was a difficult one. He uttered not a word, but went to and fro in the shop cracking nuts more vigorously than ever, and waiting patiently for the information as to the whereabouts of the Bangalu tree which Ehu and the Astronomer sought for nightly.

XII

What happened to the Princess
after the departure of the Nutcracker

I AM SURE YOU WILL BE disappointed at this tragic end to the wanderings of Ehu Dappleblock and the Astronomer, not to mention the lamentable fate which had overtaken pretty little Nikky. But the truth must be told at all costs, no matter how unpleasant it may be. The goal of Ehu and the Astronomer was actually in sight, the rich rewards which the King had promised to them were almost within their grasp, and already they had begun to look forward to a happy and prosperous old age. Now Fate had turned suddenly against them. At one stroke they had lost everything for which they hoped, and were completely ruined.

But not irrevocably. The stars clearly showed that all might yet be well, provided Nikky could accomplish the tasks that now lay before him. As for the poor Nutcracker, he realised that thrones are not to be gained, nor the hands of Princesses won, by the mere cracking of a nut. But it was no use giving in just because Misfortune had crossed his path. He would have to persevere until success at last crowned his efforts. Meanwhile he went on cracking nuts, sweeping out the shop, and dusting the toys. For Ezra, though he would have hesitated to ask his son to perform these menial tasks, had no hesitation whatever in assigning them to the servant which Ehu had brought with him from foreign parts—for such he supposed Nikky to be.

Ehu and the Astronomer lost no time in searching for the whereabouts of the Bangalu tree. This could only be done at night; and as, moreover, the stars were now frequently obscured by clouds, some time elapsed before they were able to obtain a successful horoscope.

Nikky also had something else to do besides cracking nuts. As he would have to engage the King of the Mice in deadly combat, it was necessary for him to be thoroughly prepared. Every morning Ehu gave him lessons in fencing, boxing, wrestling, high-kicking, jumping, turning Somersaults, and spinning on one toe, not to mention numerous gymnastic exercises to strengthen his limbs. But the days and nights went by, and still the stars refused to show where the Bangalu tree grew.

Meanwhile an event of great importance had taken place at the palace. You will re member that as soon as she had swallowed the kernel of the nut

Krakatuk the Princess Pirlipatine had been restored to her former beauty. Nobody troubled in the least about Nikky's fate. He and the Astronomer and Dappleblock had all been banished from the country; the troubles of the royal house seemed now at an end. The King ordered that pageants and feasts should be held everywhere throughout the kingdom for seven days to celebrate the Princess Pirlipatine's recovery.

The King himself decided to hold a magnificent banquet. As soon as he made up his mind he went to find the Queen and impart the news to her. He found her in the pantry making a light meal off seed-cake and milk.

"My dear," said the King, helping himself to a piece of cake, "my dear, don't you think we ought to give a banquet in honour of Pirlipatine's debut?"

"Certainly, my love," replied the Queen, pouring out a glass of milk for him. "What would you like to have?"

The Queen was a dutiful wife: she knew that questions like this always pleased the King.

"Oh, something quite slight," said the King nonchalantly, "a purée of liver, a chitterling or two ... and perhaps a small black pudding—provided we've got enough bacon. We might also have a roast turkey or so, and some meringues and a chocolate blanc-mange..."

"Nothing easier, my love," replied the Queen. "When shall it be?"

Having settled these important details, the King kissed her tenderly and went off to invite all the Kings and Queens and all the Royal Princes and all the Hereditary Grand Dukes, and all the most agreeable Pretenders, to a magnificent feast in honour of the Princess Pirlipatine's debut.

The day arrived. The capital was thronged with illustrious visitors. The hotels were so full that some of the Pretenders were obliged to sleep on the billiard tables. The Royal Dentist had never been so busy in all his life. For the visitors were determined that the unfortunate trial of the Krakatuk should in no wise prevent them from doing full justice to the banquet.

Yet the Chief-Nurses-Extraordinary were strangely troubled, though nobody knew why. Every morning the Princess Pirlipatine appeared punctually at breakfast looking more beautiful than ever. But it was noticed that the Chief-Nurses-Extraordinary always showed the greatest anxiety for her to go to bed in good time. At a quarter to nine every evening they hurried to her side and insisted upon her going to bed immediately. Otherwise, they said, she would lose her beauty sleep. Indeed so anxious were they to prevent this misfortune happening that upon one occasion, when the Princess insisted upon finishing a game of nap which she was playing with the King and the Court Dentist, they nearly fainted, and literally dragged the Princess out of her chair at three minutes to nine. Fortunately the King had been winning all the evening, so he only laughed good-naturedly.

Now the reason for the good nurses' solicitude was this. On the very day that she had resumed her normal shape, tired out with the excitement and noise, the Princess had gone to bed early. It happened that shortly after nine o'clock one of the Chief-Nurses-Extraordinary leant over her bed to see if she was properly covered up; and chancing to stoop down to admire her pretty little face, saw to her horror that the Princess had become once more like a mouse! The Chief-Nurse gave a stifled cry, and her companion came running up. Together they examined the sleeping Princess. There was no doubt whatever about it! The Princess Pirlipatine was a mouse once more! Sitting down by her side the Nurses burst into tears.

"Perhaps," said one of them, "she's only like this when she's asleep. Let's wake her and see."

So saying, they held a bottle of smelling salts under the Princess' nose. Pirlipatine sneezed twice and sat up. Still she was like a mouse! Her sharp little nose twitched once or twice; and then, finding a nut in her bed, she nibbled it and fell asleep again. The Nurses were in despair.

There was nothing more to be done. In the morning they would have to tell the Queen. The Queen would certainly tell the King, and all would be mourning where a few hours before joy and laughter reigned. Moreover the King would almost certainly hold the Nurses responsible for the calamity. Dame Mousekin's son must have climbed on to the foot of the Princess' bed and charmed her whilst they were folding up her clothes. The least they could hope for was perpetual banishment. Overcome by these gloomy forebodings they fell asleep.

Suddenly one of them awoke. The Princess was calling. It was now daylight—in fact the sun was shining brightly in at the windows. Hastily waking her fellow nurse, they approached the Princess' bed and asked her what she wanted. Imagine their surprise and joy at finding that the Princess was once more the beautiful girl whom they had put to bed the night before The Princess was sitting up and impatiently demanding her tea and bread and butter. Muttering excuses the bewildered nurses dashed away to execute the royal command.

It was no nightmare that the Princess' fond guardians had had. Nor was the phenomenon due to Dame Mousekin's son, who at that very moment was fast asleep inside the King's best ermine-lined crown. You will remember that the Nutcracker had stumbled just as he was finishing his task, so that the remedy had never been completed. So it happened that every night, precisely at nine o'clock, the Princess took on her mouselike shape, resuming her normal appearance at sunrise next morning.

Of course the Nurses were unaware of the cause of this; and, finding that the secret would remain undiscovered so long as the Princess was safely in bed by nine o'clock every evening, they carefully abstained from telling her mother anything about it. But secrets of this nature cannot be kept from a mother for long; they are bound to be dis covered sooner or later, and had the nurses told the Queen all about the matter at once, they would have saved a great deal of trouble.

XIII

The King sends for Dappleblock again

A t precisely ten minutes to seven the guests began to arrive. As on a former occasion, the King himself welcomed them on the front doorstep. This time there were many more visitors, for the King, having sold at consider able profit all the black puddings, chitterlings, and sausages which did not contain enough bacon to please him, was now very well off indeed. At the first stroke of seven o'clock the Grand Usher began to sound the great gong in the hall, and the King, giving his arm to the Queen, led the way into the dining room.

Here was a magnificent sight. The table was covered with gold candelabra and dishes loaded high with apples, oranges, almonds, and rare fruits; a large melon stood by itself on a superb dish in the centre; sweetmeats were before every guest's place; and the rich damask tablecloth was thickly strewn with silken crackers. Some of the Pretenders were quite dazzled with the sight, and could only repeat in a low tone just loud enough for the King to hear: "What magnificence! What superb grandeur!" The only thing that was lacking were nuts; for the Queen, being a tactful woman, thought that their presence might prove a source of embarrassment to the guests.

"For what we are about to receive," said the King reverently, and when he had finished grace they all sat down. The dinner proceeded. It was a complete success. The purée was creamy and delicious; the black puddings and chitterlings contained sufficient bacon to satisfy the most exacting epicure; whilst the turkey was stuffed so tight that it seemed to be really on the point of bursting. As for the meringues and chocolate blanc-mange, they simply melted in the guests' mouths.

At last came the dessert. Everyone was happy and smiling, and the King, carried away by his feelings and the success which the Queen and the Superintendent of the Royal Kitchens had achieved, beckoned to the Grand Butler and ordered up a bottle of the Imperial Tokay. Hardly had he done so when, with many curtseys, the two Chief-Nurses-Extraordinary entered and approached the Princess. It was a quarter to nine! But this time the King, who had dined splendidly off his favourite dishes, was seriously annoyed with the Nurses. He would not hear of the Princess leaving the table before dinner was over. Moreover her health had not yet been drunk by the assembled company. Furthermore, he announced to the Queen, in no uncertain way, that in future Pirlipatine should sit up until ten o'clock every night, and that this new regulation should come into force that very evening.

In vain the Chief-Nurses-Extraordinary pleaded. They threw themselves on their knees and with tears besought the Queen to intercede on their behalf. They even hinted that unless the Princess went to bed immediately something terrible might happen. The Queen, touched by their appeal, was about to address the King, when

DING, DONG!

The great clock on the mantelpiece began to strike nine!

Suddenly there was silence. Everyone had stopped talking and was staring at the Princess. For even before the clock had finished striking, she had begun to change. Her eyes grew larger and rounder, her nose grew longer and longer, her ears became pointed, fur appeared all over her face, and in a moment she had become a mouse!

The Queen fainted immediately. The King turned white as the tablecloth; numerous Empresses, Dowager Queens, and Hereditary Royal Duchesses collapsed on the spot. The only one who retained self-possession was Pirlipatine, whose little brown hands were darting hither and thither among the sweet meats and crackers in her endeavour to find a nut. But the two Chief-Nurses-Extraordinary were brave and capable women. Quickly they reached the Princess' chair and carried her off to bed between them, in spite of her squeaks.

The rest of the dinner, of course, was completely spoilt. The Queen and most of the Empresses and Dowager Queens and Hereditary Grand Duchesses were removed by the attendants, and the King rose as soon as he had finished his coffee. The guests all made excuses to leave early, and within half an hour the palace was practically empty. I say "practically," because some of the agree able Pretenders, who had come to the palace solely to enjoy the banquet and didn't really care in the least about Pirlipatine, returned to the dining room as soon as they could, and proved that their visits to the Court Dentist had not been in vain.

The King's first impulse was to send for Ehu Dappleblock and the Astronomer and be head them there and then. But on second thoughts he realised that even if he found out where they had gone to there was little likelihood of their obeying his command. So he went to the Queen's room instead, to talk things over with her, merely telling the Grand Usher to see that neither of the Chief-Nurses-Extraordinary left the palace.

The Queen had recovered somewhat and was sitting up on the sofa. The Court Physician had given her a wineglassful of sal volatile, and she felt much calmer. The King sat down beside her and took one of her hands in his. Together they talked the whole matter over.

Then the Chief-Nurses-Extraordinary were sent for. With fear and trembling they related how the Princess had suddenly changed into a mouse again at nine o'clock on the very evening of her restoration by the Nutcracker, how she had resumed her normal appearance next morning at sunrise, and how this changing from one to the other had gone on every evening and every morning since then.

At this the King and Queen both brightened up very much.

"It's only half as bad as we thought," said the King.

"And only at night," added the Queen.

But the King could not overlook the crime which the Nurses had committed in hiding the truth and thus exposing him to so great an affront before all his royal guests. He sentenced them both to perpetual exile on the spot. But as the Queen pointed out that there was no one else who could look after the Princess properly just at present, he granted them a permanent respite.

"We must find Ehu Dappleblock at once," said the Queen.

"Do you think he would come if I sent for him?" asked the King.

"He *must* come," replied the Queen. "At least he has cured Pirlipatine by day, and he may be able to cure her by night. But I'm afraid, my dear, that you offended him by exiling him so tersely."

"Well, well," said the King, "he needn't have taken offence at a little thing like that. I *had* thought of having his head cut off at once. However, I suppose we'd better advertise for him in all the papers."

Next day an announcement appeared in the newspapers to the effect that if Ehu Dappleblock would send his address to a leading firm of lawyers in the capital, he would hear of something to his advantage.

Ehu saw the advertisement. Before answering it he consulted the Astronomer, and together they consulted the stars. There they read that great good fortune was in store for both of them. Accordingly Ehu, who remarked to his friend that even if it were a ruse the King couldn't come and fetch him at Berylia, wrote to the address given, enclosing a stamped and addressed envelope for reply.

XIV

Ehu and the Astronomer discover the whereabouts of the Bangalu tree

THE KING WAS OVERJOYED WHEN the Lord Great Detective-Extraordinary brought him Ehu's address. Acting upon the Queen's advice he sat down immediately and wrote a kind letter to the Craftsman, telling him exactly what had happened, and asking him if he would be so kind as to take immediate steps to complete the Princess' cure. He even invited Ehu and his friend the Astronomer to come and stay at the palace ("we can always put them up somewhere for a night or two, my dear," he remarked to the Queen), promising them protection against everybody, and ended up by saying that the pension of a thousand rose-nobles, the gold-rimmed spectacles, the sword studded with diamonds, the Order of the Golden Mushroom, and the new overcoat, still awaited them. He even began "Dear Mr. Dappleblock," and ended up "always yours sincerely."

Ehu and the Astronomer read the letter through several times and even tested it for invisible ink, but could find nothing wrong with it. The stars clearly showed that no evil awaited them; but that, on the contrary, their visit to the capital would bring them nothing but good fortune.

Fortified with these hopes they set out by the mail-coach that evening, taking Nikky with them.

Arrived at the capital, they left Nikky at their hotel and made their way to the palace. The King was delighted to see them. He shook hands warmly with them and told Ehu that he was positively anxious for the Craftsman to win the new overcoat. Indeed Ehu was now really in need of a new one; for although his old yellow overcoat had been patched and repaired by the best tailor in Berylia, it still showed unmistakable signs of wear, and the patches were very much brighter than the rest of it. So Ehu thanked the King for his kindness, and replied that it would not be his fault if the Princess were not cured completely this time.

Then he went on to tell the King about Nikky's transformation; and the King, who was really a very tender-hearted man, blew his nose violently several times. But when Ehu had finished, the King remarked that although nothing would please him more than that the Nutcracker should slay the King of the Mice and recover his normal shape, yet the horoscope which announced these things said nothing about the Princess.

The Astronomer, however, assured the King that when once the King of the Mice were dead there would be no one else to cast spells (for the stars clearly showed that His Majesty was a widower with no children), and that the Princess would assuredly be rid of her trouble some ailment as soon as ever that happy event had come to pass.

There was only one thing to be done. The Bangalu tree must be discovered at all costs. The King sent at once for the Reader of the Public Thoughts and commanded that the very next day a notice should appear in all the newspapers, both at home and abroad, announcing that anyone who possessed or knew of a genuine Bangalu tree should write and tell the King immediately, and that a magnificent reward would be given.

The announcement attracted great attention; and two days later letters began to arrive from farmers, fruit-growers, nurserymen, and timber-merchants, all over Europe, as well as from several thousand private persons, offering genuine Bangalu trees at prices varying from seven and sixpence to ten guineas. Ehu and the Astronomer read them all through carefully, but not a single one described the tree indicated by the stars.

On the fifth day, tired out and their fingers sore with opening envelopes, they were going upstairs to bed when the Astronomer, looking out of the landing window, saw that it was a fine night for taking horoscopes. Accordingly they made their way to the roof of the palace. At first Ehu could not see very clearly, for he had inadvertently placed the telescope to his glass eye. But at length, written plainly in the stars, they saw that the Bangalu tree would be found only on the lower slopes of the Himalayan mountains. Moreover the spot indicated was the very one where the travellers had sat down and taken the resolution to begin their return journey!

Transported with joy, Ehu wanted to go downstairs and tell the King at once; but the Astronomer restrained him.

"My dear Ehu," he said, "after all our I exertions we are entitled to something better than a paltry pension and a new overcoat. The King is a generous man and will appreciate the difficulties of our search. Let *me* speak to him in the morning."

Ehu gladly agreed, and, regaining their room, the friends went to bed and slept soundly.

Next morning Dappleblock and the Astronomer had an interview with the King; and when Ehu hinted that the fruit of the Bangalu tree might possibly be effective—so far as the Princess was concerned—only if Nikky were her affianced husband, the King generously promised to carry out his former intention. At the Astronomer's suggestion he agreed to draw up a deed assigning the throne after his death to the Princess' husband, and promised faithfully that she should marry the Nutcracker as soon as ever he succeeded in curing her completely and in effecting his own transformation. Moreover he agreed to reinstate the Astronomer in his former post, to assign him a suite of rooms rent free in the palace, to increase his pension to five thousand rose-nobles, and to allow him coal from the royal coal cellars free of charge. As for Ehu, he should be appointed Craftsman-Extraordinary under the Great Seal, he should have a pension similar to the Astronomer's, and should have all the King's cast-off overcoats.

Satisfied with these concessions, the two friends returned joyfully to their hotel, and made arrangements for their journey. As for Nikky, he was overjoyed at the news. The people in the hotel stared at him so much that he felt quite uncomfortable; and, moreover, there was a considerable shortage of nuts in the capital just then.

XV

How Ehu, the Astronomer, and Nikky
gathered the fruit of the Bangalu tree

I WILL NOT WEARY YOU BY recounting all the adventures that befell the travellers on their journey to Ishkashim, nor by describing their long and toilsome search for the narrow path into the heart of the Himalayas which Ehu and the Astronomer had discovered on their former journey. Suffice it to say that on the evening of the one hundred and forty-fifth day after they had left the capital, the Astronomer stumbled by chance upon the very path for which they were seeking. They had followed the same route from Europe as Ehu and the Astronomer had taken on the return from their former quest, but they had taken longer to accomplish it, partly because there was no hurry, and partly because Nikky's boots were not very comfortable.

Now at last their goal was, if not in sight, at least within easy reach; and after a rapid march of ten days, during which Nikky was often obliged to run in order to keep up with his companions, they turned a corner suddenly, and there, right in front of them, stood the Bangalu tree! Eagerly they ran towards it.

Imagine their dismay on finding that there was not a single fruit upon it!

They walked round it, patted its trunk, and Nikky even climbed up into it; but not a fruit was to be seen. There was not even a bud upon it. Sorrowfully they sat down at its foot, and, overcome by fatigue and their feelings, burst into tears.

While they were sitting thus, Nikky espied a man approaching. As first Ehu and the Astronomer were rather alarmed; for they had imagined that the district they were in was quite uninhabited. So they made friendly signs, and when the newcomer approached, the Astronomer, who was a great linguist and spoke Himalayan fluently, bid him good afternoon. To their delight they discovered that the stranger was no less a person than the Wise Man of the Chinchinjunga Tribe, and that he knew all about the Bangalu tree. But their joy changed to sorrow again when they learnt that the Chinchinjungas had gathered all the fruit and had made it into jam only a fortnight before, and that the tree bore fruit only once in every seven years!

"Is there no other Bangalu tree?" asked the Astronomer, in pure Himalayan.

"Yes," replied the Wise Man; "there is one and one only. It grows on the other side of the mountain, precisely opposite this one. But this is also its year of fruit, and the Pinchinjunga tribe, like us, always make its fruit into jam. I heard recently, however, that they had had an accident with their stew pan, so it is just possible that they have not yet plucked all the fruit."

At these words the Astronomer wanted to start for the other side of the mountain there and then. But Nikky was tired out; moreover he had blistered one of his heels. So reluctantly they were obliged to postpone their departure until the following day, and the Astronomer invited the Wise Man of the Chinchinjungas to supper.

At dawn the next morning the travellers resumed their journey. The road became narrower and narrower, and after travelling for some hours they came to a place where they were obliged to go in single file. On one side the mountain rose straight up from the path, and on the other side was a sheer precipice of ten thousand feet.

They had progressed like this for some distance when suddenly, upon turning a corner, they saw an enormous tiger stretched right across their path! To pass by was impossible; and Ehu thought it would be most imprudent to attempt to step over the sleeping beast. There was no way round, and unless they proceeded at once they would lose their last hope of obtaining the fruit of the Bangalu tree for seven years They stepped back round the corner on tiptoe and, bidding Nikky stand there in order to warn them if the tiger suddenly appeared round the bend, they retired for some distance to discuss what was to be done.

At first it seemed hopeless. They could think of no plan which would rid their path of the tiger without danger to at least one of them, and the Astronomer had realised at once that both Ehu and Nikky were indispensable to his attainment of the promised reward. As for Ehu, he could not bear to part with his friend. Besides, the Astronomer had all the charts and navigating instruments in his pockets, without which they could not possibly find their way. Despondently the Astronomer opened his snuff box and took a big pinch of snuff. At this an idea suddenly struck Ehu.

"O marvellous inventiveness of human understanding," he cried; "it is thy fertile originations which shall enable us to triumph over even the most infortuitous concatenation of circumstances."

At first the Astronomer thought his friend was afflicted with sunstroke. He opened his green umbrella at once and held it sympathetically over

Ehu's head. But Dappleblock hastened to expound his plan.

Quietly they approached the corner where Nikky sat nibbling a large nut, and then, having taken off his boots and with a large square tin of his favourite snuff (without which the Astronomer never went anywhere) in his hand, the Astronomer approached the sleeping tiger on tiptoe. Twice he hesitated, but as Ehu called to him in a loud whisper to go on, he went up to the tiger and softly sprinkled snuff all round it. Then he withdrew quickly and joined Ehu round the corner.

When the Astronomer had recovered his breath and had got his boots on again, Ehu took up a stone and threw it at the tiger. After several attempts he hit the beast with a pebble right on the nose.

With a roar that made the travellers step back hastily, the tiger sprang to its feet amid clouds of snuff. Then slowly it raised its head, and . . . . A-TISH-O O! Again and again it sneezed, each time raising more clouds of snuff. At last, its eyes streaming with tears, its head reeling with sneezes, the huge beast rose up on its hind legs, and with one tremendous

A—A—C H O O!

blew itself right over the precipice.

It was an awe-inspiring sight.

The travellers were now able to continue their journey in safety; and by nightfall the next evening they espied, from a neighbouring peak, the second Bangalu tree growing at the foot of the mountain.

It was covered with golden fruit!

Joyfully they sank down on the grass beneath a large nut-tree, tired out but happier than they had been for many a day.

To describe how they reached the tree next morning, how the Astronomer carefully packed the fruit in the special air-tight boxes which he had brought with him, how just as he had finished they saw the savage Pinchinjungas coming with a huge stew pan to make the fruit into jam, and how they managed to escape in the opposite direction, Ehu having his left ear transfixed by an arrow as they ran, would be to weary you. Suffice it to say that after many hardships and dangers the travellers at length reached Baghdad. From Baghdad they journeyed to Alexandria; at Alexandria they embarked for Venice; from Venice they reached the Alps; and from the Alps they descended into the kingdom of Pirlipatine's father, hoping this time that, even if he were dead, he would at least have signed the deed appointing Nikky his successor to the throne.

XVI

Of the preparations which Ehu and the Astronomer made for Nikky's combat with the Mouse King

L EAVING NIKKY AT THEIR HOTEL, the travellers made their way to the palace. The King was overjoyed to see them, and this time he recognised them at once. After having enquired about Ehu's left ear, he folded them each to his bosom in turn, and insisted upon them staying to supper. Then when Ehu had related their adventures and the success which had crowned their efforts, the King told them that events of no small importance had happened at the palace during their absence.

Shortly after they had left the capital on their search for the Bangalu tree, a fresh calamity had overtaken the Princess Pirlipatine. It happened that one night the Chief-Nurses-Extraordinary were awakened by hearing the Princess cry out. Rushing up to her bed, they were horrified to see a large mouse, gorgeously dressed and with red top boots, standing by her side. Shaking his paw at the Princess, he cried out in a shrill voice:

> *"Though Princess proud, you spurn me now,*
> *Your love I'll gain at last;*
> *Queen of the Mouse Tribe you shall be,*
> *Ere many moons are past."*

Then, before the Chief-Nurses-Extraordinary could recover from their amazement, he darted away and disappeared. There was no doubt whatever about it: it was the King of the Mice.

All efforts to find him had been without avail. The chinks in the floor had all been stopped up, large mousetraps baited with freshly toasted cheese, bacon fat, and sweet smelling nuts, had been hastily constructed and put in the most likely spots; but all to no purpose. Every night the Mouse King appeared from nobody knew where, and continued to woo the Princess. Even the illustrious Murr and her sons had failed to locate him, and one of them had even fled on catching sight of the Mouse King.

But this was not all. Only the previous night the Mouse King had appeared as usual and had informed the Princess, in no uncertain tones, that on the following Saturday night he would carry her off, willy nilly, to his kingdom.

There was no time to be lost. It was now Friday evening, and much remained to be done. As soon as ever they had finished their coffee Ehu and the Astronomer rose and begged the King's permission to return to their hotel, promising to come back with the Nutcracker the next day. Their request was immediately granted.

It must not be imagined that during the return journey Nikky had been allowed to forget all the instructions and exercises which Ehu had taught him before they set out. As soon as ever the campfire was lighted of a morning, Ehu saw to it that the Nutcracker carried out his exercises properly. First came a quarter of an hour's fencing, then ten minutes with the boxing gloves, then a series of high kicks, besides exercises in jumping, spinning on one toe, and turning somersaults. By the time these gymnastics were over a pleasant smell of fried bacon usually announced that the Astronomer had succeeded in preparing breakfast. Nikky's appetite was large, and as the travellers seldom accomplished less than twenty miles a day, he was soon in splendid fettle. Ehu himself grew younger every day.

So there was no fear of Nikky failing to overcome the Mouse King on the score of physical weakness. Indeed he was now so lithe and athletic that he could toss a nut into the air, turn a complete somersault, spin ten times on his toe, and then catch the nut in his teeth as it fell. In fact he caused quite a lot of interest in the hotel, for in pure lightness of heart he would leap on to the mantel piece at a bound, jump high into the air, turn three somersaults, and alight on the middle of the table without breaking a single wineglass. In fact one of the guests offered him quite a large sum to join a travelling circus.

Ehu and the Astronomer returned to their hotel deep in thought. This time they were determined to leave no stone unturned in order to ensure success. Such a calamity as had occurred during Nikky's last performance at Court must be prevented at all costs; and less than twenty-four hours remained for them to concert their plans. So they went straight to the top of the house and climbed on to the roof; for although schemes of their own contriving might be brought to nought, yet the stars could not fail. Whatever may be read in the stars will come to pass as surely as night follows day. Eagerly and with trembling hands the Astronomer proceeded to cast a horoscope. At first this was somewhat obscured by a maze of tangential diaphanics, but presently it grew clearer and clearer, and to their great joy they read that not only would Nikky succeed in overcoming the Mouse King, but that he was destined to marry the Princess and, in due course, succeed to her father's throne. One thing only was to be guarded against: on no account must he eat the fruit of the Bangalu tree until he had caught hold of the Mouse King's tail.

Rejoiced by these happy auspices the two friends left the roof and regained their room.

"The question is," said Ehu, "how are we to make sure that Nikky gets hold of the Mouse King's tail? It will be a terrible combat, and the Mouse King is sure to keep his tail well out of the way."

"We must machinate, my dear Ehu," replied the Astronomer; "we must employ a stratagem. You remember the artifice Eris made use of to—"

He stopped and gripped Ehu's arm.

"Why not?" he cried excitedly. "Why should we not make use of the same ruse? Eris threw a golden apple: Nikky shall throw an orange Bangalu."

"My dear fellow," said Ehu, "your ingenuity is perfectly astounding. But—if the Mouse King succeeds in getting hold of the Bangalu fruit first, won't it upset our plans a little?"

"Of course," replied his friend; "but it's not bound to be a real Bangalu, is it? I don't suppose the Mouse King has ever seen a real one, and I'm quite sure you could contrive—"

"Say no more, my dear friend," said Ehu hastily. "I will go and find a carpenter's shop immediately after breakfast tomorrow."

Satisfied with their plan, the two friends went to bed; and presently nothing but Ehu's bass snore was disturbing the quiet of the night. But before he went to sleep Ehu revolved the plan in his mind, and determined that the shop which he would visit next day would not be a carpenter's one.

XVII

How Nikky combated with the Mouse King, and with what result

N EXT DAY THE TRAVELLERS WERE up betimes, and immediately after breakfast Dappleblock went out into the town in order to set about making the imitation Bangalu. The Astronomer saw that Nikky went through all his exercises properly, and then told him precisely what he was to do. He even took off his coat and went through part of the performance with the Nutcracker, practising particularly that stage of it where the Mouse King's attention was to be diverted by the orange Bangalu. At the third trial, however, Nikky performed his part with such skill and agility that the Astronomer spun through the air and fell heavily upon his nose. Nikky was anxious to practise it once more, but the Astronomer felt that he was now proficient enough.

At lunch time Ehu returned, and handed a small cardboard box to his friend. The Astronomer opened it carefully, and inside, surrounded with pink tissue paper, was a perfect and most inviting orange Bangalu.

"Really my dear Ehu," said the Astronomer, "you surpass yourself. We had better not show it to Nikky until just before it is to be used; otherwise he might treat it like the Krakatuk."

"It wouldn't take a Nutcracker to crack that, ha, ha!" replied Ehu mysteriously.

Then he took the Astronomer's ear between his finger and thumb and whispered into it.

"No! Have you really? Is that so? Capital, my dear fellow," said the Astronomer; "that should put the matter beyond all possible doubt."

Just before tea time Ehu, carrying a small bag, set out for the palace with Nikky and the Astronomer. The King received them courteously, and himself led the way to the Princess' room. Here they examined the door, took up the carpet and stamped on the floor, poked their penknives underneath the skirting-boards, and examined carefully every chink and crevice through which it would be possible for the Mouse King to enter or leave the room. Then they carefully rehearsed the part they were about to play, the Astronomer persuading Ehu to personate the Mouse King upon this occasion.

At half past nine that night one of the Chief-Nurses-Extraordinary came downstairs and announced that the Princess was now tucked up in bed. So Ehu, taking up his bag and followed by the Astronomer, Nikky, and the King (who insisted upon being present on so historic an occasion), made their way upstairs to the Princess' room.

All was in darkness. They entered on tip toe, and Nikky felt so excited that he could hardly keep still, and was obliged to nibble a nut all the time to keep himself quiet. How long they were there I am unable to say, but whether it was the darkness or the warmth, or merely because it was bedtime, certain it is that they all began to feel sleepy. First the King yawned twice and then began to nod, then Ehu felt his eyes closing, the Astronomer was wondering whether there was time for forty winks, and Nikky was curling himself up among the cushions in his chair, when suddenly there was a strange noise.

They all woke up with a start. The King could hear Ehu breathing heavily. Then all at once they heard a high thin voice, and next moment the Princess cried out. Nikky was the first to regain his self-possession. With one bound he was in the middle of the room, and next instant he and the Mouse King were locked in a deadly struggle!

The Chief-Nurses-Extraordinary came hurrying in with lights; the King drew his sword and seized a cushion with which to defend himself; whilst Ehu and the Astronomer danced excitedly round the combatants.

Nikky had seized the Mouse King round the middle and was rolling him over and over in a vain endeavour to grasp his tail. But the Mouse King, knowing that everything was at stake, was fighting magnificently, and kept swishing his tail from side to side just out of Nikky's reach.

I will not weary you by describing in detail every incident of that historic fight. Suffice it to say that at the critical moment Ehu, making a pre-arranged signal to Nikky, allowed the imitation Bangalu fruit to fall close to the King of the Mice, at the same time exclaiming:

"Look out! There goes the Orange Bangalu!"

The Mouse King made a furious effort, grabbed the fruit, and plunged his teeth into it!

For an instant his caution was relaxed, and Nikky grasped his tail firmly in both hands.

Instantly the Mouse King began to grow smaller and smaller and smaller!

At the same moment the Astronomer, deftly abstracting a genuine fruit from the air-tight box, rapidly stuffed it into Nikky's open mouth. Nikky took three hard bites on the luscious fruit and the Astronomer's finger.

Immediately there was a change in the situation. Nikky grew larger and fatter and stronger, his legs became shapely and muscular, his arms thickened, and with a terrible grip he squeezed the Mouse King with all his might. For one moment the Mouse King threw back his head and would have cried out, but his teeth were firmly embedded in the artificial Bangalu fruit, which Ehu had cunningly constructed of caramel toffee. And so, unable to utter any further malediction or pronounce a single charm, he sank lifeless upon the ground. Nikky had squeezed the life out of him.

At this moment the King gave a shout and they all looked up. The Princess had risen from her bed and was standing beside her father, looking more lovely than ever. She was a young and exquisitely beautiful girl once more! Then she too gave a little cry, and they all looked at Nikky. No longer was he like a mouse; for he stood before them all, strong, lissom, and well, a handsome youth with curly chestnut hair and ivory teeth.

"Oh!" said the Princess, "there's the handsome young man whom I saw at the Krakatuk tournament! I do like him so much, father."

Even the King was amazed. Nikky was such a handsome fellow and so dignified and well-mannered and quiet. The King held out his hand to him, and Nikky advanced hesitatingly. But though he took the King's hand he never took his eyes off the Princess the whole time.

"My dear," said the King, "let me present Mr. er—Nikky to you. He has done us a very great service indeed, and I'm sure you will like to add your thanks to mine."

Nikky dropped on one knee and pressed the Princess' hand respectfully to his lips. As for the Princess, she blushed so prettily and could only stammer: "Thank you *so* much, dear Mr. Nikky."

Just then the Queen entered the room. She took in the situation at a glance.

"You had better sleep with me tonight, my dear," she said to Pirlipatine; "these things are so disturbing." Then turning to the King, she said: "My dear, I'm sure Mr. Dappleblock and his friends are hungry after all their exertions. Won't you take them downstairs and give them some supper?"

This course seemed to all a wise one. Whilst they had been talking the Lord Great Scavenger (who had been sent for in haste by the Chief-Nurses-Extraordinary) had entered, picked up the Mouse King by the tail and carried him out. It was all over, Nikky had triumphed, the Princess was completely cured, and the anxieties of Ehu and the Astronomer as to their future were entirely Set at rest.

Little remains to be told. On the following day the King held a Privy Council at which he announced that the Princess Pirlipatine was about to be betrothed to the Royal Prince Nikky of Krakatuk and Bangalu, Hereditary Prince of Chinchinjunga, and Grand Archduke of Pinchinjungaland. All the bells were rung, and the whole kingdom was soon en fete. The same day he held an Investiture at which both Ehu and the Astronomer were decorated with the Grand Cross of the Order of the Golden Mushroom. The King's own tailor had measured Ehu for a new overcoat immediately after breakfast, and the Royal Eyeglass-Maker was already busy fitting the Astronomer's face with a pair of gold-rimmed spectacles. Ehu's diamond studded sword was taken in hand by the Court Jeweller at once.

But the King went even further. He caused Royal Patents to be drawn up creating Ehu a Peer of the Realm by the title of Lord Dappleblock of Berylia, and granting the Astronomer a Marquisate in Pinchinjungaland. Nikky, of course, was knighted there and then, invested with twenty-eight Orders simultaneously, and formally introduced to everyone as heir to the throne.

In the midst of this shower of honours Ezra Dappleblock suddenly appeared at the palace and demanded to see his son. But as he was unused to Court life and insisted upon eating asparagus with a knife, the King got rid of him with a pension of five thousand rose nobles and the monopoly of making toys within the Kingdom.

The Queen was not forgotten. The King was a sensible man, and he realised that her advice was really indispensable to him. So he gave her a pearl necklace worth all the rest of her jewels put together. In return she told him that as the pork harvest seemed likely to be the heaviest on record, it was her intention to make, with her own hands, as many black puddings, chitterlings, and sausages, each containing a double quantity of fat bacon, as would last them until the next harvest.

As they crossed the hall arm-in-arm they caught sight of Nikky wandering about disconsolately. He blushed when he saw them.

"She's in the rose garden," said the Queen. "You'd better go and join her."

And as Nikky and the Princess had been in love with each other from the very moment they had each resumed their normal shapes, I will leave you to imagine what they said to each other among the roses.

A Note About the Book

Bringing together one original story and three subsequent retellings, *The Nutcracker Treasury* features the work of two influential storytellers—E.T.A Hoffman, who is recognized as a leading figure in German Romanticism and a pioneer of science fiction and fantasy; and Alexandre Dumas, who was one of the most universally read French authors and is known his extravagantly adventurous historical novels—as well as the renowned composer Pyotr Ilyich Tchaikovsky, whose work made him the first Russian composer to attract international acclaim; and a children's book author, O. Eliphaz Keat, whose only listed work is *Princess Pirlipatine and the Nutcracker.*

A Note from the Publisher

Spanning many genres, from non-fiction essays to literature classics to children's books and lyric poetry, Mint Edition books showcase the master works of our time in a modern new package. The text is freshly typeset, is clean and easy to read, and features a new note about the author in each volume. Many books also include exclusive new introductory material. Every book boasts a striking new cover, which makes it as appropriate for collecting as it is for gift giving. Mint Edition books are only printed when a reader orders them, so natural resources are not wasted. We're proud that our books are never manufactured in excess and exist only in the exact quantity they need to be read and enjoyed. To learn more and view our library, go to minteditionbooks.com.

bookfinity & MINT EDITIONS

Enjoy more of your favorite classics with Bookfinity,
a new search and discovery experience for readers.
With Bookfinity, you can discover more vintage
literature for your collection, find your Reader Type,
track books you've read or want to read,
and add reviews to your favorite books.
Visit www.bookfinity.com, and click on
Take the Quiz to get started.

Don't forget to follow us
@bookfinityofficial and @mint_editions